Extraordinary Praise for Jim Geraghty and The CIA's Dangerous Clique Series:

"Geraghty has hit another homerun! *Hunting Four Horsemen* is an absolutely electrifying thriller. Fantastic plot, pacing, and characters. Bravo!"

—Brad Thor, #1 *New York Times*-bestselling author of *Near Dark*

"A thoroughly researched thriller [*Between Two Scorpions*] with a threat vector I wish I'd come up with—and a bite of humor rarely seen in the genre."

—Brad Taylor, author of *Daughter of War* and the *New York Times*-bestselling Pike Logan series, retired U.S. Army Special Forces Lieutenant Colonel

"Powerful, real, and relevant, Jim Geraghty's *Between Two Scorpions* is a well-written and dynamite page turner and a welcome addition to the thriller genre."

—Mark Greaney, #1 *New York Times* Bestselling Author of *Mission Critical*

"Jim Geraghty is one of the most insightful and cutting writers in the country.

—Ben Shapiro, author, *The Right Side of History* and founder of The Daily Wire

DUELING SIX DEMONS

Also By Jim Geraghty

The CIA's Dangerous Clique Series

Gathering Five Storms

Saving the Devil: A Dangerous Clique Story

Hunting Four Horsemen

Between Two Scorpions

Other Books

Fiction

The Weed Agency

Nonfiction

Voting to Kill

With Cam Edwards

Heavy Lifting

DUELING SIX DEMONS

A DANGEROUS CLIQUE NOVEL

JIM GERAGHTY

This is a work of fiction. Names, characters, places and incidents either are the product of the author's imagination or are used fictitiously, and resemblance to actual persons, living or dead, businesses, companies, events, or locales is entirely coincidental.

ISBN: 978-1-7337346-5-3 (paperback)

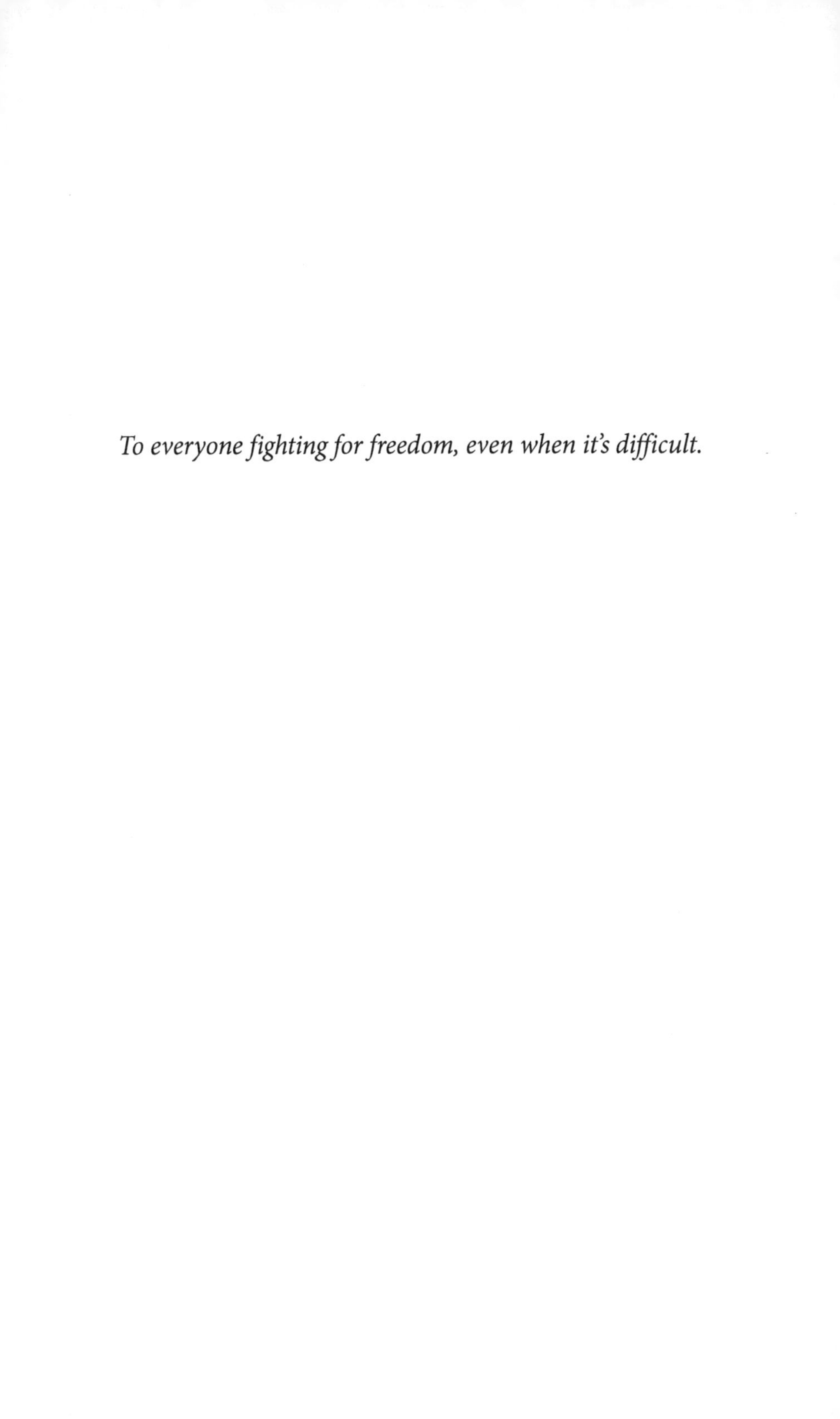

To everyone fighting for freedom, even when it's difficult.

TABLE OF CONTENTS

CHAPTER ONE

A BACK ROAD ROUGHLY PARALLEL TO THE
E-40 HIGHWAY
BETWEEN LVIV AND KYIV, UKRAINE
AUGUST 8, 2023

The first sign that the mission had gone spectacularly wrong was the Russian-manufactured FAB-1500 M54, a high-explosive bomb, landing and exploding on the road about a half a kilometer in front of them. The Range Rover slammed on the brakes and just avoided skidding into a shallow ditch by the side of the road, as small pieces of shrapnel and earth pelted the hood, windshield, and roof.

The three occupants of the vehicle stared at what was left of the road ahead. The exploding bomb had left the mother of all potholes, a flaming crater with little bits of fire burning around it.

Within the Range Rover, the giant smoking bowl of blackened dirt and torn-up asphalt reminded Katrina and Alec a bit of their encounter at "the Gates of Hell," the ever-burning Darvaza Crater in Turkmenistan, a few years ago.

The Ukrainian foreign intelligence service SZRU had originally planned for their American guests to travel the road through the Lviv region in an "infantry mobility vehicle" that would offer some combination of armor and speed. Since the war began, the Ukrainians found themselves the new owners of a suddenly much larger hodge-podge fleet of wheeled military vehicles donated from Western allies. But those had all been sent to the front, and the two high-priority guests from the CIA, Katrina Leonidivna and Alec Flanagan, had to make do with a basic civilian Ranger Rover and the driving skills of Pavel Koval, a junior sergeant in the Ukrainian military who had been reassigned as a gofer for SZRU.

They had been instructed to follow behind a Ukrainian military convoy at a safe distance—no one had really specified what a "safe distance" was—while heading west toward Kyiv. And for venturing into a country that was attempting to fight off an invasion by nearly one million Russian soldiers, the journey had seemed safe, right up until the moment the road exploded ahead of them.

Inside the Range Rover, Katrina slowly loosened her fingers' grip on the dashboard, from where she had reached out at the moment of the blast. She belatedly noticed that no passenger-side airbag had deployed.

"That is as close as I ever want to get to a Russian bomb," Katrina exhaled.

"Everybody who told us that two parents shouldn't go into a war zone together is starting to look pretty vindicated," Alec whispered, wide-eyed and breathing heavily.

"Rarely see Russian air force this far west, must be feeling *zhavvy* today," Pavel observed, as casually as if he was noticing rain clouds ahead. Pavel had an oddly deadpan way of speaking that suggested either he was being slyly sarcastic to his American guests, or the past year of war had left him numb and blasé about anything going on around him.

On either side of the road were fields of sunflowers. So far, the drive into Ukraine had taken the married couple from the Korczowa–Krakovets border post to a highway through forests, before emerging into long stretches of cornfields. Alec observed that driving through Ukraine didn't look all that different from driving through Iowa or Indiana, before bright fields of yellow sunflowers replaced the corn.

The three of them intensely surveyed the skies ahead of them and behind them. "Is that MiG going to come back around? Would we be safer out of the car?" Alec asked.

"So far in this war, the Russians have been lousy at 'dynamic targeting.'" Katrina exhaled, leaning low and wondering if the MiG had disappeared into the clouds or was returning to its base, most likely a military airfield on the Belarussian side of the border.

"In other words, they're a lot worse at hitting moving targets." She looked over at Pavel and glared. "That means it would be a good idea to get moving!"

Pavel nodded. After a few moments of the wheels spinning, Pavel managed to rock the Range Rover back and forth, get some traction, and begin the process of driving around the smoking crater that replaced the road ahead of them.

As the view of the smoking crater got smaller in the rearview mirror, Alec grappled with what his one-year-old twin sons' lives would have been like if the bomb had landed closer. He and Katrina had recognized the risks of going back into the field—or at least, they had thought they recognized them—and they had been assured that traveling in this part of Ukraine would be relatively safe.

Frustrated with himself, Alec redirected his irritation toward Pavel.

"I thought you guys said this road was the safer route!" Alec muttered. "What did the other route have? Land mines? Snipers? Maryland drivers?"

"Russians aimed for convoy in front of us, missed." Pavel's English was fine, but he made gestures with his hands to demonstrate anyway. Alec wished Pavel would keep his hands on the steering wheel.

After an awkward quiet moment, Pavel piped up. "Sure would be nice to have more air defenses around right about now. But no rush. Your Congress can take its time debating whether we need more." There was Pavel's dry sarcasm again.

"Where's the Ghost of Kyiv when we need him?" Alec replied.

Pavel shook his head sadly. "My government conceded that the Ghost of Kyiv is mythical," he explained. "The stories grew out of the exploits of Stepan Tarabalka, who shot down several Russian planes before losing a dogfight."

"So, he really is a ghost, then."

The three heard some sort of heavy firing off in the distance ahead of them. Either the convoy ahead of them was trying to fire into the air to discourage the Russian fighter-bomber from attempting another attack, or some Ukrainian air defense system in the distance had detected the MiG and was belatedly swinging into action.

Whatever Russian jet had dropped the glider bomb to this spot likely hadn't even known their vehicle was approaching. Nothing about their gray civilian Range Rover indicated it would be a valuable target, compared to the five military modified Toyota Hiluxes driving ahead of them, spread out to minimize the odds of getting hit in the same barrage. Then again, Katrina knew, Russian cruise missiles had slammed into apartment buildings, their tanks had fired into homes, and their soldiers had executed ordinary citizens in the Kyiv suburb of Bucha without any hesitation. The Russians had demonstrated they could kill civilians, targets without any military or tactical value, without blinking an eye.

"You know, when we ran around Salzburg, and those Russian Iron Wolf mercenaries tried to kill us, I had a gun!" Alec fumed from the back seat, venting irritation. "When we ran into them the second time in Budapest a few months later, and you spayed Sergei Markov, I had a gun! But here I am, in a country with the whole damn Russian army invading with everything they've got, and some MENSA candidate back at headquarters concluded that if you or I had a gun, it would be *unacceptably dangerous*!"

He laughed at the absurdity of the CIA's assessment of danger.

Katrina shook her head. "The Russians are using Su-34s and Su-35s, some of the best warplanes they've got. You or me having a handgun isn't going to make a difference." She scanned the skies, still a little shaken from the near-miss with the falling bomb. "And the policy of us being unarmed is because if anybody saw you or me taking shots at the Russians, that would make the United States a combatant in this war."

"Can somebody fire me?" Alec shot back. "I still don't see how us shooting back at Russians trying to kill us changes the calculus of things. This whole war is a proxy fight between NATO and Russia, and at least half of what the Ukrainians are firing at the Russians says 'made in the U.S.A.'"

"Yes, we thank you very much for all of that," Pavel interjected. "Nothing makes my brothers in arms more confident than opening up a crate to see another delivery of the very best American weapons from the 1990s, instead of your newest top-of-the-line stuff. The last shipment of Howitzers had no GPS, but had a Backstreet Boys CD in it, so it all balances out. Attacking the Russians with the most advanced targeting technology and most firepower would be too easy. Must give Russians a fighting chance, keep it fair."

"Pavel, as I said before, Alec and I gather intelligence, we don't advise the president," Katrina said, betraying just a bit of frustration. "Let's just go see the Tattooed Man and get this over with."

CHAPTER TWO

The lone area where Ukrainians and Russians had managed to engage in some form of productive diplomacy during the war so far was the regular exchange of captured prisoners. The Ukrainian government's attitude was, as long as a captured Russian wasn't suspected of war crimes, they were worth trading to Russia to get some of their own men and women out of captivity.

The country's largest prisoner-of-war camp was an old fortress outside of Lviv, relatively far from the front lines. During World War Two, both Russian and German prisoners had been involuntary guests. Today, the sand-colored high walls featured posters of ancient Ukrainian rulers—an in-your-face declaration to the arriving prisoners that the country's independence was not some quirk of the Cold War's finale. The afternoons featured mandatory viewing of documentaries about Ukraine's history as an independent country—in Ukrainian, not Russian. This meant some of the Russian prisoners didn't understand the narration, but their lack of understanding reinforced the point that the Ukrainians wanted to emphasize: *This is a different place. We are not the same. And you will never get a chance to rule us again.*

The Range Rover waited in a short line of cars at the military checkpoint. Pavel turned to Katrina.

"Why is the CIA so interested in the Tattooed Man?"

Katrina didn't want to answer the question, so she countered with another question. "You've heard of him?"

"Everybody in Ukraine has heard stories of him," Pavel said, as his eyebrows jumped up upon his forehead. "Captured near Bakhmut, whole body covered in tattoos. Stories say all the rest of his platoon were killed, but not by Ukrainians. Some say he was found eating the flesh of his fallen comrades. He's given up no secrets, but he growls like an animal, speaks in tongues no one can translate. Other prisoners refuse to stay in the same cell as him. They say during prisoner exchange negotiations, the Russians refused to take him back."

Katrina smirked. "Who's 'they'?"

Pavel shrugged. "Military rumor mill. The wildest stories say he's not a soldier or even a Russian at all, he's *Azhdaya*, a Russian devil or dragon in the form of a man."

Katrina shook her head, chuckling at the absurd legends springing up around one captured Russian. "The Russians are evil enough as is, they don't need any help from demons."

"Amen," Pavel nodded, but then he eyed the American married couple carefully. "But must be something to the rumors if the CIA wants to talk to him," he concluded.

Katrina and Alec exchanged a look.

"Might as well tell him, he won't believe you anyway," she shook her head and smiled.

Alec took a deep breath. "About a year and a half ago, our team uncovered a strange pattern among some of our past enemies. People knowing each other, making references to events that they couldn't have known happened."

"They were working together?" Pavel asked.

"Eh, something like that," Alec nodded. "Do you remember about a year and a half ago, those militia guys who snuck a giant bomb into the Freedom Tower in New York?"

Pavel stared back in confusion.

"It was the same week that the Taliban took over Afghanistan, so everybody forgot about it," Alec sighed. "Anyway, those guys knew things about the Atarsa attacks that were never publicly disclosed. And that was, what, five years ago now, before the pandemic?"

"And you think the Tattooed Man or the Russians are connected, too?"

"That's what we're here to find out."

The last car was cleared through the checkpoint, and Pavel slowly drove up, and the three removed their forms of ID.

***

The fortress was old and cold, but it did the job. Steel doors painted green creaked as they opened. A room full of garbage bags held the possessions of the most recently captured Russian soldiers.

Once inside, Katrina and Alec were greeted by Major Igor Danyluk. The Ukrainian major didn't know exactly why two CIA officers had shown up and wanted to speak to one prisoner, but his superiors had informed him that these were important guests from Ukraine's vital and irreplaceable ally and deserved complete cooperation. The rumor was they were key members of some notorious American covert team, called the "Daredevil Pack" or something like that.

"The State Penal Service of Ukraine has set up fifty-one prisoner-of-war centers across the country, and this largest camp here near Lviv," Danyluk began, as if he was giving a standard tour. "Our facilities are well guarded, and no one has escaped so far. But our prisoners are given appropriate living conditions, and access to health care. We are not brutes or animals, the way the Russians abuse their prisoners. We even give prisoners the opportunity to call home, although obviously all the calls are recorded."

Danyluk boasted the fortress had even allowed a BBC camera crew into the facility, eager to demonstrate to the world that they were upholding human rights even in the most difficult of circumstances. The BBC were not allowed to show the prisoners' faces, as that would have violated the Geneva Conventions.

They turned a corner, and Danyluk gestured in the direction of a line of prisoners moving into a room down the hallway. "We realize many of the Russians, particularly the younger ones, were tricked into fighting this war. Some of them were told they were on a training mission. One realized the mission was real before he left, and he said he was issued a road atlas from 1974 instead of proper maps. He and his team wandered around the suburbs in Irpin, asking civilians where the forest was."

Katrina let out a bitter chuckle. She had heard enough stories from her parents, Bukharin Jews, who had horror stories of living as Jews in the Soviet Union, and the unique combination of malice and stupidity that permeated the Red Army.

As they passed a doorway, Danyluk gestured for them to peer through the window, where a group of pale Russian men, wearing black knit caps and identical blue uniforms, sat around a table, seemingly whittling. "We have given the prisoners work programs, but not exploitative. They are doing woodwork and doing things for the benefit of the Ukrainian society."

Alec looked through the window skeptically. "You sure it's such a great idea to put sharp instruments in the hands of captured Russian soldiers and hope for the best?"

Danyluk furrowed his brow. "We haven't had any incidents yet. Our psychological analysis of the captured prisoners indicates—"

"That's fascinating," Alec lied. "What can you guys tell us about the Tattooed Man?"

Danyluk's expression shifted. "Prisoner 656768, Yuri Voronin, a.k.a. 'the Tattooed Man' has been our guest for five weeks now."

He began the process of unlocking a giant steel door, painted green. Katrina read the sign above the door: "Odynochne uv'yaznennya"—"solitary confinement."

"Bad behavior, huh?"

Danyluk grimaced as the last lock finally opened. He led Katrina and Alec into yet another cold, stone, hallway. The cells nearest the door were all empty.

"Last door at the end," Danyluk announced. "It's both Voronin's behavior and his effect on the other prisoners. He seemed to stir up trouble wherever he went. Put him in a group of previously cooperative prisoners, and fights and accusations would start. He put everyone on edge, fearful, suspicious. It's why his reputa—"

The officer's voice stopped, and he gasped as they turned the corner and saw the cell.

The body of the Tattooed Man lay on the floor, throat slit, lying in a large pool of his own blood.

CHAPTER THREE

The guards at the fortress had wanted to clean up the bloody mess immediately, which struck Katrina and Alec suspicious. They urged some staff to photograph the scene, while Alec took out his cell phone and began taking pictures.

"We're going to need all your files on this guy," Katrina said to Danyluk. "And to speak to the Warden."

Danyluk nodded. He seemed to have a hard time tearing his eyes off the prisoner's body.

"I had never seen all of his tattoos like this," Danyluk explained.

Yuri Voronin's body covered, from neck to toe, with every kind of tattoo imaginable, an interwoven tapestry of images that must have taken years to accumulate. It was as if he had a nightmare shaped by the works of Hieronymus Bosch, and immortalized it on almost every square inch of his own skin. The images ranged from beautiful women and succubus demons, figures with skulls for faces, snakes, spirals, devilish-looking smiling faces, eyes staring out from complete black stretches, all kinds of seemingly occult symbols, zig-zag lines, triangles, an owl, beetle-like insects, and, around his shin, calf and ankle, a stretch of seemingly abandoned high-rise buildings.

Alec pointed with a pen to the abandoned buildings tattoo. "Does that remind you of any place?"

Katrina nodded. "Varosha, Cyprus."

Danyluk shook his head. "Have you ever seen anything like this?"

Katrina and Alec exchanged a look that confirmed they had.

"Years back, a chemist named Francis Neuse was kidnapped by the Atarsa terrorist group and drugged, and he drew his hallucinations in his diary," Alec murmured. "His drawings looked a lot like this."

A few minutes later, Danyluk received a phone call and informed Katrina and Alec that someone at the Foreign Ministry wished to speak with them immediately.

***

After Danyluk's phone call, he and several prison guards politely but firmly insisted that Katrina and Alec had to leave. Katrina couldn't tell if it was because the Ukrainians were worried that whoever had murdered the Tattooed Man could strike again, or that they had been mortified that a prisoner the CIA wanted to interview had been murdered, right under their nose. Someone did not want the Tattooed Man talking to the Americans.

After a few moments of waiting in the car, Pavel was given instructions on which route to take into the city.

"No worry on rest of trip," Pavel assured his American guests. "Much safer from here to Kyiv."

Alec smirked. "Not exactly the highest bar to clear."

Coming up on twenty years as part of the Dangerous Clique, Alec had been in several lifetimes' worth of dangerous places, but he had never been in a country at war; Katrina had begun her agency career as essentially an armed translator of the Uzbek language for U.S. forces in Afghanistan.

Alec found the sprawling city of Kyiv a bizarre combination of the shocking and the mundane. The city at war still had traffic jams, still had pedestrians walking the streets, shoppers in the stores, diners eating in the restaurants. The outskirts of the city had plenty of old-school Soviet brutalist architecture, gargantuan stacks of gray-tan boxes that seemed to suck the soul out of anyone who looked at it for too long. But the closer they drove into the heart of the city, the more Alec could see one of Europe's spectacular capitals, full of onion domes of cathedrals and grand, classic architecture, and its beleaguered but determined residents somehow soldiering on.

Some of the statues in the public squares were surrounded by a protective barrier of sandbags. The twenty-seven-story, modern Samsung skyscraper still had plenty of windows blown out from when a Russian missile had exploded nearby.

They had passed through many military checkpoints, although once they entered the city limits, none had bothered to stop them. And while they were well on schedule, Katrina and Alec had been instructed they would need to be in either their hotel or the U.S. embassy by midnight; the entire country was under a curfew from midnight to 5 a.m. Even the strip clubs closed at 11.

Pavel drove under an overpass and told his American guests that the location marked the farthest Russian troops had advanced into the city in February.

"That spot is past the U.S. embassy," Alec observed.

"No tanks, only troops," Pavel clarified.

They passed a restaurant, and Alec read the awning's words in English: "Enjoy every moment. Life is beautiful."

"When a Russian bomb could fall out of the sky any minute, that's not just a cliché," Katrina observed.

Pavel finally brought them to the Ukrainian Foreign Ministry.

***

A woman in a military uniform offered Alec and Katrina tea, and then invited them to wait inside a room in the basement of the foreign ministry. This was clearly an old storage room that had recently been repurposed for meetings and a bomb shelter.

All kinds of old, seemingly Soviet-era office furniture and equipment had been pushed against the back wall—chairs with hideous pea-soup-green imitation leather seats, Cyrillic typewriters, a mechanical calculator, and what must have been the first computers, from either the Soviet days or right after.

"You're right, my dear, old Soviet habits die hard," Alec observed. While Katrina had no memory of her first year of life in Soviet Uzbekistan, the habits of her parents, necessary adaptations for survival while living between the twin scorpions of Soviet authorities and virulently antisemitic Uzbek Muslims, had been intricately wired into her thinking and worldview.

Alec reached out and pressed a key on one of the typewriters.

"We would chuck this old stuff decades ago, but I guess when you've lived under Communism, you hold onto everything, never knowing when you might be able to use it again," Alec observed. "Reminds me of my grandparents—they lived through the Great Depression, and they would never throw out a piece of string."

"I read that some of Ukraine's state-owned businesses used typewriters until 2015 or so," Katrina observed. "I'm surprised they didn't start using those again, typewriters can't be hacked. Ah, that makes sense—these keys are in Russian. Obviously, everybody around here's speaking Ukrainian, even if like me they grew up speaking Russian."

She pointed as Alec studied the keys closely.

"There's no letter 'G,' which looks like a Greek Gamma. The Soviets banned the letter in 1933 because it was too nationalistic."

Alec looked back at her incredulously. "Killing all those Ukrainians wasn't enough, Stalin had to go and liquidate letters of the alphabet, too?"

Katrina shook her head. "Ukraine's fighting this war with whatever they can scrounge," she sighed. "The anti-drone stations on rooftops in this city are using machine guns manufactured during the Second World War. I heard they've got some Supreme Court justice manning the guns."

Alec was about to speculate about Clarence Thomas's marksmanship skills when the door to the office opened. Katrina and Alec were greeted by Maryan Kovalenko, a senior officer in the SBU, the federal security service of Ukraine. The SBU functioned as the equivalent of the FBI, as well as a national counterterrorism unit, and some intelligence-gathering duties.

"An honor to meet you, Ms. Leonidivna—and your husband," Kovalenko said with seemingly genuine awe, bowing his head and extending his hand to her. Alec shook his head.

"I'm always Steve Trevor," he sighed to himself.

"In a world full of secrets, your exploits against the world's evil men are too legendary to be completely hidden," Kovalenko said. Katrina almost blushed.

Kovalenko paused, as if internally debating whether to ask something. He leaned in and lowered his voice.

"If you are indeed the woman who killed Sergei Markov, I have a bottle of vodka I wanted to give you."

Katrina had tangled with Markov and his Russian mercenary team, an offshoot of the infamous Wagner Group, twice before. Markov, the team's leader, and Dimitri Guryanov, the team's gargantuan muscle, had met an untimely end at the hands of Katrina and their teammate Ward in Budapest a year earlier.

"I'm slightly tempted to see that bottle, but as far as we know, the Chechens killed Markov," Katrina lied with a straight face.

Kovalenko stared, smiling, and decided he wasn't done. "We were thrilled to hear that two of the notorious 'Iron Wolves' were killed in a Budapest brothel. But an operation like that seemed too difficult and precise for the Chechens," he added. He paused and decided to reveal a bit more. "And our intelligence did confirm that you and your team were in Budapest that week."

"Sightseeing," Katrina said with a smile. "I was close to going on maternity leave."

"You know what they say about pregnant women." Alec smiled. "They're always *Hungary.*"

Katrina couldn't completely suppress her groan. Guryanov completely missed Alec's pun, and nodded, accepting that his American guests weren't going to let him in on any secrets.

"Very well. The Russians did send the remaining members of the Iron Wolves against Zelensky. What was left of their team slipped into Ukraine with a backup leader, right before the invasion. Thanks to some intelligence from your NSA, we successfully ambushed them."

Katrina nodded, with a bit of satisfaction that the rest of the notorious Russian mercenary team had met up with fierce karma. "Well, we were plugged in to Russia's plans from the start. Did you take any alive?"

Guryanov held her stare, and declared, "They wanted to help Putin occupy Ukrainian soil. Now they are part of the Ukrainian soil."

Alec chuckled. "Well, as they sang in *Hamilton*, 'That's one less thing to worry about.'"

For some reason that prompted Guryanov to let out a laugh, and they settled into their chairs.

"What can you tell us about the Tattooed Man?" Katrina began.

"Our investigation is proceeding well, we've narrowed the suspects to everyone who has ever met him," Kovalenko declared in a dark deadpan.

He dropped a thick file onto the table and announced, "The story of Russia's Tattooed Man is a dark one, and I've seen plenty of darkness, even before the war began. This is everything we have on Yuri Voronin, which is being shared with you as a demonstration of our appreciation for all the American help in defending our country."

Katrina nodded appreciatively and started flipping through the files, the new ones written in Ukrainian and the old ones in Russian. Alec listened intently.

"Voronin was trained as a butcher in the industrial city of Samara, Russia, in the dying days of the Soviet Union and served briefly in the Russian army," Kovalenko reported. "It turns out he was a butcher in more than one way. Right before the pandemic, he was convicted on two counts of murder, two sisters who lived alone in a rural area."

The file had a newspaper clipping.

"Actually, that's not everything we have," Kovalenko corrected himself. "Some Russian websites published crime scene photos that were—well, trust me, no one needs to see that. The Tattooed Man was suspected in several other murders—homeless and prostitutes, mostly. Central Russia's own Jack the Ripper. After Russia ran into its manpower problems in the war, this beast was offered his freedom in exchange for six months of paid military service under Wagner's command."

Alec couldn't hide his shock and horror. "Wait, you're telling me they let a *serial killer* into their mercenary unit?"

"I'm sure Wagner was eager to hire an experienced killer," Kovalenko responded, poker-faced. "Reportedly, Putin pardoned a cannibal from Sakhalin so he could join the war effort. Russia will let anyone out, as long as they're willing to kill Ukrainians. Tens of thousands of inmates have taken the deal in the past year. Thankfully, my colleagues have ensured that for most of them, their new careers have been short."

"How'd this lunatic end up with you?" Alec asked.

"They gave him a rifle and sent him to attack Bakhmut," Kovalenko continued. "After that, we're not sure what happened. When our forces found him, he was surrounded by dead

Russians. The rumors are half-true. Some of his unit members appearing to have been shot by the enemy, but some stabbed. Those on scene strongly suspected the Tattooed Man had turned on his comrades and killed some of them."

Alec shook his head in disbelief.

"He surrendered, but apparently everyone wished they had just shot him when they found him," Kovalenko added. "No one thought he had any value to the Russians and wouldn't be worth much in a prisoner exchange. They sent him further west, and it's around then he acquired his notorious reputation. Speaking in tongues, starting fights with other prisoners. Hardened men who have seen combat found him odd and unnerving. He would talk to interrogators, but his stories kept changing. But we passed along the transcripts to the Americans, seeing if he said anything useful to you. Judging from your presence here, he did."

Katrina nodded. "We have software that is constantly scanning intelligence reports for words and phrases connected to one of our ongoing investigations. Apparently, the Tattooed Man said during one interrogation, 'I hear the Voices, and serve the Voices, and the whole war is a *bol'shoy prazdnik* for the Voices.'"

"Grand feast," Kovalenko translated, still a little confused. "Who or what are 'the Voices'?"

Alec exhaled.

"That, my friend, is a really big question. How would you react if I told you it was the Dark Side of the Force?"

CHAPTER FOUR

Katrina Leonidivna's first year of motherhood ensured that she had an overwhelming desire to wring the neck of some terrorist.

After giving birth to twins Harold and William—she and her husband Alec Flanagan constantly had to explain that no, they were not big fans of the British Royal Family—Katrina hit pause on her spectacular career as a senior case officer with the Central Intelligence Agency, assigned to a small, secretive group nicknamed the "Dangerous Clique."

Her friends were overjoyed at the arrival of Katrina and Alec's new twins, but many quietly predicted she would go insane dealing with breastfeeding, dirty diapers, sippy cups, spills, breast pumps, spit-up, and constant visits to the pediatrician. Alec had taken two months of paternity leave but went back to work and he now attempted to balance his new life as a daddy of two twin sons with duties with predictable hours, a slow-moving but methodical investigation, attempting to discern the meaning of newly discovered ties among several terrorist attacks in recent years.

But for about the first nine months, Katrina found motherhood, for all its stresses, headaches, and sleepless nights to be a welcome relief from the stresses of her old life. She even endured indignities like sore nipples when one of the twins chose to bite down with a gummy jaw. Katrina said she couldn't describe the feeling as relaxing, but a realization that for nearly three decades now, she felt like she had been running on an invisible treadmill, an endless game of whack-a-mole against the world's terrorist groups and support networks. Now her actions had immediate, concrete results. Harry and Will would sleep, or coo, or gurgle, or gaze back at her eyes.

Katrina had always been a type-A personality, driven to succeed by the guilt trips of Bukhari Jewish parents who had immigrated to the United States when she was one. Some of her exhaustion with her career reflected that the Dangerous Clique's work in the past few years had lived up to its label, taking on everyone from an obscure Turkmenistan cult that had initially been mistaken for Islamist terrorism, to a mad virologist who was offering genetically engineered pathogens that could target those with particular genes, and then, during her pregnancy, a long-forgotten foe hell-bent on revenge for the team's first mission.

Compared to all that, spit-up was a mild inconvenience.

Since March 20, 1995—the day that then-foreign exchange student Katrina had witnessed the sarin gas attack upon the Tokyo subway system, committed by the doomsday cult Aum Shinrikyo, Katrina felt a calling—no, an obligation—to protect others who couldn't protect themselves. Normal, happy, well-adjusted people preferred to not think too much about the likes of Shoko Asahara, Osama bin Laden, Abu Bakr al-Baghdadi, Vladimir Putin, or Tiffany and Madison Strauss—maniacs consumed by ambitions that could only be satisfied by mass death and suffering on a grand scale, constantly plotting to turn their visions to reality. The fact that you live in a world that has people who want to kill you, for reasons you can barely comprehend, is too frightening and unnerving a thought to contemplate even rarely, never mind regularly. Most people just put it out of their minds.

But by early adulthood, Katrina realized that she couldn't put it out of her mind. She would find the threats and put them out of business, one way or another.

Now what Katrina sought to protect was no longer abstract like "the public" or "innocent people" or even "the United States." She had two babies to protect, alongside Alec. And for a little while, Katrina wondered if she wanted to go back to the Agency.

But week by week, the itch to return to the office grew stronger. Alec's description of his investigation in partnership with the FBI, which had seemed like a wild goose chase with supernatural overtones, started to bear fruit. Katrina's sabbatical started shortly before the Russian invasion of Ukraine, and the news was full of reports of Chinese saber-rattling about Taiwan. Katrina knew the CIA would be almost as busy as it had been during the height of the War on Terror.

And she didn't like the idea of the Agency, her teammates, and her friends, charging into a dangerous world without her.

***

Katrina and Alec's one-year-old twins, Harry and Will, seemingly settled into the new routine of day care, although Katrina knew that their trip to Ukraine had disrupted the twins' nascent rhythm of life. Harry and Will had enjoyed the care of the quartet of the world's best babysitters, all four grandparents—Abraham and Ziva Leonidivna, and Joseph and Aneta Flanagan. The Leonidivnas had flown up from Miami Beach, Florida; the Flanagans from Nags Head, North Carolina.

The grandparenting quartet relished their duties. Alec remarked, with subtle sarcasm, that his sons were blessed with dual servings of state-of-the-art mid-1970s Bukharan Jew and American philosophies of childcare.

But God had blessed Katrina and Alec with children relatively late in life, and this meant their parents became grandparents later than usual.

Both sets of parents had always gotten along, but now the Flanagans seemed a little concerned when Abraham held one of the children. Katrina surmised that one of the two one-year-olds had nearly squirmed out of his grandfather's grasp at one point—most likely Harry, who was the squiggly little inchworm who was so flexible he could seemingly bend in half backward. Alec had noted that his younger son, by a matter of minutes, had a bad daredevil habit of suddenly thrusting himself backward with wild abandon.

"He gets that from you," Alec cracked.

Meanwhile, Abraham and Ziva pointed out that both Joseph and Aneta seemed to be having more memory lapses—forgetting what they came into a room to get, taking longer to remember names, and dates, and places.

"Dad, you do that too," Katrina observed.

But she mentioned it to Alec, who said he had noticed the trend as well.

Was this just another sign of getting older or a sign of Alzheimer's? Was that little wobble as they walked—normal aging or a worry for a potential fall?

Katrina realized that one of the reasons she spent so much time thinking about terrorists and other foreign threats is that the problem they presented was much simpler—find them and arrange an appropriate drone strike. Deciding when it was time for a parent to give up their car keys, and having that conversation, was much more difficult.

CHAPTER FIVE

LIBERTY CAMPUS
TYSON'S CORNER, VIRGINIA
AUGUST 14, 2023

Katrina drove to Liberty Campus for the first time since returning from Ukraine. It felt like preparation for the trip to Kyiv began almost immediately after she returned to the Dangerous Clique's office at the Liberty Crossing Intelligence Campus at 1500 Tysons McLean Drive, home of the National Counterterrorism Center, the Office of the Director of National Intelligence, and in the federal office building just across the complex, the incongruously located U.S. Farm Credit Administration. Alec liked to joke that someday some confused spy was going to break in and steal a bunch of USDA loan documents.

Katrina arrived early, well before almost all of the building's other workers—but to her surprise, Ward Rutledge had arrived in the locked office—the "vault."

"You still work here?" Katrina joked. "I thought you never left Williamsburg anymore!"

"It's a special occasion," Ward said with a laugh. Katrina's stocky teammate rose from his seat a little slower than she was used to his moving and enveloped her in a bear hug.

"I'm so relieved you and Alec are in one piece," he said, holding her in the hug. "I don't like you guys being out there without me watching your back." He didn't want to say it, but he had heard about their near-miss with the Russian missile on the road to the fortress, and it had shaken him.

"We're very careful when you're not watching our back, Ward," Katrina said with a smile.

"Hey, gunfights, knife fights, fistfights—I'm your man. But some giant Russian bomb falling out of the sky?" Ward murmured. "Not even I can knock those away." After a moment, he defused the tension of his genuine worry. "Hey, I got you something. Welcome back!"

Katrina opened the small box and removed a coffee mug with the label "World's Second-Best Mom."

"Second Best?"

Ward smiled. "I'm married, and Marie and I four kids ahead of you! You and Alec are off to a good start, though."

"Two is plenty, thank you!" Katrina exclaimed. She knew at her age, the odds were strongly against another successful pregnancy; God had delivered two miracles simultaneously, and it would be greedy to ask for more.

"Where is everybody, anyway?" Ward grumbled. "I come all the way up here into the office, and everybody's out?"

"Alec dropped off the twins at day care, then he and Elaine have meetings at the Bureau, then they're coming over here. I think Dee was at Fort Meade again this morning, and I guess Raquel's late."

Ward chuckled. "I'm sure Alec's having a blast tagging along with the FBI."

Katrina unlocked the door to her office. "He keeps complaining they don't stop for cherry pie like he thought they would."

***

FBI HEADQUARTERS
AUGUST 14, 2023

Alec had spent much of his teenage years dreaming of being an FBI agent, even before his junior year of high school, when his friend Sarina Locke seemed to disappear without a trace. His image of the Bureau had been shaped heavily by the portrayal of the FBI in popular culture—smart detectives in suits, the men with all the answers, the guys who could walk into any situation, from a serial killer who paired livers with chianti to the murder of the homecoming queen in a small town, and follow the clues, methodically and relentlessly, until they get their man.

But the disappearance of Sarina Locke was never solved, and the more Alec learned about the reality of the FBI, the more he saw it as just another unresponsive bureaucracy. Alec had seethed about how his hometown had chosen to believe Sarina had run away, and he concluded the Bureau was one more institution bound by rules and regulations and the status quo, all too comfortable with allowing cases to go cold, filed away in the basement. No, Alec concluded he needed to work someplace where the rules were more malleable, the mission came first, and no one ever had to worry about persuading a jury.

And now he was working alongside an FBI special agent who sometimes got teased for an appearance and demeanor reminiscent of Dana Scully, a comparison that Elaine Kopek didn't particularly appreciate. Working as the FBI's liaison to the Dangerous Clique had been among the most fulfilling, consequential, and unpredictable work of her career. But within the halls of the Bureau, the team was considered reckless, far too secretive, poorly supervised by the CIA management, and far too casual about operating and using deadly force on American soil.

Elaine learned she had a reputation within the Bureau as the Clique's designated driver, circus ringmaster, and enabler.

And now she was alongside Alec, investigating whether the team's enemies over the past decades could have had some sort of connection that was not easily explained, perhaps something even supernatural, otherworldly, or divine. Elaine Kopek realized she was never going to escape the Dana Scully jokes.

But on this day, Elaine was required to check in with various superiors to ensure this project wasn't the wild goose chase that she had been warned about—meaning she and Alec, freshly returned from his short jaunt to Ukraine, had a long morning of meetings. And those meetings meant long stretches waiting outside the offices of the higher-level FBI officials. They had been sitting outside the office of the executive assistant director for the national security branch for twenty minutes.

"Busy day?" Alec asked the assistant director's secretary, flashing a little irritation.

"It always is," the secretary responded. Her tone suggested she would be content to see Alec grow old in the waiting room.

"Well, I understand you guys have gotta investigate everybody running for president these days," Alec sighed.

The secretary glared at Alec as if he had just belched "The Star-Spangled Banner." Elaine cleared her throat and decided to distract Alec by asking a question that had been on her mind for a while.

"Does Raquel have Ward down in Williamsburg training a team to replace you?"

Alec turned in surprise and forgot about how he was irritated by the secretary. He sat down next to Elaine and lowered his voice.

"I thought my team was supposed to be good at keeping secrets."

"I thought you knew your team's FBI liaison is good at uncovering secrets," Elaine shot back.

Alec sighed and stared out the ceiling.

"Yeah, even before our field trip to Ukraine, Katrina and I were talking more seriously about downshifting into something closer to desk jobs," he sighed. "I mean, we've got kids now. God forbid, we're out on some mission together, and something happens to us, we're leaving orphans behind." For a moment, he thought again about that Russian bomb that had landed far too close to their Range Rover.

Elaine nodded. "That sounds like a difficult choice, but a sign you have your priorities in the right place."

Alec erupted a variety of sounds, groans, grunts and mumbles that never quite turned into actual words.

"Eloquent," Elaine observed dryly.

Alec knocked his fist against his thigh and tried again.

"Half the time I can't wait for Katrina and me to pass the baton to someone else," Alec muttered. "Just sweep it all off my desk, all the terrorists, all the threats, all the lunatics, just dump it all on somebody else's desk and let them deal with it! Coming up on twenty years of the Dangerous Clique? We've done more than our share to keep the world from spinning off its axis."

"Two babies that just turned one will do that to you." Elaine chuckled. "What's going on the other half of the time?"

"What if whoever we pass the baton to isn't as good as us?" Alec asked. "I mean, can you imagine it? Katrina and I retire from the team, settle into cushy desk jobs with normal hours, get to live as one big happy family... and then one day Capitol Hill gets hit with sarin, or Manhattan gets nuked, or somebody figures out Hell-Summoner's biological weapons formula for Jews-Be-Gone. What's left of our normal life like then? Knowing that maybe if I had stuck around, maybe things would have turned out different? I'd have to go live as a hermit in the woods—assuming I could live with myself at all."

Elaine made a mental note about the vague but dark allusion by Alec.

"So, you think that if you change your job, the world might blow up," Elaine summarized skeptically.

Alec sighed. "Well, the other part of me worries that whoever replaces me will actually be better than me, and I'll be forgotten. The world just keeps going on without me."

"So you want to rest, and you want to be irreplaceable."

Alec thought for a moment and concluded Elaine had efficiently summarized his dilemma.

"Yeah, I guess."

Elaine shook her head, as if Alec were being ridiculous.

"Pick one."

Alec was about to object when the secretary finally said the assistant director was ready to see them.

CHAPTER SIX

Katrina looked over Ward's shoulder, as he sat at his now-almost-abandoned desk, and the family portrait of Ward, Marie, and their six kids, now several years out of date.

"You know, it used to be when I asked how you're doing with those kids on the farm, I meant your kids on your farm," she said with a chuckle. "Now I mean those other kids on *the* farm."

Ward laughed.

"I thought this was a good time to be on sabbatical from the action," Ward sighed, marveling at the way the world could change without warning. "Changing of the guard, you can almost feel the earth shifting under your feet."

"And here I naively thought we had stopped those gathering five storms that Sanai kept rambling about," Katrina sighed.

Ward turned in his chair.

"Hey, we did!" Ward snickered, raising an eyebrow. "Instead of dealing with the Strauss sisters blowing up New York City, the world is only facing a Russian invasion of Ukraine, a global food shortage because the ports are blocked, a global energy crisis making everything more expensive, crackdowns from Tehran to Beijing, and now these panics about hackers and some massive breach every few weeks."

As Ward listed them off, he counted on his fingers, and when he reached five, he mockingly opened his eyes wide, and mouthed, "uh-oh!" Katrina laughed.

"We saved the day, and the five gathering storms arrived anyway," Katrina lamented.

Raquel finally arrived, seemingly overflowing with exasperation and eager to put down a heavy grocery bag and her usual satchel of wallet, keys, breath mints, and other accoutrements of the cornucopia of necessities kept in women's purses.

"Welcome back!" Raquel exclaimed, trying to find a clear patch of desk to place the grocery bag.

"I had planned this a big welcome-back lunch for today, but apparently today is First-Time Driver Day on the Beltway, and all of them decided to learn how to merge right in front of me," she fumed. "Simultaneously."

Katrina nodded. She realized that on mornings like this one when Alec left early, she would be calculating the earliest possible moment to drop off Harry and Will at the day care, recognizing that each passing minute increased her likelihood of getting stuck in Washington's notorious commuter traffic. Throughout her year off, she had watched spy thriller movies with Alec and they scoffed each time there was a car chase in the Washington area that careened through strangely empty roads. In real life, the escaping spies would have hit gridlock and a bumper-to-bumper virtual parking lot at the first on-ramp and been apprehended with ease.

"I'm glad you've remembered at least one of your log-in passwords," Raquel observed. "After that bomb in Ukraine, I may want to crazy glue you to that desk. How did it feel to be back in the field?"

Katrina tried to soften the blow, but her joke let slip what was on her mind.

"Honestly, I still don't feel a hundred percent back to what I was before maternity leave, but if we came back in one piece, we must have done something right," Katrina sighed. "Beyond that... it feels like the world's falling apart. I thought you said you would take care of this place while I was gone!"

Raquel grimaced. She and Katrina had been friends for so long, that the chain of command had effectively disappeared; Katrina could vent her grievances and not sound insubordinate. From Katrina's tone, Raquel could tell she was *mostly* joking... but she had returned to find a bunch of fires the thought had been extinguished had reignited.

"When you say 'this place,' do you mean our team, the Agency, the country, or the world?"

"Any of them, all of them," Katrina answered dryly. "Take your pick."

"Hey, our team is still operating!" Raquel said. "And that was not an easy magic trick to pull off under Stern. We're just in more management-friendly low-key assignments. You were out on maternity leave, I sent Alec out with Elaine to Mulder-and-Scully the weird pattern among our enemies. Ward's out training your younger replacements. As for the CIA itself, I can't help it if management changes come out of the blue!"

The resignation of the most recent CIA director, Barbara Stern, was a quiet concession that she had always been an awkward fit for the job. The initial public statement about Stern's departure included the Washington boilerplate declaration that Stern was resigning to "spend more time with her family." However, members of the media noted Stern was unmarried, had no children, no siblings, and her parents had long since passed away—raising the question of just what family Stern was so eager to spend time with, since they apparently didn't exist. In response to reporters' inquiries, the Agency's public affairs office identified some distant cousins.

The factors forcing Stern's departure were a bit like Ernest Hemingway's description of how he went bankrupt—gradually, and then suddenly. Stern had feared turning into the administration's designated scapegoat for the chaotic images of withdrawal from Afghanistan, as well as the botched investigation of an attempted truck bomber at the front gate of CIA headquarters. The successful disruption of the Strauss Twins' plot to bomb the Freedom Tower was quickly forgotten in the aftermath of the fall of Kabul. While the Agency had scored enormous amounts of actionable intelligence about Russia's invasion of Ukraine, the administration found that conflict growing into a persistent headache with no quick fixes.

And then there was the mysterious "Kobold" attack. From the moment Katrina came back, it seemed like everyone in the Agency had heard about it, but no one seemed to know anything specific about it.

Stern's replacement, Jonathan Boyles, was a distinguished career diplomat whom all of Washington had expected to be named Secretary of State in the new administration. Boyles brought to the job years of experience negotiating with Russians, the Chinese and the Taliban, but had absolutely no experience in the world of intelligence. Before his confirmation hearing, a senator from the opposition party was overheard asking Boyles, "Are you absolutely sure the president didn't mix up his cue cards, and you were supposed to be running the State Department?" Boyles laughed, but the senator didn't.

And so far, the new director seemed ... fine. He ran meetings smoothly, hadn't yet taken any crazy or controversial stances, and seemed to genuinely listen when others briefed him. But a lot of intelligence officials, at home and abroad, wondered if the new guy would have the stomach for the rougher parts of the job.

Over the years, Katrina and Raquel had fallen into the habit of greeting new directors with a shrug. They came and went, each one arriving with some bold vision and new plan to modernize the Agency, which usually meant reorganizing directorates and mission centers; almost all of them retired after a couple of years, with the planned reforms usually half-enacted and soon to be scrapped by the next director. Raquel once cracked that all

CIA organization charts should be drawn on Etch A Sketches, so everyone could just shake it and redraw new charts as needed. Most of the time, these proposed, debated, half-enacted, and abandoned plans had little impact on her team anyway. Ward once summarized the Dangerous Clique's philosophy as, "Just stay out of everybody else's way and focus on killing the right bad people."

But Katrina concluded the sense of anxiety in the halls that remembered before she went on maternity leave had worsened in her absence. The U.S. mission in Afghanistan had ended about as badly as possible. Some exceptional intelligence-gathering work hadn't managed to prevent a brutal Russian invasion of Ukraine. A particular former president kept railing that the Agency was part of a sinister "deep state." Not to mention the Strauss twins nearly blowing up lower Manhattan, a narrowly avoided catastrophe that the country had forgotten with almost ludicrous speed.

CHAPTER SEVEN

LIBERTY CAMPUS
AUGUST 14, 2023

Shortly before lunch, Dee had returned from Fort Meade, and after lunch, Alec and Elaine arrived.

Katrina and Alec kissed, and Alec asked how her morning had been.

"Same as usual, the world's on fire," Katrina gushed, in a cheerful tone that didn't match her words. "How were your meetings over at the Bureau?"

Alec shook his head in frustration. "I miss the peace and quiet of Ukraine."

Raquel gestured for Ward and Dee to take seats around the small conference table in the adjacent room.

"With Ward up here, and all of us together in the office for the first time in—God, it seems like weeks — why don't you two walk us through what you've got so far?"

Elaine and Alec exchanged glares of frustration as they settled in their seats.

Elaine spoke first. "Well, the first problem is that the further we get in our investigation, the further apart our interpretations of the evidence get."

"The only thing Elaine is wrong about is everything," Alec chirped.

Elaine shot him a look of weapons-grade condescension. "Traditionally, when the FBI engages in pattern analysis, the Bureau's assessment will stick to the planet Earth."

"There are more things in heaven and earth, Horatio, than are dreamt of in your philosophy." Alec tried not to sound condescending and failed.

Elaine turned to Katrina. "Your husband remembers one Shakespeare quote and he thinks he's Sherlock Holmes." Katrina laughed.

"Okay, what have you learned?" Dee exclaimed. "The seventh floor and NSA have me up to my neck in Kobold stuff, I haven't been in the loop."

"What's the Kobold stuff?" Katrina asked pointedly. Dee exchanged a look with Raquel, as if asking for permission to tell her.

"We'll tell you later," Raquel said, slightly curtly. "I've been working on getting you all cleared to hear about that." Katrina responded with a look of incredulous exasperation.

"Should I start or not?" Elaine asked Alec.

Alec gestured with his palm, as if offering the floor. "Sure. You go first, and I'll respond in the form of a Battle Rap." He went over to a computer and opened up a secure file, full of images, transcripts, and grainy security photos, and transferred the display on the large screen on the wall.

"A bit less than two years ago, shortly after we wrapped up our fun at the Freedom Tower, I determined that four of this team's enemies over the past twenty years—oceans and decades apart, with no known connection to each other—have separately referred to 'the Voices.'" Elaine began. "Not just referring to voices in their head, but '*The* Voices.' The 'the' is important. It's like part of the title, like 'the Batman' or 'the *National Review*.'"

"It's just *National Review*," Alec muttered behind her.

Elaine ignored him. "The first reference was in March 2003. Linus Strauss, shortly before he died, shouted, 'The Voices were right, the throne is empty, which means I can sit upon it.'"

Elaine used the mouse and opened up a file, playing a short snippet of audio from a toppled video recorder that had been left running in an adjacent room. Strauss sounded unhinged, thrilled, in the throes of a combination of rage and ecstasy.

Dee squinted. "Strauss was nuts, what he said back then—"

Elaine ignored the interruption and pressed on. "April 2, 2019, Atarsa sleeper cell member Norman Fein, while being interrogated by Ward, said, quote, 'The Voices need it this way.'"

Dee turned to Ward, who nodded. "I had asked the twisted bastard why he and his lunatic buddies weren't shooting people or building bombs. Apparently, whatever Atarsa worshipped, it—or *they*—wanted people stabbed."

Dee recoiled in horror. "*Jesuchristo!* Did he say why?"

Ward rubbed his beard. "I got the feeling they wanted people to die slowly."

Before Dee could let out another exclamation at the pitch-black motivations of their old enemies, Elaine continued.

"The third case was Alec's account of Atarsa leader Sarvar Rashin in Cyprus. 'Let me give you a final lesson from the Voices: There are no consequences, no cosmic justice. Only chaos.'"

"She didn't say any more?"

"Her monologue was interrupted when I shot her in the head," Katrina declared, with just a hint of satisfaction.

Dee nodded, like Sarvar had just offered an acceptable excuse.

"In the fourth case, the American mercenary Cody Washington, while part of the Strauss sisters' attack on the Freedom Tower. Shortly before he died, he said to Ward he was being told to do something by 'the Voices from Cyprus,' which I admit it is a pretty spectacular coincidence," Elaine concluded.

Dee's mouth was open, shocked at the implications of four of their enemies, going back nearly two decades, all describing some sort of demonic commanding force.

"Dee, I can see your tonsils," Alec quipped. "Now, I know you're wondering if it's just us who heard our enemies describing the Voices. The answer is no; Elaine and I found at least two other cases. The first was Yuri Voronin, the Tattooed Man in Russia, who either slit his own throat or had it slit for him shortly before we arrived. Yeah, that's suspicious to me, too."

Raquel shook her head. "I realize dead men tell no tales, but the trip didn't generate any useful leads?"

Alec and Katrina exchanged a look.

"We're still reviewing all those tattoos on him, look for some sort of symbols or messages, but ... so far, not much."

Raquel grumbled a bit. "Oh, I'm going to love justifying the cost and risk of sending you two to Ukraine to get 'not much.' What else do you have?"

"The other case was in Libya," Alec said, bringing another file to the screen. "Back during the glory days of ISIS, there was this rising star in their ranks called Arslanbek Murgen. An Iraqi Turkman, ruthless, merciless—picture Abu Musab al-Zarqawi on Weight Watchers. Then after a few years, his comrades excommunicated him."

"Excommunicated?" Ward asked incredulously. "Just what the hell do you have to do to get thrown out of ISIS? What, did he join a Bible study? Serve red wine with fish?"

"You're close — blasphemy!" Alec said, pointing. He enlarged the CIA's files on Murgen on the screen—a passport photo, a few grainy photos from a drone, a psychological profile completed by his targeting officer. "One day instead of worshipping Allah and all the usual Islamic State stuff, his ISIS buddies discover he's been leading a small group in secret rituals worshipping something he called ... 'the Voices.'"

Elaine picked up the narration. "So Arslanbek Murgen and his followers get exiled into the desert, and they set up operations in Libya, where they formed their own offshoot splinter faction, which they call 'al-Aswat'—which is Arabic for 'the Voices.'"

"Sounds like we need to talk to this Arslanbek Murgen character," Ward said.

"Well, that's going to be tough without a Ouiji board," Alec quipped. "About a year after al-Aswat formed, they deployed out of their base of operations in a convoy, and the U.S. Air Force spotted them and thought they were ISIS. A whole bunch of Hellfire missiles turned Arslanbek Murgen and all his followers into vulture chow."

Ward grinned. "Hooah! Glad the Chair Force is pulling their weight! At least that story has a happy ending."

"Everything we know about Murgen and al-Aswat comes from accounts of captured ISIS members, interviews at Gitmo and black sites, that sort of thing," Elaine summarized. "The weird thing is, his old ISIS buddies liked him a lot—they talk about him leaving like the breakup of the Beatles."

Katrina stared at the work of her husband and Elaine. "If we tell anyone this, they'll think we're nuts."

"Yes, it was absolutely delightful to talk vaguely around all this in the meetings today," Elaine smiled.

Raquel leaned back in her chair and looked pensive.

"Before he died, Merlin told me he thought our work had stumbled across something—something beyond ... mortal men and women," she said, her eyes drifting to the picture on the wall with the late CIA deputy director Harold Hare, an unusually colorful personality in the history of the Agency's leadership. "Something like ... God and the Devil, or angels and demons, or maybe something we don't have names for yet. That over the course of human history, something had been trying to lift us up, above our worst impulses, toward something greater, and something else was trying to steer all of humanity to a very bad end."

"Satan?" Dee asked.

"Maybe," Raquel replied. "Some of us would use the term 'The Adversary.'" Dee didn't pick up on that particular reference.

"My theory is that it's less of a conscious being than an intermittent-to-constant psychokinetic tug in the moral wrong direction," Alec declared. "The Dark Side of the Force. A form of temptation and inspiration to malevolence that becomes so intertwined with a person it's hard to tell where they stop and the dark side begins. Like two globs of chewing gum stuck together, the person's original malice and this ... " He paused, wondering how everyone would react to the next word. " ... *demonic* influence become really hard to separate."

"That's some pretty heavy theological implications to put into a PDB," Katrina dryly observed.

"All of our enemies had their personal demons," Alec declared coolly. "Maybe not all of them were metaphorical."

Katrina turned and studied Raquel's contemplative face. "You're not seriously thinking of sending a report up a chain contending there's a supernatural link amongst some of the world's terrorist groups?"

"My dear, are you any more reassured to think that everybody who joined al-Qaeda, ISIS, Atarsa and the Brotherhood of Eblis just chose to be that way?" Alec countered.

He turned to Raquel. "The English word 'Satan' comes from a Hebrew term, 'Hashatan,' which roughly translates to 'the Adversary,'" Alec said, revealing he understood Raquel's word choice. "We've spent years going toe-to-toe with terrorists and aspiring mass-murdering maniacs. Why is it so unthinkable that our adversaries are, in one form or another, shaped by *The* Adversary?"

Raquel waved her hand. "I know, I know, you think old Merlin was going senile by then—"

"Actually, I'm afraid he wasn't," Katrina corrected. "And the old man had to go and die of Covid before he could explain any of this to us."

DRAFT COPY—DO NOT FORWARD
ELAINE KOPEK
FEDERAL BUREAU OF INVESTIGATION

Ideas can spread as virally as any organism. Based upon what we have uncovered, the most likely explanation for multiple terrorist group members and leaders, with no easily identifiable connection, separately making verbal references to "the Voices" is that "the Voices" have become something of an urban legend within the criminal and terrorist underground.

Of the half-dozen figures recorded referring to "the Voices," five of them are dead, four killed in conflict shortly after making those statements. Yuri Voronin, the Russian known as the "Tattooed Man," was killed shortly before Alec and Katrina could interrogate him. At this time, there is no clear evidence he was killed to prevent him from answering our questions.

The remaining individual, Norman Fein, is currently serving a life sentence in the U.S Penitentiary Lee near Pennington Gap, Virginia, on convictions for murder, attempted murder and providing material support or resources to a terrorist organization. He pled insanity, and

during the trial his legal team's psychological experts contended Fein was hearing voices that urged him to join and support the terrorist group Atarsa. The jury did not find that argument convincing. Fein's lawyers have repeatedly filed appeals.

An interview with Fein at the penitentiary did not offer much additional light on the subject, and certainly nothing that was verifiable. He contended that he heard "the Voices" shortly after going through the Isoptera counseling program, which was secretly a recruitment operation for the Atarsa terrorist group. He said the Voices pledged to empower Fein to overcome all of the challenges and injustices in his life, in exchange for blood sacrifices; Fein's first sacrifice to the Voices was his grandmother, who he lived with. Fein said the Voices required him to kill her with a knife, and that it was important to feel fear before her death. Fein described the Voices as otherworldly beings who were fed by the human sensations of fear, terror, rage, and sadism.

The research onto the psychology of terrorist group members largely lacks substance and rigor; the better studies have concluded that there is no one personality type or trait that indicates someone is likely to join a terrorist group. Israeli psychology professor Ariel Merari is one of the few people in the world to have collected systematic, empirical data on a significant sample of suicide bombers, and he concluded, "In the majority, you find none of the risk factors normally associated with suicide, such as mood disorders or schizophrenia, substance abuse or history of attempted suicide."

Schizophrenia has been diagnosed in one individual who attempted to join ISIS, and Jerry Drake Varnell, who attempted to detonate a vehicle bomb in an alley adjacent to BancFirst in downtown Oklahoma City. But most schizophrenics are not terrorists, and most terrorists are not schizophrenics.

With that said, terrorist ideologies provide a set of beliefs that justify and mandate certain malevolent and antisocial behaviors. While a terrorist may feel compelled to blow up a bus full of commuters, some part of him—they are more often, but not exclusively, men—may feel some residual guilt, doubt, or inner conflict about the harmful consequences of his actions. It may be easier for the terrorist to believe that someone else is making them take violent and destructive actions; references to "the Voices" could just be an updated version of "the Devil made me do it."

At some point, likely shortly after 9/11, someone in the global terrorist underground invented or hallucinated the existence of these "Voices," which he shared with his colleagues. The concept spread, like a game of telephone, to groups as disparate as "al-Aswat" and domestic extremists like Cody Washington.

Now numerous terrorist groups and extremists believe that a malevolent supernatural force is

their ally in their efforts to commit mass-casualty attacks.

***

DRAFT COPY—FORWARD WHEREEVER YOU LIKE, I DON'T CARE
ALEC FLANAGAN

With all due respect, the analysis of my colleague, FBI special agent Elaine Kopek, is so far away from the most plausible answers that the distance may be best measured with the Hubble Space Telescope.

The available information points to four possible scenarios:

Possibility one: While I realize this will be incomprehensible to those in our government who are secular rationalists who choose to dismiss all organized religions as superstitious mumbo-jumbo with no basis in reality, "the Voices" are the demon Legion, described in Mark 5:1 to 5:13. (Jesus asked him, "What is your name?" He replied, "My name is Legion; for we are many.")

Possibility two, a variant of possibility one: "The Voices" are some other demonic figure or force.

Possibility three: "The Voices" are some other extradimensional or extraterrestrial force, connected to the unidentified flying objects that the U.S. Air Force has investigated on and off over the past decades.

I would note that during the events of the Atarsa terrorism attacks, there was a noticeable pattern of hallucinations and visions of giant insects:

- In Turkmenistan, Atarsa had a secret underground altar with a creepy giant insect statue.
- The Atarsa agent that Katrina and I ran into in Turkmenistan contorted his body in disturbing, insect-like ways.
- Katrina described nightmares of a giant insect preparing to attack me.
- During his fight with Fabrice Vuscovi, my colleague Edward Rutlidge briefly believed she had transformed into a giant termite-like creature.
- After Atarsa poisoned former CIA director William Peck, during his drug-induced hallucination, he cried, "We've got thousands of people coming into our country every day, any one of them could be a bug."

Perhaps the true form of one of "the Voices" is something resembling an insect. But I would note that based upon everything we have seen, "the Voices" do not have a tangible physical form or presence. If "the Voices" exist and they are alive, they are a form of life we do not have the capability to observe or measure yet.

But we've discovered life existing in forms that we once thought impossible. There are several forms of bacteria, such as Shewanella or

Geobacter, that are "electric bacteria"—that is, they consume electrons harvested from rocks and metals to live instead of sugars or proteins or other nutrients. Strain 121 bacteria can reproduce at 250 degrees Fahrenheit and survive up to 266 degrees—temperatures once thought impossible for sustaining life. Tardigrades are microscopic multicellular animals that can survive 1,000 times as much radioactivity as most other creatures, live for a decade without water, briefly survive temperatures lower than liquid nitrogen and hotter than boiling water, and even survived exposure to the vacuum of space.

And that leads me to…

Possibility Four: The Voices are a conscious, communicating form of life that previous generations described as demons, and their relationship with humanity is parasitic.

What if the closest thing the Voices have to a physical form is the electric signals between the neurons of the human brain? What if the Voices are in fact a form of life that only physically manifested in those hard-to-measure electrical signals in the human brain, and whose effect is measured in human thoughts?

People might ask, "If the Voices exist, why haven't I heard them?" But…what if you already have? What if you've ever been tempted to do something malevolent but resisted the temptation? Where did that thought or temptation come from?

As for Norman Fein's claim that the Voices are "fed by the human sensations of fear, terror, rage, and sadism," those sound like the emotions that result in the stimulation of the amygdala and hypothalamus, resulting in the release of hormones like adrenaline and cortisol. What if to the Voices, those brain chemicals are like bread—a necessary form of nourishment? Or something more like potato chips—a particularly enjoyable form of sustenance where the appetite becomes hard to control? Or what if the fear and rage and sadism brain chemicals are something akin to cocaine to the Voices—something they're addicted to?

For decades, the United States and the world have lived with a terrorism problem. But what if all along, we've been trying to deal with a Voices problem?

CHAPTER EIGHT

Alec completed his counter-presentation, which included connecting through to the Internet and using clips from *Aliens*, *Invasion of the Body Snatchers*, the bug-man from *Men in Black*, pantomiming and mimicking a demonic possession, and images of a giant and a dwarf from an old television show.

At its completion, a flabbergasted Dee asked, "And you believe all that?"

Alec stopped short and thought for a moment.

"I don't believe it, but I suspect it," Alec declared firmly. "You're a bit younger than me, Dee, but I'll bet you feel it too. I feel like I grew up in a flawed but generally sane world. We won the Cold War. The Berlin Wall came down. History had ended, Francis Fukuyama told us so. China was opening up. The U.N. actually did something about Saddam Hussein! And then somewhere along the line, somebody opened up Pandora's Box. At this rate, my sons are going to grow up in a worldwide circus of chaos. Terrorism, viruses, wars, extremist ethno-nationalist movements at home and abroad—what the hell is this? This isn't the future we were supposed to get! I mean, these Millennials and Gen-Z... they don't realize how bright the future once seemed!"

Ward closed his eyes, and sang, *"Right here, right now, watching the world wake up from history! Oh, I saw the decade in, when it seemed the world could change in the blink of an eye!"* Raquel and Dee laughed as Alec nodded and joined in.

An exasperated Katrina turned to Elaine. "You realize we're going to go brief the seventh floor, and we're going to start with *The X-Files* and conclude with a musical number."

Alec chuckled, recognizing how absurd his presentation sounded to skeptical ears. "I don't know how, and I don't know when, but somebody broke the world—they cracked it open, and something else was able to slip through," he continued. "Maybe it's like *Stranger Things* or something. Evil has always existed, but something let more of it in at some point—we've been living with it on steroids lately."

Raquel froze, thinking of her own thoughts when Merlin had first told her his theory that something beyond man was influencing their efforts to stop terrorists. She had momentarily wondered if something about the worst terror attack in American history had somehow altered reality in ways humanity couldn't quite measure, that some hidden capacity for good and evil had been unlocked on that dark day—that the rule book for human behavior had been rewritten in the face of such vivid, unforgettable horror and heroism.

She shook herself away from the thought, as Katrina asked Alec when he would be leaving for day care.

"Wait, I did drop off, so you're supposed to ... " He belatedly realized which day of the week it was. "Ah, that's right, I'm on drop-off *and* pick-up duty on Mondays! Time zone change has me not knowing what day it is!" He grimaced. He checked his watch. "Considering traffic, I should leave ... eh, fifteen minutes ago." He kissed Katrina, then turned to Elaine.

"You think I'm nuts, don't you?"

"I've always thought you were nuts," Elaine shot back, with a smile. "What's different in this case is that now I'm hoping you're nuts."

***

Before Katrina left for the day, she thought she had heard a commotion in the office down the hall. To be heard through a vault door, whatever was happening inside had to be loud. She realized that door led to a small office that had been temporarily loaned to the Director of National Intelligence's Office of the Executive Secretariat.

Patrick Horne's office—the man who had once been Alec's best friend, who had quit the Dangerous Clique midway into its first mission, and who had turned into her team's intermittent rival and critic.

Katrina knocked on the door. "Everything okay in there?"

Patrick Horne opened the door. He looked disheveled, like he had grabbed the sides of his head and tried to pull out his hair. His tie was loosened, one shirt flap was out of the front of his pants, and he was a little flush.

"Katrina! I didn't know you were back in the office!" Patrick's face cycled through the emotions of surprise, embarrassment, and elation in a matter of seconds.

"Back online, back on duty," she said with a shrug. "You doing okay in there?"

Patrick looked down and realized he was a mess.

"Oh!" He chuckled. "Oh, yes. Well, I guess it's pretty obvious. We just got word that an op went south. Nobody's dead, thank heavens, but it's a major setback. Lot of work down the drain. I was..."

He opened the office door a bit more and showed he had swept everything off his desk in a rage and thrown books around the room.

"I blew my stack," he admitted. "I just lost it, and just... had a tantrum. This is really embarrassing."

Katrina looked at Patrick and realized he could be likeable when he was willing to show a little vulnerability instead of constantly boasting and trying to prove he was the best at everything.

"It happens to all of us," Katrina said reassuringly. "We don't work in low-stakes jobs."

"Tell me about it." Patrick chuckled. "Now I have to clean my office before anyone notices."

"Take it easy, Patrick," she said.

"Good to see you back," he said, and Katrina was pretty sure she sensed genuine affection cracking through his jerky exterior.

On the drive home, Katrina heard Bloomberg radio excitedly talking about a topic, and wondered if it had any connection to the failed operation Patrick was so upset about.

"Shocking news out of Zurich today, as a group of Swiss banks issued a statement admitting their secure financial records systems had been breached. UBS, Credit Suisse, Julius Baer, Pictet, and Vontobel—five of the largest and most highly regarded banks in Switzerland—say they have contacted Swiss authorities after 'a significant amount' of account holders' personal financial data was hacked and stolen. At this point, the banks and Swiss authorities say they have no clues about the perpetrator, but the brief joint statement from the banks stated that none of them had been contacted with any ransom demands. This is particularly eye-opening because the cyber-security of these institutions is considered to rank among the best in the world, and Swiss banks are known for their privacy—in fact, under Swiss law, it is illegal for a bank to disclose any information about an account, even its existence, except in cases of severe illegal activity. The markets have been taking a dive since this news broke—"

CHAPTER NINE

LIBERTY CAMPUS
AUGUST 15, 2023

When Katrina returned to the office the next day, she decided she was down to her last ounces of patience. She asked Dee to join her in Raquel's office—still inching closer to resembling the home of a hoarder—and burst once the office door was closed.

"What is Kobold?" Katrina demanded. "My security clearance should be high enough for me to give guided tours of the Roswell alien spacecraft in Area 51, but for some reason I'm locked out of every file connected to Kobold!"

Raquel and Dee exchanged a look, and mutually decided Katrina could now be read in.

"They're playing all of this extremely close to the vest," Dee sighed. "We've had leaks before. We've had moles before. But this hack . . . " Dee shook her head and sighed. "This is like nothing anybody in the intelligence community had ever seen before. Somebody got past the very best firewalls the U.S. government could build—the kinds of encryption where if you gave me a team of the best of the best hackers on earth, we couldn't crack if you gave us a bunch of Cray supercomputers and decades of time to crack it. This is like somebody broke into Fort Knox and decided to host the Burning Man festival inside."

Katrina felt a twist in the pit of her stomach. So that's why the building seemed so tense and gloomy since she returned.

"They think it was the Chinese?"

Raquel shook her head. "That's the thing! Whoever hit us didn't stop with us. NSA intercepts revealed the main headquarters of the Ministry of State Security in Xiyuan got hacked, too. For the past six months, every eight weeks or so, one of the most secure sites in the world has been cleaned out of secrets. First us, then the Chinese, then the FSB in Moscow about two months ago."

Katrina's eyes widened. "Wait, those Swiss banks—"

"Sure looks like hack number four, by the same perpetrator," Raquel declared. "Those banks are legendarily secure and secretive. If the Illuminati ever had to take out a mortgage, these are the banks they would use."

"No electronic fingerprints, no ransom demands, no hackers bragging in chat rooms about pulling off the job," Dee rattled off. "It's the hacker equivalent of an alien abduction. These guys just strolled through firewalls that are supposed to be impenetrable. Your first thought would be some sort of inside job, somebody who knew the right passwords, but this hacker's got double-agents from us, *and* the Chinese, *and* the Russians, *and* a bunch of Swiss banks? Really implausible."

Raquel, who had been increasingly reluctant to use computers even before this Mother of All Hacks, dug through a massive pile of folders and handed Katrina a printout of a relatively terse agency memo about the hack.

Katrina read the memo. "Huh." She leaned forward in her seat and lowered her voice, as if just expressing the thought aloud was taboo: "So what did they hack from us?"

"That's what has everyone so freaked out," Raquel murmured. "Very few people know, and no one is saying exactly what information got compromised. Apparently, it makes the Office of Personnel Management hack back in 2014 look like somebody stealing your Netflix password. Whatever they got… it was bad enough that Director Stern submitted her resignation two days later."

That revelation was surprising enough to get Katrina to gasp. "Wait, *that's* why she resigned?"

A knock on the office door interrupted their discussion. Dee opened it, revealing Alec.

"Why is everybody hiding in here?" he asked.

Raquel and Dee brought him up to speed.

"As for Stern's departure, the rumor is that the hack was the straw that broke the camel's back," Raquel clarified. "With her, there was a buffet table with many different varieties of bad leadership, so you can pick and choose which forms of incompetence made her intolerable."

"And nobody's going to miss her!" Alec said with a grin. "I'm already enjoying our new era under an unreadable sphinx. I hear Director Boyles' personalized license plate is a random sequence of letters and numbers."

Katrina cleared her throat. "So, why is it being called the Kobold hack?"

Raquel furrowed her brow. "Do you know Vanessa Barron?"

"Only by reputation, but it's a sharp one," Katrina answered. "Sharp up-and-comer, she exposed that Russian penetration of the German government a few years back."

"Barron is running the Agency's investigation into the hacks, and nicknamed the perpetrator 'Kobold,'" Raquel explained. "Allegedly that's short for 'Key Operation Bold,' but I know she did a lot of work in Berlin tracking hackers over the years, and she's into central European folklore."

Dee sighed. "Barron was great when this started, but she's getting a ton of pressure from Boyles and the frustration is getting to her. For the past few months, every couple of days, I get invited to a meeting of the Kobold Working Group. We get a little information, we try to come up with potential avenues of investigation, and then they close the meeting by screaming at us about how highly classified all of this is. They are really freaked out about this."

"Kobold," Alec said, closing his eyes and trying to remember something from his past. "For some reason I'm flashing back to Dungeons and Dragons—little reptile people who lived underground or something?"

"Something like that." Dee nodded. "I looked it up myself, a goblin that sneaks into people's houses and steals things—appears and disappears, walks through walls, impossible to keep out of your house. A fitting metaphor for whoever hacked our systems."

Dee looked at her teammates, as if measuring them for something. After a moment she asked, "You want to know my current working theory?"

"When have we ever not wanted to know?"

"Somebody cracked quantum computing, and now they've got a skeleton key for just about any secure computer system in the world."

Dee was about to explain when there was another knock at the door. It was Ward.

"Why are the bunch of you meeting in here?"

***

Dee retold everything to Ward.

"Sometimes I feel like the last sane man in an insane world," Ward muttered.

Alec nodded. "We are indeed a shrinking minority."

"Do you know what a quantum computer is?" Dee asked. Alec nodded, but Dee studied his eyes carefully. "No, you don't. You think it has something to do with Ant-Man."

Alec raised an eyebrow. "I don't think you can prove that it *doesn't* have something to do with Ant-Man."

Dee rolled her eyes. "Okay, quantum computing 101. Almost all computer code operates on a binary system—all instructions, all programs, in the end, they're all a giant pile of ones and zeros in particular orders that tell the computer what to do. It's like a coin, heads or tails."

She took out a quarter and flipped it.

"What is it?"

"Heads," Alec answered.

She put the coin down on its side on the table and flicked it, sending it spinning like a top.

"Now what is it? Heads or tails?"

"I can't tell yet, it hasn't stopped."

"It's both, simultaneously," Dee explained. "In a quantum computer, it's not just a one or a zero, it can be both, which means all the things a computer does can be done much, much faster. Exponentially faster. Not just a little faster; something like 150 million times faster than the most sophisticated supercomputer we have in the world today. A quantum computer could do in four minutes what it would take a traditional supercomputer ten thousand years to accomplish."

Alec emitted a surprised "huh."

Ward raised his hand. "Okay, I feel pretty good getting my Smart TV to work, so I like to think that I'm smart, but aren't today's computers really darn fast?"

"Sure, but this is a bigger step than moving from the Wright Brothers to modern fighter jets," Dee said, shaking her hands, trying to think of simple ways to illuminate the stakes.

"Almost all modern computer security, from your home network to the NSA, operates on a password or code that would take a really long time to figure out through trial and error. If I gave you a three-digit bicycle lock, you could crack it, right?"

"Sure, it would just take a while," Ward answered. "Start at zero, zero, zero, and then try to open it. Then zero, zero, one, and try again."

"Yup, you would have to try up to a thousand possible combinations of numbers—it would take a lot of time, but you could eventually do it," Dee said. "But that approach just isn't feasible for most computer or online security; it would take decades or centuries or even longer to try every possible combination to most modern encryption programs. Except if you develop a really good quantum computer, you can run through all the potential combinations to the 'lock' really fast because it's not doing them one at a time. A quantum computer does not have to wait for one process to end before it can begin another, it can do them at the same time. It's like trying every combination from 0-0-0 to 9-9-9 on that bicycle lock at the same time."

"This is why China and Russia are dumping enormous resources into developing quantum computing," Raquel noted gravely. "Whoever discovers this gets an unparalleled strategic and tactical advantage in everything connected with computers for a generation."

"If this is so important, and everybody's chasing it, why hasn't anyone discovered it yet—assuming that Dee's theory is wrong?"

"People have built very simple versions of this, but the race is to build more advanced ones—remember, we're talking about manipulating molecules. To do this, you've got to operate at extremely cold temperatures, just above absolute zero."

Dee read Alec's face and determined he didn't know what that meant. "Negative four hundred sixty degrees Fahrenheit. Your freezer at home can probably get to about negative thirty or forty degrees."

Ward rubbed his beard. "So if somebody's discovered how to make a quantum computer, could this person just hack the nuclear codes or something?"

Raquel offered a reassuring negative shake of her head. “Nuclear launch codes and other extremely sensitive intelligence are protected via symmetric encryption where both sender and receiver share a key. This can be a nearly unbreakable form of encryption, but it does require the physical exchange of new code sheets or digital keys, often via truck, helicopter, or hand courier.”

“You want to know something neat?” Dee asked with a flash of glee, revealing a glimpse of the fascination and wonder that brought her to the world of computers all those years ago. “If and when we develop quantum key distribution, we will have a way of sharing information on a quantum channel, which will be extremely secure at two ends, but delicate in between—which means attempting to listen in will collapse the quantum state.”

Alec and Ward stared back, trying to maneuver their minds around the concepts.

Dee sighed. “Okay, you didn’t understand that. Picture a telephone with one wire, and the moment someone tries to attach anything to that wire to eavesdrop, the wire disintegrates. Somebody could disrupt your communications, but they could never intercept, listen in, or hack into it.”

She could almost see the light bulbs going off above their heads.

“I’m starting to see the appeal of this,” Alec said with a nod.

CHAPTER TEN

LIBERTY CAMPUS
AUGUST 17, 2023

A few days of relative normalcy passed, until Raquel requested Ward to make the drive up from Williamsburg again.

"Vanessa Barron and the Kobold Working Group want to meet with us," Raquel announced, alongside a grimacing Dee. "Apparently, they've gotten nowhere, and now she's desperate and wants to see what the whole team can do for her." She asked if Ward could stick around until the late afternoon, and he agreed.

Katrina noticed Dee's less-than-enthusiastic response.

"What's the problem, Dee?"

Dee looked around and let it out.

"No offense, I love you all, and I'd trust you with my life. But this is a cyber issue, and none of you are cyber people. You're all smart, but you don't have backgrounds in this area. How many years have I been trying to explain what I do to you, and getting blank stares in response?"

Alec and Ward looked at each other.

"She thinks we're dumb," Alec concluded.

"I didn't say that!"

"She definitely thinks we're dumb," Ward concurred, more playful than offended.

"Trust me, we're up to this!" Alec boasted. "You know why they want to bring us in, Dee?"

Dee answered honestly: "Because they haven't found anything, they're desperate, and there's no way bringing you in can make it worse?"

Alec scoffed. "No, it's because none of our enemies ever come back for the sequel."

"How about Jaguar?" Katrina asked. Alec winced, conceding that point.

"We didn't take out the Iron Wolves the first time we ran into them in Salzburg," Raquel added.

"Do the Strauss twins count?" Dee asked.

"We never caught Iraj Khansari, that Iranian intel guy who ran off from Norway," Ward remembered.

Alec frowned, as his teammates had, off the top of their heads, punched holes in this self-flattering narrative.

"Okay, *very few* of our enemies come back for the sequel," Alec corrected himself. "Most of them are either six feet under or they're rotting in Supermax. Nearly two decades, we've cut a path through the international criminal and terrorist underworld like Sherman marching through Georgia. I'm not gonna say everything worked out perfect, but there's a reason nobody worries about Atarsa or Hell-Summoner or the Shedim anymore."

"Everyone I've ever killed has stayed dead!" Ward cackled. "Zombie-free since ninety-three!"

Alec paused, and his expression became almost wistful. "You know, I've never had a Belloq."

"A Belloq?"

"*Too bad the Hovitos don't know you the way I do, Belloq!*" Alec growled with a grimace, impersonating his favorite movie character. "Indiana Jones' archenemy, his top rival, the Moriarty to his Sherlock Holmes! None of our enemies ever stick around long enough to become our archenemies! It's like Reagan and the Soviet leaders of the early eighties, he couldn't get very far in negotiations with them because they kept dying on him."

"That is such a not-problem, it doesn't even qualify as a first-world problem!" Dee snapped.

"I'm just saying, as much as people tease us for being a so-called 'Dangerous Clique,' when we solve a problem, it stays solved."

***

Five of the six core teammates in Dangerous Clique had been invited to the Kobold briefing. Elaine was working in the Bureau that day, and the CIA was extremely touchy about discussing its most catastrophic hack in front of anyone employed by a rival agency. The briefing also invited CIA psychologist Rhiannon Street and had asked her to write up a profile of the kind of person who could pull off a hack like this. Rhiannon had argued that as confident as she was in her profiling skills, there was no way she could discern key personality traits or other personal qualities from lines of code.

"The Kobold Working Group really is reaching the bottom of the barrel," Dee muttered. Dee was attempting, and failing, to hide her offense that the Agency was now bringing in every Tom, Dick, and Harry to hunt down a hacker, which was the sort of role she excelled at.

"I would have bet a significant amount of money that you, of all people, would have been able to devise some traceroute program," Alec remarked.

"Oh, I have!" Dee shot back. "As soon as I heard this, I deployed my own home-cooked, jury-rigged, traceroute program. I was going to call it Artemis, but apparently everybody calls their traceroute programs after the goddess of hunting, so I'm calling my program 'The Bloodhound Gang.'"

Alec raised an amused eyebrow, thinking he recognized the reference. "Nothing but mammals?"

Dee shook her head. "Three-two-one Contact! 'Whenever there's trouble, we're there on the double!' Anyway, my program is going to work, too. The problem is, it's like looking for a needle in a haystack, over and over and over again, until you get the location of the hacker at that time. Sometimes my program can find the needle fairly quickly—a day or two—and sometimes it takes a week, week and a half. And I don't actually know how many haystacks there are. There could be hundreds." Dee looked disappointed. "I had to tell Barron that my program would find the location of hacking program sometime between tomorrow and the year 2097."

"Less than ideal," Katrina concurred.

Vanessa Barron was a striking professional of the Agency, with stints in both the Directorate of Operations and the Counterintelligence Mission Center. She had long black hair and wore the sort of eyeglasses that inevitably spurred "hot librarian" jokes. She began the briefing, misread her notes, and said "root vegetable" when she meant "rootkit enabled."

"I'm sorry," she said, dropping her façade. "I have not been myself lately. I'm sure Dee has told you horror stories about how I'm losing my well-cultivated cool. This is ... unlike anything I've ever worked on before. Everything else I've ever done in my career, there's been some promising leads, some clue or evidence, some path to follow. The Kobold nickname is all too accurate, this is like a hacker with magical powers or something. At this point, my best hope is that Dee's Rube Goldberg search program spits out a result before the end of the century."

Dee smiled and nodded in satisfaction. "I will beat that deadline."

Katrina found herself sympathizing with Barron. The CIA could, at times, be the best place to work in the world. And it could also feel like a massive, unresponsive bureaucracy that demanded the impossible—and that it was particularly demanding, and unbending, for the women that worked there.

"Just tell us what you can, and we'll see if there's anything we can do," Katrina offered.

Barron smiled, exhaled and started again. The good news was that Barron got through her twenty-minute "introduction to quantum computing" briefing without a single stumble, demonstrating her fluency with every known aspect of the hack.

The bad news is, Alec, Ward, and even Katrina and Raquel stared at the complicated diagrams and formulas in confusion.

Rhiannon sat with folded arms. "From what you've shown me, I can conclusively determine, in my professional opinion as a psychologist, that the perpetrator is the kind of person who types on a computer a lot."

Dee shook her head. "I warned you."

"Well, I didn't need to know what the Death Star plans were to know they're important," Alec snapped.

"Alec is right, you don't want us to unravel the mystery of quantum computing, you want us to find a trail leading back to the person who appears to have built a quantum computer and used it to hack the Agency," Katrina added.

Katrina laid out the sheets in the briefing packet in front of her and studied a map of the world on the wall.

"I think you guys are right that it's extremely unlikely to be a foreign government," Katrina began. "Something like this would be too big, complicated, and expensive to hide. It's not quite a nuclear reactor, but it's close. You can't just cook this up in your garage. It's expensive, you need specialized equipment, and a lot of smart people. Or at least a handful of absolutely brilliant people. This agency and our partners watch all the usual suspects and a bunch of the unusual suspects pretty closely."

She got up, walked closer to the map, ran her finger over North America, and then Europe.

"But what about allied countries?" she asked.

Everyone else in the room exchanged uncomfortable glances.

"You think one of our allies hacked some of our most sensitive files?" Barron asked, revealing how disconcerting she found the thought.

"It's not like we haven't angered our allies over the years. We abandoned the Kurds," Katrina began. "We abandoned the Afghans. We demonized Saudi Arabia, then we turned around and begged them to make more oil. We loved NATO, then we were ready to walk away from NATO, now we love NATO again, but nobody knows how long that will last. Over the past few administrations, our schizophrenic foreign policy has announced to the world that we're not a reliable ally. It doesn't seem quite so unthinkable to me that one of our shaken allies might feel like taking us down a peg."

Raquel nodded in agreement. "If you really have nothing from looking at the usual suspects, start looking at the unusual suspects. Look for someone who you crossed off the list early. Someone who initially seemed like they were on our side. Remember, Hell-Summoner was one of the British heroes of the pandemic."

Barron exhaled. "I see the logic of what you're saying, but man, even bringing this up with Director Boyles is going to stir up a hornet's nest."

Katrina picked up the thread again. "Someone who doesn't seem to know enough to have a breakthrough but might have gotten lucky. Or someone who seemed too nuts to find a genuine breakthrough."

"Someone who dropped off the radar screen, maybe presumed dead or enjoying a quiet retirement." Alec thought of his experience with the twin daughters of Linus Strauss. "See if any of your usual suspects who came up clean have any ambitious children."

"Absolutely nothing led to any useful leads?" Ward inquired, even though he knew the answer was no, otherwise the Kobold Working Group wouldn't have called them in. "It couldn't be that Russia or China faked it to look like they were hacked, too?"

Barron shook her head. "If it were Russia and China, it would mean hacking themselves, and they're reacting with a level of panic that just doesn't look like it can be faked. I know Russians have gone to extraordinary lengths to fool us, but there are reports that they either beat up or beat to death the head of the FSB's cyber-security."

Ward nodded.

"Then you're not dealing with anybody the U.S. intelligence community has ever looked at before," he speculated. "Somebody with a clean record, above suspicion, no criminal record or ties, no suspicious financial ties, or links to hostile foreign governments. Someone who only recently decided to hit us, or, even worse . . . " He paused. "Somebody who's been playing a long, long game, who has spent their entire adult life working themselves into a position where they would be above all suspicion."

Dee cleared her throat. "I can create an algorithm to go through public records, news articles to find anybody with money who's ever expressed an interest in quantum computing."

"And once we've compiled a list of these too-crazy suspects, what would you recommend we do?" Barron asked.

"Knock on their door and have a chat," Ward answered.

"Or even better," Alec chirped. "Ask the Dangerous Clique to knock on their door and have a chat."

CHAPTER ELEVEN

Raquel returned to her office, sat in her desk, and stared at the portrait of her mentor, former deputy director Harold Hare, on the wall. Somehow it had slanted, and she straightened it.

"You shouldn't have died on us, Merlin," she muttered as she returned to her desk.

"I'm sure he feels the same way," Katrina said from the doorway, startling Raquel. Katrina still had the useful and somewhat annoying habit of moving so quietly no one ever heard her approaching.

"Barron didn't exactly paint a flattering picture of Director Boyles, did she?" Katrina asked.

"Nope," Raquel said, taking a swig of coffee from a mug that had grown stone-cold since the morning and wincing. "Merlin had his quirks, but we knew he always had our backs when it counted."

"Barron's younger than I pictured," Katrina observed. "I guess we're now at the age where the 'senior' in 'senior case officer' isn't just for decoration."

"I feel like the prime of our careers started twenty minutes ago," Raquel said dryly. "Now all of a sudden we're yesterday's news."

"Hey, you think you have it bad? I had a 'geriatric pregnancy!'" Katrina chuckled, still offended at the term, which medically applied to any woman thirty-five or older but that Katrina felt spurred visions of *The Golden Girls*.

Katrina shook her head and thought for a moment. "Maybe that's what feels different—maybe since Director Stern, or maybe since I came back from maternity leave," she sighed. "For almost our whole careers, we had somebody older than us, more experienced than us, and hopefully a little wiser than us watching our back. Remember that sense of security, knowing that even if we screwed up, there was somebody else out there who was watching over it all, and who could step in to help? Where did that go?"

"All the good old ones are retired or dead now," Raquel said with a shrug. "The ones who are left are the ones who just hung on and hung on and were determined to sit in the big chair, and they seem hell-bent on staying there until they die. They don't actually know how to lead, and they're afraid to actually lead. Because that involves risk, and they've gotten to the top by avoiding risk."

Her eyes slid from the portrait of Merlin to the chaotic piles of papers strewn all over her office.

"It's on us now," she declared.

***

LIBERTY CAMPUS
AUGUST 18, 2023

Having been bummed by the gloomy tone of her conversation with Katrina the previous day, Raquel announced the team should take a "field trip."

"We're going to Williamsburg," she announced.

What she meant was Camp Peary, a 9,000-acre U.S. military reservation in York County that served as the primary site for training CIA case officers, complete with a fake town square, woodland, and buildings designed to look like embassies. There, case officers were trained in every skill from surveillance and counter-surveillance, firearms, explosives, evasive driving and pursuit, and methods for withstanding torture.

A few months ago, seven promising individuals in the past two classes of recruits had been notified that they were selected for "additional training" and consideration for membership in a particular team whose existence was so secret, most members of the Agency had little idea of their actual work exploits. Those recruits had asked around and found that no one had any memory of anyone else being selected for this particular team. One rumor was that they had started as "Dick Cheney's personal assassination squad."

The Dangerous Clique had never recruited directly from the Farm before, but seven had stood out to Raquel, with either enthusiastic endorsements or begrudging acquiescence from Alec and Ward.

Katrina, Dee, and Elaine had barely heard anything about them so far, and Raquel felt like everyone would feel a bit energized by seeing promising younger potential teammates.

"It's like the NFL combine for spies," Alec observed.

"Meet our replacements," Ward said with a chuckle.

Inside a large gymnasium-like building, the seven were practicing judo-like personal defense moves on each other, separate from about twenty-four other recruits on the other side of the gym. A Farm instructor occasionally paused them and made recommendations, but all of them seemed more than competent.

"On our budget, the seven rookies are listed as the Terrorism Neutralization Group, or TNG."

Alec shook his head. "You named them after *Star Trek: The Next Generation*, and I will not accept alternate explanations."

Raquel smirked. "I can neither confirm nor deny that accusation. As we discussed, TNG consists of seven trained case officers, all from the two most recent classes from the Farm, all ages twenty-three to twenty-six."

"Babies!"

"The tall one is Benedict Vermeulen. From his size, you would think he's the bruiser, but look at those fluid, smooth motions."

When one of Benedict's teammates attempted to get him in a chokehold from behind, Benedict simply grabbed hold of his assailant's arm, straightened it, and flipping the assailant over his shoulder, throwing him down upon the mat with a loud *thump*. Benedict made it seem effortless, like tossing dirty laundry over his shoulder into the basket.

"Vermeulen's the oldest, came to the Agency after qualifying for explosive ordnance disposal teams, so he's got off-the-charts technical know-how and nerves of steel. He's our Wirecutter. Guy could have been a rocket scientist, but he wound up here. NASA's loss is our gain."

"Who just got tossed?" Katrina asked.

"Oh, I'm saving that one for the end," Raquel said, chuckling. Unfolding her arms, she gestured to where two similar-looking women were squaring off, like wrestlers, each patiently waiting for the other to make the first move.

"Meet the Navars. The taller and older one is Belina. Photographic memory—she's the Recorder. Show her a page full of numbers for a minute and she can recite them in order a month later. She apparently doesn't forget anything—she's a flesh-and-blood recording system, which is going to come in handy for moments where we can only get a moment's glimpse at some sensitive document."

"If she's so terrific, how did we get her?"

"Brilliant people tend to have challenging personalities, but I'm sure none of you would know anything about that," Raquel remarked.

Katrina, Alec, Ward, Dee, and Elaine all agreed and assumed that Raquel was talking about everyone on the team except themselves.

"Belina puts a lot of pressure on herself, sometimes has friction with others. It was a two-for-one deal, she applied to the Agency with her sister, Sonia, about a year and a half younger. The Firecracker. Little sister's feisty. She's got that gleam in her eye. She wants somebody to mess with her, just so she can show what she can do."

"I recognize that personality type," Katrina murmured. "I'm glad I have boys."

"The one waiting to get next is Emma Gallier, the Chameleon. She just disappears into cover identities. Language, accent, mannerisms, even her walking gait. She's going to be a master of disguise—mistress of disguise?"

"Use Emma to get Belina into a sensitive spot, and then let Belina's brain photocopy all the secret documents," Katrina envisioned.

"You get what I'm thinking," Raquel nodded.

A little farther away, two younger men were enjoying tossing each other around like tackling dummies. One had slightly messy hair and a forehead scar.

"Who's the Harry Potter over there?" Dee asked.

"You ever read Encyclopedia Brown? As a kid, Braden Ravid actually started a neighborhood detective agency. By twelve, he had led his town's police to the guy who was running the local car theft ring, by determining the whole thing was tied into some insurance scam. His mind's always working. Everybody thought he should apply to the FBI, but apparently his mom works for us as an administrator. He's the detective."

Braden charged at the other younger man, but his opponent simply crouched down, and bounced up and forward, like a linebacker tackling a running back—Braden tumbled to the mat and bounced.

"Okay, that was a good one," Braden wheezed.

"Knocked the wind out of him," Ward assessed.

"And a few internal organs, too," Alec added.

"The guy who just tossed him around like a rag doll is Christopher 'Chip' Brauer. He's the Tinkerer. One part Bond's 'Q,' one part Animal from *The Muppet Show*. Mechanical engineer, the guy's always either putting something together or breaking it apart. He's got the soul of a percussionist, little bit of a mad scientist to him."

"Did you say mad scientist or hockey goon?" Alec asked.

They were distracted by another loud *thud* as the tall lean body of Benedict Vermeulen came crashing down to the mat, after his opponent had swung his leg directly into the back of Vermeulen's knees.

"Finally, there's Zachary O'Connell."

"The problem child," Alec muttered. "Why'd you give him the code name Climber? How about 'Headache' or 'Little Punk,' or 'Juvenile Delinquent'?"

Raquel continued. "O'Connell's got serious hacking skills *and* he's a black belt. Rock climbs. Marksmanship's terrific too, apparently, he was a few slots away from qualifying for the U.S. Olympic archery team."

Katrina studied the young man and wondered if her sons would grow up like him.

"If he's that good at that many skills, what makes him a problem child?" Katrina asked.

Alec scowled. "He thinks he knows everything, and that I'm an old fogey."

Katrina smirked at Alec's bruised ego. "Well, you're not exactly a young fogey anymore. Have you told him that his mouth is writing checks that his body can't cash?"

Alec just fumed more. "Yeah, but he's a Generation Z, he doesn't even understand Top Gun references! He just told me nobody writes checks anymore!"

CHAPTER TWELVE

The trip to Williamsburg and getting-to-know-you dinner with the TNG "kids" as Alec called them had lifted everyone's spirits. And the following Monday, after tossing around the idea with Katrina, Alec proposed a new direction for his investigation of "the Voices."

"Following up on the Tattooed Man in Ukraine... I want to know what that ISIS reject Arslanbek Murgen knew about the Voices," Alec announced.

"I thought you said he's dead," Ward replied.

"He's toast like Elvis Patterson," Alec confirmed, although no one around the table appeared to remember the former NFL cornerback who was infamous for getting "burned" by fast wide receivers. "But that doesn't mean Murgen didn't leave anything that could tell us something useful."

He pressed a button and opened a new file on the computer monitor.

"Back in the bad old days of ISIS in Libya, Arslanbek Murgen and his crew took over an ancient fortress out in the Sahara Desert, called Qasr Al-Hājj," Alec declared. "Nomadic Berbers used to use that place for storage of grain and other food."

The monitor displayed satellite and other photos of a large light auburn-colored bleached stone circle with high walls and a lone arched doorway. Inside the wall was a giant rounded courtyard with more than a hundred cave-like storage rooms, arranged in four levels.

"It looks like something out of *Star Wars*," Ward observed.

"Yup, Tatooine." Alec nodded. "The locals are the same Berber architects as the ones you're thinking of in Tunisia. Anyway, as far as I can tell, what's left of the Libyan government never sent in anybody to investigate after Murgen and his guys got blown up. So, there's probably still some useful evidence about Murgen's crew in there, but it's not exactly safe territory. Libya's not exactly stable, and this corner of the country's got it bad. This site could be infested with anything—bandits, gangs, ISIS leftovers." Alec paused. "Bounty hunters, Tusken Raiders, Jawas . . . "

Elaine, who had been watching the briefing with her arms folded, shook her head with mild exasperation.

"The Libyan desert is a little outside of my jurisdiction," Elaine said. "I can't go over there without looping in my bosses, and if I do that, they're going to ask a lot of questions about my investigation with Alec, and I'm just not ready to explain that he thinks that demons or the Dark Side of the Force are creating terrorists. If you guys want to go digging in the sandbox, go ahead. I'll be waiting here for you when you get back."

"No, Elaine, you're right, this isn't a job for the FBI. This is the job for the Pentagon."

She turned to Alec and Katrina. "The last time I sent you two new parents of twins into the field, you nearly had a Russian bomb dropped on you," Raquel reminded them, a flash of irritation in her voice. "If you guys are taking a field trip to Libya, I'm sending you in there with every kind of backup imaginable."

Alec and Katrina exchanged a look and nodded.

"No objections," Katrina said. "We're not the same charge-into-the-fight, guns-blazing couple we used to be."

Raquel rubbed her chin.

"And maybe it's a good time to see what TNG can do in the field."

***

For once, the U.S. Navy proved remarkably cooperative with the Agency's request.

The U.S. Sixth Fleet was patrolling the Mediterranean and was already scheduled to be conducting exercises in international waters off the coast of Libya; many within the Pentagon wondered if the administration wanted intervention or rescue options available in case the domestic unrest in Libya grew worse or threatened American citizens. Technically, Libya had endured two separate civil wars since an angry mob executed the notorious dictator Muammar Gaddafi in Sirte in 2011. Gaddafi met his grisly end at the hands of a young Libyan in a New York Yankees baseball cap. (Alec had headlined his report about the assassination, "YANKEES BEAT PIRATES, 1–0.") In practice, life in Libya had never been all that stable, although so far Americans had barely paid it much attention with other deadly crises on the world stage eating up most of the limited attention for foreign news.

Four members of the Dangerous Clique—Katrina, Ward, Alec, and Dee—flew to Rome, then Aviano Air Base, where a U.S. Navy helicopter transported them to the USS *Bataan*, a Wasp-class amphibious assault ship that looked like a small aircraft carrier that carried Ospreys and other aircraft.

"Sure would have been nice to have all this during Benghazi," Ward observed.

The irony was that the Dangerous Clique would be the third team on the ground at the Libyan target site, and only after the Navy and Marines had shown off their many ways of bringing force to a potential target. Satellite and drone footage indicated that the site was abandoned, but no one in the chain of command wanted "another Benghazi." First a pair of McDonnell Douglas Harrier II fighter jets would make a test run over Qasr

Al-Hājj. They would be followed by a pair of Bell Super Cobra attack helicopters. Then an Osprey tilt-rotor craft would arrive with two dozen Marines from the special-operations-capable 26th Marine Expeditionary Unit. Then, once the Marines had declared the site clear, a Bell Venom helicopter, carrying the Threat Neutralization Group or TNG team would arrive on-site. Only then, when everyone was certain the site was secure, would a second Bell Venom helicopter with the senior members of the Dangerous Clique arrive.

"Pentagon really wants to show off, huh?" Alec remarked when the briefing concluded.

"They think we're too old and the TNG kids are too young," Katrina concluded.

Alec glanced at her. "Or after our couples' getaway to the shooting gallery in Ukraine, everybody's paranoid about having the mom and the dad of twins on the same mission."

The one pleasant surprise was that the second Bell Venom helicopter would be flown by two adjunct members of the Dangerous Clique, Thomas Wells and Alejandro Serrano de la Verde. When the team absolutely, positively needed to get somewhere in one piece, Raquel called this pair, and their piloting skills had gotten the team out of a particularly thorny jam in Serbia a few years earlier.

Thomas Wells boasted, only half-jokingly, that he could fly anything and had yet to be proven wrong. Katrina was happy to see them but surprised to spot a few gray hairs in Tom's mane, and crow's-feet around his eyes. She figured the fact that Tom wore Ray-Ban aviator sunglasses as often as the president would have prevented that. She realized that when she had met Tom, he looked like Tom Cruise in the original *Top Gun*. Now he was aging into Tom Skerritt without the mustache.

She realized that none of her friends looked as young as they used to appear.

Alejandro had closed down his boutique private security firm in Dallas shortly after the team's adventure in Serbia. The U.S. government always seemed to need someone either flown somewhere, driven somewhere, or trained to do the same. Over the years, Alejandro had earned all kinds of delivery- and transport-themed nicknames and jokes—Federal Express, the deliveryman, "see what Verde can do for you"—but after one official had jokingly called him the U.S. government's version of the title character of Jason Statham's *The Transporter*, Alejandro chose to start wearing Armani suits and cutting his hair just short of shaved. If he was going to be a deliveryman, he was going to be the most stylish and glamorous deliveryman possible.

After this assignment, the pair were scheduled to help train Ukrainian pilots.

"My favorite Uber drivers," Alec greeted Tom and Alejandro.

"Hey, Alec, glad to see you're in one piece after getting tied up by the Barbie Twins," Alejandro shot back. "Some men pay good money for that kind of thing."

Alec shook his head in exasperation. The more the tale of his kidnapping by the Strauss Twins worked through the Agency's rumor mill, the less menacing it sounded. In the initial stages of their trial, the lawyers for Madison and Tiffany Strauss tried to portray the pair as bimbo spoiled brats who didn't recognize the moral consequences of their actions. Few legal analysts thought the pair's defense would work, but that didn't mean Alec didn't stress over the possibility of two women he considered sociopaths being let back onto the street by a gullible jury.

"The prosecutor, McCarthy, is tough as nails and smart," Elaine had tried to reassure him weeks earlier. "They're guilty as sin and the prosecutors have a mountain of evidence."

"I'm pretty sure they said the same thing about O.J."

The Strauss Twins had recently won the argument that they were not a significant flight risk, and were willing to give up their passports, but bail already had been set at more than two million dollars for each of them. With their assets seized by the U.S. government, the pair remained in custody.

Alec rolled his eyes at Tom and Alejandro's teasing about his abduction by the Strauss twins.

"Yeah, but when somebody hires two hot young women to tie them up, there's not usually a mountain of ammonium nitrate rigged to explode one floor above them!"

"Oh, yeah, that," Tom said with a chuckle.

"Many wives wouldn't appreciate everyone joking about her husband's abduction," Katrina interrupted. Tom and Alejandro looked sheepish and guilty for a moment, but then Katrina giggled. "Of course, I'm not most wives. Sure, Alec was in danger, but with me looking for him, the Strauss twins were in worse danger."

The Bell Venom took off from the deck and headed south. The azure of the ocean beneath them quickly was replaced by the ochre, beige, and dark red sands of the Sahara.

"TNG has the site secure. One individual detained, being interrogated now."

CHAPTER THIRTEEN

QASR AL-HĀJJ
ABOUT 80 MILES SOUTHWEST OF TRIPOLI, LIBYA
AUGUST 31, 2023

The Bell Venom kicked up a small sandstorm as it landed alongside the other helicopter and the Osprey tilt-rotor craft, close to the entrance of Qasr Al-Hājj.

Katrina, Alec, Ward, and Dee climbed out. The ancient granary, often mistaken for a fortress with its featureless, three-story circular wall, was already a beehive of activity, with Marines assisting in the search of the 119 chambers inside. Benedict Vermeulen, who had stepped into the role of the leader of the TNG team, ran up to greet Katrina and the others.

"Who's the detained individual?" Katrina asked.

"Just some guy who turned the place into his home, they're interrogating him now," Vermeulen reported. "Probably no significance, but there's always a chance he may have found something they left behind. Bellina's sitting in with the Marines and their translator."

"Belina speaks Syrian Arabic?"

"No, but she read an Arabic-English dictionary on the way over."

Dee peered up at the ancient structure.

"These guys don't look like the type to leave a lot of computers behind," Dee observed. "I may have crossed the world for nothing."

"Eh, you never know when we'll find a thumb drive, disk, old laptop," Katrina said.

They entered through the archway into the ring of the ancient structure. O'Connell approached.

"Delinquent," Alec greeted him.

"Old man," O'Connell shot back. "The Marines found a metal trapdoor in one of the chambers, sealed shut. We've got Braden and Chip working on it with an arc welder. At this rate, they should be open in eh, maybe five, maybe ten minutes."

"Anything in any of these chambers pointing back to Murgen or al-Aswat?"

Connell nodded. "Bits and pieces, but it looks like the scavengers picked over everything and stole anything useful. An old banner, torn up. Empty ammunition clips. No signs of traps."

Katrina nodded and walked into the nearest chamber. It was mostly empty, other than someone who had carved a crude image of a giant skull in the back wall.

"Punisher fans," Ward quipped.

"So, what was 'al-Aswat'?" Dee asked. "What made these guys any different from any other terrorist group?"

"At first the Agency thought they were just another ISIS splinter faction," Katrina began, moving to the next chamber and finding it similarly empty. "The U.S. started bombing ISIS in Libya from 2016, did it on and off for three years, and by 2020 they had been driven out of Sirte and were reduced to roving gangs. Al-Aswat just seemed like the most psycho and massacre-hungry faction in a convention of devils."

"Tell her about the video declaration," Alec prompted.

Katrina shook her head. "Back in early 2019 or so, when we were chasing Atarsa, Arslanbek Murgen issued his video manifesto, and this was our first clue there was something different about these guys. No reference to Islam, no quoting the Koran. It was like the usual ISIS terror videos, but scrubbed of the religious rhetoric."

Katrina paused, remembering, and feeling a sense of unease as she remembered the precise phrases that the bearded Murgen had chanted, almost drone-like, into the camera.

"Murgen boasted that they love death more than the rest of us love life," Katrina continued. "He said they weren't afraid to die and took joy in killing. He said they saw visions of a new earth, scrubbed clean of the vermin of humanity, and a great silence replacing our bickering voices."

She concluded, "He said they feared nothing but hellfire."

Alec smiled. "Which is pretty ironic, because that's exactly the kind of missile that turned them into barbeque."

"Yeah, yeah, jihadis, Atarsa, these clowns, it's all the same big talk," Ward scoffed, making a vulgar gesture. "We eat Hot Pockets straight out of the microwave because the roof of our mouth fears no heat. We drink milk three days after the sell-by date. We wipe our asses with sandpaper because we're just that tough, blah, blah, blah. Bigger they are, harder they fall."

The Navar sisters approached. Belina and Sonia both had a satisfied look on their faces, like they had found something important.

"The guy who's been living here says his name is Mohammed," Belina began.

Alec turned to Ward. "What are the odds?"

Sonia looked like she was ready to burst. "Mohammed says that when he moved in, he found this, and he thinks it belonged to Murgen."

She held up a filthy, torn-up leather journal with yellow pages that looked like it had been buried underground for a while. Katrina took the journal and opened it, finding that the pages had no words, just pages and pages of nightmarish doodles and illustrations—crooked tree branches, skulls that seemed to smile, serpents, beetles, men and women blindfolded and bound with leather straps, and other dark, hellacious landscapes.

Alec looked over Katrina's shoulder. "Ah, eighties heavy-metal album covers meets Hot Topic. Say, my dear, does this remind you of anybody's tattoos?"

Katrina looked up at him, not yet ready to concede that Murgen and the Tattooed Man of Russia could have had some sort of shadowy spiritual connection.

"This doesn't prove—"

Dee was already convinced. "Katrina, these guys are devil worshippers!"

Belina cleared her throat. "And Mohammed said something else that you really need to hear."

Katrina nodded.

"Mohammed said some nomad came through a month ago and told him to move out, because Arslanbek Murgen was still alive and might come back some day!"

"No way," Alec insisted. "The U.S. Air Force shot up his convoy like the climax of a Mad Max movie! I watched the videos! A nice clean line of big orange fireballs and shrapnel flying all across the desert! They put so much ordnance on those trucks that you would have thought Ward was directing the operation! Nobody survived that."

"Did they ever recover his particular body?" Ward asked. "We've learned the hard way that guys reported dead aren't always dead."

Katrina shook her head. "If Arslanbek Murgen survived, where's he been all these years? A guy like that doesn't just go get a job at Walmart or something. He's a wanted terrorist! He's wanted by us, and his old buddies in ISIS hate him, too."

"Yeah, but ISIS isn't what it used to be, thank God," Ward added. "But sometimes terrorists just disappear, fall off the radar screen. It's a big world. There are al-Qaeda guys we never found. Sometimes guys just pull a D.B. Cooper or a Whitey Bulger and vanish."

Katrina folded her arms. "Well, we've got some rumor from some nomad, against the footage of the shot-up convoy with no survivors. Occam's razor would suggest this is the same crazy conspiracy stuff that we see every time some leader gets killed. There are Iraqis who say Saddam Hussein is still alive, and everybody saw him hang. A certain former president retweeted a claim that the Navy Seals had killed one of Osama bin Laden's doubles. It's been years and there's no trace of his survival. I'm not going to lose a lot of sleep over the possibility that Arslanbek Murgen is alive. If he is alive, he's hiding."

Before the debate could continue, Braden Ravid came over, excited.

"We've almost got that steel trapdoor open!"

***

In one chamber, farthest from the entry arch, the center of the room featured a large metal trapdoor that looked like it dated from some uglier, heavier era of the industrial age.

Chip Brauer flipped off wielding goggles. "Took a while, sucker's thick, but I knew how to cut through it."

"This was added," Katrina concluded. "Relatively recently. This was a grain storage facility, and a storage locker for those on pilgrimage for centuries. That thing in the floor was installed, no earlier than the mid-twentieth century. Welded shut for a reason."

"Somebody didn't want anyone rooting around down there," Ward agreed.

It took two Marines and Benedict Vermeulen to lift the heavy door. The hinges creaked loudly.

"Like Howard Carter opening King Tut's tomb," Alec remarked.

Two other Marines quickly pointed their rifles down into the hole, with the others waving flashlights. From what they could see, it looked like an empty stone room.

"Or like Geraldo Rivera opening up Al Capone's vault," Ward muttered.

"Alright, O'Connell, Braden Ravid, you're with me going down in there in the first wave," Benedict ordered. "Belina, Sonia, Emma, you're wave two once we've secured this chamber. After we—"

Katrina cleared her throat and smirked a bit.

"Benedict, that's appreciated, but I'm going down in the first group," Katrina said with a smile. "We're middle-aged parents, not handicapped."

Benedict shifted uncomfortably. "Miss Leonidivna—"

"Call me Katrina."

"Okay, Ms. Katrina. Ms. Holtz ordered us to minimize any potential risk to you and Mr. Flanagan—"

"Oh, for God's sake, kid!" Alec exclaimed. "This is not our first rodeo! The bunch of us were getting into gunfights in Petra when you guys were in diapers!"

Behind him, Ward rolled his eyes. "As I recall, you didn't even fire a shot."

Alec patted Benedict on the back, and then gently nudged him aside. "Ward, Katrina and I will go down first, and make sure it's safe for you kids," Alec cheerfully announced. "Mom and Dad and Uncle Gunshow have got this one, okay?"

Benedict shifted uncomfortably and winced.

"I feel like you guys going down there first would violate our orders—"

"Somebody get some ropes or cables!" Katrina ordered. "Flashlights. My Glock should be fine."

***

The first chamber beneath the trapdoor had been empty, just a round circle carved out of rock, about the size of a living room. But it had two carved doorways with wooden doors on hinges pounded into the rock.

"Silent as a tomb," she whispered.

Katrina picked the north door first and had found a similarly sized room full of about a dozen crates, most of them pushed up against the walls, but a handful in the center of the room.

"Great, as if being terrorists wasn't bad enough, they're pack rats, too," Ward quipped.

The first crate Katrina opened—the lid was closed, but not nailed shut—was half-filled with uniformly shaped, colorful stacks of paper, yellow with age.

"Money," she declared, removing a wad. "Libyan dinars, mostly. Some Iraqi dinars, some Syrian pounds. A couple stacks of euros."

Ward gave it a cursory look. "Old currency," he concluded. "Most of the ISIS bands and groups were thieves as well as being murderers and rapists. Guess we found the Al-Aswat safe-deposit box."

Alec looked inside the crate, then counted the other crates in the room, and did math in his head.

"There must be hundreds of thousands of dollars down here, maybe more than a million," Alec calculated. "Good thing the Air Force blew Murgen and Al-Aswat to Kingdom Come when they did, they were building up the resources to do something really terrible."

"And don't forget, we still have that south chamber," Katrina said.

Alec turned around and crossed the initial chamber.

"Just be careful!"

"Nobody's been down here in years, Katrina, I think we can—"

Alec never finished the sentence. As he opened the door, the top of the door scraped against the rock ceiling above—and then, without warning, all the rock and stone started to crumble to sand above his head, and even the usually unflappable Katrina screamed as a torrent of dark, shiny objects suddenly fell upon Alec, landing in his hair, his neck, shoulders,

Scorpions!

Alec screamed in a pitch that was slightly less masculine than he would have liked, and began frantically trying to brush and shake off the two hundred or so shiny black predatory arachnids that kept coming, like some horrific clown car of creepy-crawlies.

"Ahh! Getemoff! Getemoff! Getemoff!"

Ward raised his gun, but Katrina reached out and lowered it, suddenly realizing something as her husband jumped around and howled that one had fallen in his shirt.

"SCORPIONS!" Alec screamed. "Ahh! They're deadly! Get them off me before they sting!"

"They're not moving!" Katrina shouted. "Alec, they're all dead."

Ward looked to the floor and realized that Katrina was right—none of the scorpions were moving. Whoever had set the trap had left hundreds of scorpions in the ceiling chamber, ready to fall when the door was opened, and hadn't bothered to think about what those scorpions would eat.

A few more dead scorpions fell from the ceiling where the process of opening the door had triggered the trap.

Alec ripped off his shirt, popping buttons, determined to get the cold, hard creepy sensation of a scorpion away from his back. His shouts were only halfway coherent, a tapestry of profanity with "little" "buggers" "off" "creepy" "sicko who built this."

Ward approached and helped brush them off Alec.

"You're fine, buddy," he said, stepping on them. "See? They're not moving. Let's just make sure you don't get pricked by any stingers."

"Pricks built this trap!" Alec shouted angrily. "Or maybe this is God telling me that I should have let the kids come in here first."

"Alec," Katrina gasped, pointing through the doorway.

Alec looked up from his frantic brushing—even though all the scorpions were off him, his fear made him feel like they were still crawling on him. He saw Ward was staring in horror at what was within the south chamber.

Alec turned and gasped himself.

It was a statue, seemingly carved out of the same stone that made up the walls. It depicted two humanoid figures—one male, one female—except the male had six limbs and the lower body of a beetle or cockroach, and the female's naked breasted torso morphed into the body of a giant centipede, her long chain of segments and legs forming a ring around them. The figures' faces were also a morph between an insectoid form and some classical human features. The two figures were in an embrace, their mouths open, insect-like antennae extending from their mouths like split tongues. It was almost a grotesque parody of Rodin's statue *The Embrace*, featuring two giant bug people.

"After what I saw during Atarsa," Ward said softly. He paused and began again. "When I hallucinated Fabrice Vuscovi turning into an insect, I started reading up on whether anybody else had ever had a vision like that. I learned Edward Gorey had written about a malevolent insect god. I learned about Anansi, the trickster God of West Africa. I learned about the role of scarabs in ancient Egypt. I relearned about the locusts in the Ten Plagues. But I never got any good answers, any good sense of why I hallucinated that particular image."

Katrina noticed small, organized piles of bones at the foot of the statue.

"Please tell me those are animal bones," she whispered. Ward stepped closer—they all felt the uncanny, illogical fear that at any moment the horrific statue might come to life—and winced.

"I'm not going to tell you anything about those bones," Ward declared. He looked up at the statue again. "Have you ever seen anything like that?"

Katrina shook her head, which many people would have interpreted as a "no." But Alec knew better. He knew his wife was concluding that the coincidences were piling up a little too high.

"Yeah, we did," Alec declared. "In Turkmenistan. This little village called Erbent. It had this monument to a handful of Soviets killed when the Soviets were squashing a rebellion in the 1930s. And right underneath it was this underground altar to this kind of a creepy bug man."

They heard some tense shouting above them. Much to their surprise, it was Dee who was doing the yelling, and so frantic and insistent in her instructions to the Marines and the TNG team that everyone seemed to be shocked into obedience.

Katrina, Alec, and Ward ran back to the central chamber with the trapdoor in the ceiling and grabbed the climbing ropes.

Ward shouted, betraying concern: "What the hell is going on up there?"

Dee looked down in the hole, as if she had seen a ghost.

"We need to get all of these guys out of the country, immediately!"

CHAPTER FOURTEEN

There hadn't been time to explain. Dee was adamant that the TNG team get into their Bell Venom helicopter first, and then she insisted Katrina get into the helicopter piloted by Tom and Alejandro. Katrina noticed that Dee didn't give similar instructions for the Marines. In Spanish, she shouted instructions at Alejandro that included a frantic "Andale!"

Once they were strapped in and airborne, they headed north, low and fast, back toward the blue of the Mediterranean and the USS *Bataan*.

"DEE!" Katrina shouted. "What's the danger?"

Dee's expression turned from frantic concern to sadness.

"Well, we now know what Kobold hacked from us!" she shouted, pointing to her laptop. "Kobold just posted everything they stole—which included the personnel files for the most recent three classes to come out of the Farm! That includes all the Clique Babies!"

Katrina, Alec, and Ward suddenly realized why Dee had been so panicked. At that moment, every hostile spy agency in the world was reading those files. The entire TNG team had just had giant bull's-eyes tattooed to their backs.

"And get this—whoever it was... they signed it 'Kobold'!" Dee roared in a combination of shock and outrage.

Katrina looked horrified and started adding up the ramifications. "Meaning they know our internal code name for them, which Barron came up with *after* the theft...we didn't just get hacked once, they're still hacking us!"

***

It was there, all around the Internet, worse than the WikiLeaks revelations. The TNG team weren't the only CIA personnel records leaked; the Kobold hack had apparently obtained three classes' worth of personnel records of the youngest case officers, nearly two hundred officers in total. And as they scanned the list of names they popped up, one by one:

Christopher Brauer
Emma Gallier
Belina Navar
Sonia Navar
Zachary O'Connell
Braden Ravid
Benedict Vermeulen

The leak included photos, resumes, evaluations, and all kinds of paperwork. Hostile governments now knew all kinds of details—from specialties and grades, to who had their tonsils, appendix, or wisdom teeth removed, who had distinctive scars and where.

Within a day and a half, the CIA had suddenly had to organize the emergency evacuation of nearly two hundred case officers from dozens of countries, all around the world. A few were still working at Langley. For those in friendly countries, it was simply a matter of booking a ticket on the first available flight back to the United States. But for those working in places like Venezuela, Cuba, Russia, China, Belarus, and other countries under nonofficial cover, getting out of the country and back to

U.S. soil was a matter of life and death. The two dozen or so working under official cover as U.S. diplomats were immediately declared persona non grata and ordered to leave the country by host countries.

So far none of the young case officers had been arrested or killed, but three operating under deep cover, far afield from normal communication channels, hadn't yet reported in.

Years of work were destroyed instantly. Even worse than the sudden involuntary early retirement of the case officers, now hundreds of agents—the foreign citizens recruited to steal secrets from other governments—were now at risk of being exposed from their meetings with known CIA case officers.

For each of the nearly two hundred exposed case officers, their career as a spy was over. They could still work in the Agency, but their real names and faces were public, and traveling to a lot of foreign countries would now be dangerous. There was always the chance that China's Ministry of State Security, Russia's FSB, Iran's Intelligence Organization of the Islamic Revolutionary Guard Corps, or some other hostile foreign intelligence service would try to grab them and see what secrets could be squeezed out of them. And the world had no shortage of organizations who would gladly murder anyone known to be CIA, just to settle an old score—the Taliban, what was left of ISIS and al-Qaeda.

***

Ward had arrived, after spending a few additional days with the TNG case officers, each still grappling with the consequences of exposure.

"How are the kids taking it?" Alec asked. Katrina noticed that for all his complaining about Connell, fatherhood had cultivated his paternal, protective perspective toward the younger agents.

"Badly," Ward answered. "They're troopers, but they've spent years of their lives training to be case officers. I mean, they'll find other jobs. Skills like theirs are always in demand. Braden's probably a more natural fit for the Bureau, anyway. But you know this isn't a job, it's a mission. We get to travel around the world and kick the asses of terrorist scum and arms dealers and see the fear in their eyes when they realize they're not going to get away with it this time. That's an adrenaline rush that a million dollars a year can't buy."

"Taking the TNG out of commission also means we won't be able to pass the torch for a long while," Katrina observed. She and Alec looked at each other, each one grappling with warring emotions within. They wanted to move on to less dangerous assignments, and they wanted to still be needed, to defy Father Time.

"Was there something we could have done to prevent this?" Alec asked. "Some clue we missed, some preparation we should have—"

Dee interrupted him. "Kind of hard when the seventh floor refused to give us any hint of what had been hacked!" She spat, with a bitterness so intense it even surprised her. "They could have called back everybody! Instead, they kept all those case officers out there, hoping their luck wouldn't run out!"

Katrina exhaled in defeat and frustration. "There's no way to bring two hundred case officers back in from the field quietly and subtly, even over the course of a couple months. Our friends and enemies would have noticed—and everyone would know we had suffered an epic breach." Off Dee's skeptical look, Katrina added, "I'm not saying Boyles and the rest of them made the right choice, only that every other option had drawbacks, too."

"Yeah, but making hard choices with no good options is the job," Ward added. "Don't ask for that responsibility if you're not ready to handle it. We've got a lot of plates spinning on our own down here. We've got our Voices hunt, and we've got our Kobold hunt—this world rarely throws just one problem at you at a time."

Raquel approached, realized the tension in the moment, and waited a minute or two before interrupting.

"Patrick wants a meeting," Raquel mentioned to Katrina.

Alec rolled his eyes. "Haven't we suffered enough?"

When Patrick arrived, he was tense, and on edge. He offered he most cursory greetings to Katrina, Raquel, and Dee, and just barely nodded at Alec and Ward. Katrina noticed Patrick avoided eye contact with Ward—which was just as well, because Ward's body language made clear he wasn't interested in anything Patrick had to say.

Patrick looked at the empty chair around the table. "No little friend from the Bureau today?"

"Nah, she's busy acting out a Tuesday night prime-time drama for CBS," Alec deadpanned.

Patrick announced that he wanted to talk Kobold. He had barely gotten started when a knock on the office vault door revealed that someone had brought a hand-delivered memo to Raquel. She promptly disappeared into her office.

"You set up a meeting with Patrick and then abandon us?" Alec snarked as the door closed. "Coward!"

Patrick shot Alec a contemptuous glare, cleared his throat, and restarted his opening pitch.

"I had really hoped that Barron and the Kobold working group had asked you to do more than just consult," Patrick fumed. "We need to hunt these bastards down now and shut them down before they open up Pandora's Box even wider!"

Alec and Katrina exchanged a look, furrowing their brows at Patrick's sudden urgency. What was his angle in all this?

"Patrick, we've just gotten our pants pulled down by Kobold," Katrina observed. "Kobold's already done their worst to us. The biggest threat is now to everyone else they hacked."

Alec grinned. "And if Kobold's about to embarrass the crap out of Beijing or Moscow or a bunch of Swiss bankers, my biggest concern is going to be having enough popcorn while I watch and laugh."

Patrick exhaled with seething exasperation. "I see your ability to grasp the big picture is as strong as ever. Pop quiz, Alec, how calm do China and Russia seem these days? Xi Jinping shut down whole cities for months every time somebody sneezed! If those nuclear-capable Chinese bombers fly any lower over Taiwan they're gonna start scraping the roofs! And how steady and rational does Russia's leadership seem lately? Putin hints at leaving Ukraine all aglow every couple of weeks. You really want to see what a humiliated Russia does, when it's backed into a corner?"

Alec began to begrudgingly nod.

"Let me spell it out for you," Patrick continued. "Putin and Xi are not the kinds of laid-back guys who will just kick the cat when their dirty laundry gets exposed for all the world to see! And what if the next hack is of the Iranians? Or the Norks? This Kobold character doesn't realize that he's juggling nitroglycerin. All these regimes are run by paranoid maniacs who are terrified of looking vulnerable in front of the people they rule. They'll lash out and start rattling sabers. If we're lucky, nobody starts another war over this. If we're not lucky, we'll get strikes on Taiwan and Russian strikes on the Baltics and everybody's running duck-and-cover drills again."

Alec sighed. "This is unbelievable," he muttered. "Patrick just made a good point."

They were interrupted by Raquel emerging from her office; her face and body language indicated she was beside herself with anger and frustration.

"The exposure from Kobold just got a lot worse," she fumed. "The good news is we're now sure we got all our case officers out, but we've lost a ton of agents and informants. We lost high-value sources within Hezbollah, Hamas, Iranian intelligence, the old VEVAK, the Russians, the Syrians, the Chinese ... "

"Lost, as in ... " Dee's voice trailed off.

"As in executed or scheduled to be executed, Dee. Seventeen that we're sure have been executed, twenty-nine that we suspect. Whole rings of spies, rounded up and shot in the head. Kobold might as well have pulled the trigger himself."

The group offered various groans and sounds of frustration and defeat.

"Wait, believe it or not, there's an even worse part. We've still got a whole bunch of captured intelligence sources who are scheduled for execution, which means every hostile state in the world just collected a big pile of bargaining chips."

"Every one of those people risked their lives to help the United States," Katrina firmly declared. "We owe it to people like that to do whatever we can to get them out."

"Director Boyles is working the phones like a general manager at the trade deadline, trying to see which ones of our people we can save."

"In exchange for what?" Alec asked, with rising concern.

"In exchange for whom," Raquel corrected. "Everybody wants a rerun of the Viktor Bout trade. By the time this is done, they're gonna clean out Federal Medical Center Carswell. The Iranians want the Atarsa recruiter Fabrice Vuscovi."

"Oh, hell no!" Ward roared. "That woman tried to kill me! You do not get to play a key role in a series of terrorist attacks on American soil and then waltz off to enjoy a cushy retirement in Tehran!"

"Wait, I'm not done," Raquel continued. "The Syrians want Shedim mastermind Shakira Eribat, and the Russians asked for Allen Pittman, a.k.a. Hell-Summoner. I presume they want to see if he could design a virus that would only wipe out Ukrainians. Or maybe just because it would piss us off."

"The Syrians want Eribat?" Alec asked in confusion.

"She's Lebanese heritage, they see her as one of theirs," Raquel said with a shrug.

"You're saying everyone we worked so hard to put behind bars might be set free in a prisoner exchange, and left to take another shot at killing innocent people and unleashing chaos?" Katrina seethed.

"Ya see, this is why I kill people," Ward boasted, in a tone that made it hard to tell if he was joking. "Every terrorist I've ever shot is still dead. You know who I'm willing to trade to the Russians and Iranians? All the corpses. Knock yourself out, comrades."

CHAPTER FIFTEEN

When Boyle and other senior CIA officials couldn't work out a trade, they stalled for time. Rescue plans were discussed, but universally dismissed as unlikely to succeed. After a week, four more agents had been executed after talks broke down, and roughly a hundred more were imprisoned, and often beaten and harshly interrogated, in prisons from Moscow to Damascus to Tehran to Beijing.

Katrina wasn't sure she had ever seen the mood within the Agency worse—until one day the entire building seemed to simultaneously exclaim excitement, as obscure websites and chat boards around the world were suddenly all full of a small mountain of highly classified Chinese government documents.

Kobold had released the treasure from his second big hack, a massive trove of documents from Beijing's Ministry of State Security. The CIA suddenly knew the identities of at least two hundred Chinese spies, and now it was Beijing's turn to panic.

Dee burst into the offices with a gleeful smile, brimming with excitement.

"Did you see in the second Kobold leak? They just exposed the Nine-Tailed Foxes!"

Katrina and Raquel reacted with delight and satisfaction, while Alec and Ward looked at each other, the name ringing some vague bell in the back of their minds. Elaine, who had been at Liberty Campus to argue with Alec in person some more, was also trying to place the name.

"Okay, I remember that term from my CI days," Elaine said. "Remind me, who are the 'Nine Tailed Foxes'?"

Raquel erupted with an uncharacteristic "Yes!" and fist pump as she scrolled through the first summary of the hack. Finally, one of America's enemies was being bitten in the ass by bad luck.

"China's version of us, the 'Hulijing,'" Raquel explained. "Technically off-the-books, a small team that Beijing uses for covert missions abroad. They've been a nasty thorn in the side of us, Taiwan, Japan, South Korea for, oh, at least a decade, probably a decade and a half. They're scary good. Couple years back they got all the secrets of the Taiwanese president's security detail."

"Funny, I would have figured our paths would have crossed by now," Alec observed.

"Mine almost did," Katrina murmured, reading the first internal agency bulletin summarizing the latest Kobold leak on her computer. She paused and leaned back, and half smiled.

"Picture it: Thailand, 2015," Katrina began.

"You learned storytelling from Sofia Petrillo," Alec said with a laugh. "I've been rubbing off on you more than you want to admit."

Katrina winked back at her husband. "This was when we were chasing Bengali ISIS, and their money men were traveling in the same circles as the Nine-Tailed Foxes," she said in a tone reserved for the peculiar kind of nostalgia for a difficult time sufficiently past to seem not so bad anymore. "Right before I arrived in Bangkok, some Thai official known for opposing closer ties with China had fallen from a window of a high-rise hotel. But the Foxes didn't even bother to make it look like a suicide. Everybody knew they threw him through the window. Lots of signs of struggle in the hotel room, he'd lost a lot of blood before he fell. The Thais thought it was the Chinese being sloppy. I figured they wanted us to know they did it—and they wanted everyone to know that this guy's final hours were terrible. Deterrent effect on anybody else in the Thai government thinking of taking the same stance."

Ward nodded grimly. "And here I thought China had so much leverage over southeast Asia because of their charming diplomats."

"A few weeks later, I was in Malaysia, similar story," Katrina continued. "Some Malaysian Navy official, might have been some guy on track to be admiral, been making noise about the South China Sea, arguing for a tougher line against Beijing. One day he just disappears, without a trace. Six months later, they found one of his fingers—his middle finger. In Chinese culture, a middle finger is even more contemptuous than our culture."

"Well, if they're exposed, they're out of business, right?" Alec asked hopefully.

Katrina nodded. "Exposure like this means letting them out of the country is an enormous risk for China. Everybody will have them on watch lists, maybe even an Interpol Red Notice. Lots of governments will want revenge. This forces them into early retirement."

"Ruthless Chinese assassins get to retire early?" Elaine asked. "Not exactly my definition of a win."

They were interrupted by Raquel, slamming her hand down on the desk, in excitement and surprise.

"No kidding!" Raquel exclaimed, leaning so far toward Dee's screen she nearly tipped over her rolling office chair. "Katrina, did you see who was running that team?"

"I haven't read that far yet—wait... William Yen Wen?"

Raquel nodded, smiling as if she had just found evidence of the Loch Ness Monster. "Better known in the halls of Langley as 'Waldo.'"

"That guy?" Katrina's eyes widened in recognition. "Waldo! We were so close, so many times!"

Alec, Ward, and Dee exchanged confused looks.

"Who's Waldo?" Dee asked in bewilderment.

"Nobody disappeared in a crowd better than this guy," Katrina said with a combination of wonder and frustration. "I remember guys on the China desk complaining about him—Beijing, Hong Kong, Macau, Tokyo—time and again, they'd have this guy under surveillance, dead to rights, whole teams on scene, and he'd just disappear. One moment he's there—" She snapped her fingers. "Next moment he's gone. After a while, we were pretty sure he was toying with us. I've seen the videos, it's like a magic trick—he's staring at the camera, someone walks in front of him, and when they pass, he's gone. Pure Houdini."

"Did you try looking for the striped shirt and glasses?" Alec asked.

Raquel read off the leaks detailing the other five members of the Nine-Tailed Fox team.

"Okay, we've had files on a bunch of these folks, we just didn't have anything connecting them to the Foxes. Chen Zhang—hard to nail down his role on the team because he's so versatile. He's big for a Chinese, tough and strong, so he can be their bruiser. But he was also often the getaway driver. Highly rated marksman, but also charming."

Ward studied the summary and smiled. "So, basically Chinese me."

Raquel let out a laugh and then looked thoughtful. "When I read about this guy, we thought he was tied in with the Chinese criminal underground. That must have been his cover."

She scrolled down the screen.

"They've got a hacker, Jin Goh. Suspected of cracking and hacking at least two secure Pentagon systems and basically all our allies, to say nothing of every security system in any place the Foxes have ever gone."

Alas, the leaked ID photo of Jin Goh looked terribly awkward—thick glasses, poor teeth, overweight with a baby face.

"That is the face of a man who never gets up from his computer," Ward observed.

Dee offered a smug smile. "You guys have no idea how lucky you are to have me."

"Oh, we know," Alec said with a nod.

The next image, of a strikingly beautiful Chinese woman, spurred reflexive "wow"s from Alec and Ward. Katrina wasn't offended or threatened, but smiled and made a mental note of it.

"This Nine-Tailed Fox is an actual fox," Alec joked.

"Ren Xiulan, who, as you can see, probably could have been a supermodel if she had wanted that path," Raquel continued, with a slight roll of her eyes. "Don't let her looks fool you. Off-the-charts intelligence, speaks a dozen languages, trained in close-quarters weapons, not afraid to slit somebody's throat."

"Chinese Katrina," Alec concluded.

"Needless to say, if any of the Nine-Tailed Foxes' plans required seducing or luring some poor schmuck into a compromising position, chances are Ren was the one to do it."

"So, she's like me, without standards," Katrina said with a laugh.

The next file was another woman, younger than Ren, in a Chinese military uniform.

"Peng Xiaodan, newest member of the team. Ironically transferred after a sterling start to her career in the Intelligence Bureau of the Joint Staff Department of the Central Military Commission—Chinese military intelligence. She's probably a big factor in why the Nine-Tailed Foxes were never caught. Thinks like a cop, which keeps them one step ahead of the cops. Another jack-of-all-trades, she can fight, drive, sneak around, charm and distract a guard."

Everyone at the table glanced over at Elaine, then looked down. Elaine seemed oblivious to any similarity between herself and Peng.

Alec scrolled up and down the electronic document.

"Hey, wait, there's no Chinese me!"

He looked up, revealing a disappointment deeper than the Mariana trench.

"Raquel, you said these guys were the Chinese version of us! Why don't the Nine-Tailed Foxes have their own version of the forensic accountant and terrorism financing analyst with the sharpest wit and funniest one-liners, who's more competent than he looks and who goes into a berserker rage when his family is threatened?"

Katrina, amused by his not-entirely-acting sense of offense, kissed him on the forehead.

"Because you're one of a kind," she purred.

Raquel shook her head. "Nope, Beijing went in a different direction for their last member. Zeng Zongying. Yes, tough martial artist and field agent, but specializes as an interrogator. More than a little psycho. Fanatically loyal to the state."

"Still... you would think they could have tried to find a Chinese me," Alec muttered, only half-joking. "They're called the Nine-Tailed Foxes, you would think they would have nine team members."

"Dueling six demons is plenty, partner," Ward warned.

CHAPTER SIXTEEN

Despite the good news, Dee entered the office, fuming.

"Remember a few weeks ago, when we told Barron and the Kobold Working Group we would come up with a list of unlikely suspects to check out? My algorithm came up with forty-seven possible suspects. I sent the whole list to the Kobold working group. Barron told me they did investigations of the first forty-five and came up empty. She said they weren't even bothering with the last two."

"They skipped the last two? Gee, with a work ethic like that, how could anyone possibly elude such relentless sleuths?" Katrina asked dryly.

"Man, that's kind of bitchy," Alec exclaimed. "They have some setback in the investigation or something?"

Dee looked a little sullen. "Well, she had asked how my program the Bloodhound Gang was going. It's still working, and I said I still didn't know when it would finish. I think that put her in a bad mood."

"Pressure's getting to them," Raquel sighed. "Our leak, China's leak, Russia leak likely coming next—it's all making people outside this building wonder if someone has a working quantum computer. The speculation and rumors are already out there."

Alec suddenly looked serious. "Who were the last two?"

"The last two leaks?"

"No, the last two names on your list of potential suspects."

Dee typed quickly, bringing up two files and displaying them on the large monitor.

"Amaja Rai, retired tech CEO entrepreneur," Dee began. "Born in India, immigrated to the U.S. at age ten, went to Yale, Harvard MBA, her resume basically glows. McKinsey Consulting, stints at GlobeScape and IBM, ran some R&D departments, was a big deal in the Davos conference circuit for a few years, promoting women in tech, that kind of stuff. Then around 2017, she just went quiet. Some people thought it was burnout, but there are a few rumors she's been working on some project. And before she went quiet, she was asking a lot of questions about the potential of quantum computing."

"She certainly piqued my interest as a suspect," Raquel remarked.

Alec furrowed her brow. "And the Kobold Working Group didn't want to check her out?"

"If it's not just laziness, then she probably seems too clean. Super-wealthy, lot of lawyers on speed dial," Katrina observed.

"She owns a bunch of houses, but is currently living in her luxury beachfront estate in the Maldives, out in the middle of nowhere," Dee said, bringing up an image from Google Earth.

"Once the Kobold Group said they didn't want to look any further, I tried to dig into her financial records. First, she's got cybersecurity tricks that I've never even seen before. Second, her finances are complicated, lots of holding companies, offshore accounts, LLCs. Not a certain indicator that there's something sinister going on, but it's the sort of mess you would use if you wanted to hide money going somewhere. Third, what I could find is that she spends a lot—probably too much—on a private security firm for her Maldives estate and travels. Like, Salman Rushdie level security."

Alec stared back skeptically. "Is that a lot? Because he got stabbed."

Ward perused the file on the security firm she had under contract. "These guys tout themselves as heavy hitters, and they don't come cheap. You don't hire guys like this unless you think somebody's coming after you."

"Who's the other one?" Katrina asked.

Dee tapped a button on her keyboard and brought up the second file.

"Vadam Balan. The biggest quantum computing geek in Transnistria."

Ward and Alec exchanged a skeptical glance.

Alec asked, "Is that big, or like being the tallest skyscraper in Des Moines?"

Ward looked closer at the map. "I'm pretty good at geography, and I'm pretty sure Transnistria isn't a real country."

Dee nodded. "In the eyes of most of the world, it isn't. Transnistria is a breakaway region of Moldova, a thin sliver of land up against the border of Ukraine, that insists it's an independent country. The place loves Russia and acts like it's a colony of theirs. The second-biggest company in the country is a conglomerate formed by two former KGB guys. The nephew of one of them is into computer science, has his own company, state contracts, the works. But in the past few years he's been really into quantum computing."

Katrina looked closer at the picture of Balan, a Slavic combination of Mark Zuckerberg and Justin Timberlake. "How is this guy not higher on the suspect list?"

"Remember, FSB got hacked shortly after we did," Raquel observed. "A pro-Russian Transnistrian with KGB in the family would be taking a massive risk trying something like that."

"Unless you've built something amazing and you want the whole world to know you can hack anyplace," Alec countered. "Hitting us and the Russians and the Chinese points to having a lot of nerve, or a serious lack of judgment. Look at that face.

Look at these portraits—fancy furniture and t-shirt and designer jeans that are a little too perfectly torn up? A snot-nosed punk like this? He's definitely bold and dumb enough to do something like that."

"If this place is basically a satellite state of Russia, that's going to make knocking on the door of this guy a lot more challenging," Ward warned.

Raquel shook his head. "Eh, not really, he's in Transnistria, not Russia, and either way, we're still not explicitly at war with Russia."

"We're not *not* at war with Russia, either," Alec shot back.

Raquel looked around the room.

"Tom and Alejandro were supposed to be helping train Ukrainian pilots, but apparently that program is delayed getting the Ukrainians up to speed on English. Katrina, I'm going to have one of them fly you and Ward to the Maldives."

Ward studied the satellite photo of Rai's beachfront estate.

"You think we should storm the beaches?" he asked Raquel.

Raquel nodded. "I trust your judgment, but yes, at first glance, that's what I'd recommend. She'll have security guards all around the perimeter, doors, gates, but that beach and bay is huge—very tough to watch all of that."

Katrina and Alec picked up separate phones to see which parents could get to northern Virginia on short notice to watch Harry and William.

CHAPTER SEVENTEEN

VAADHOO ISLAND
THE MALDIVES
SEPTEMBER 8, 2023

"Ward . . . why is the beach glowing?"

Amaja Rai's estate on Vaadhoo Island in the Noonu Atoll of the Maldives belonged on the cover of a travel magazine. The property was sprawling but seemed to blend in with the jungle. On the north side of the property was a long dock, several small boats, a luxury yacht, and seaplane. During the day, the view in every direction looked like it came from a postcard; at night, the sky and the land were spectacularly dark, other than a handful of lights in the house.

But the sea was not dark. Instead, the beach incursion was complicated by the fact that the tide coming in seemed to be glowing an eerie aquamarine, almost like the water was saturated with blue neon. The satellite photos, taken during the day, had not detected that the waters off Vaadhoo Island were full of swarms of bioluminescent ostracod crustaceans—flat aquatic creatures carried in by the tides that were about one millimeter in length. The orstacods glowed like fireflies but blue instead of yellow. They didn't bite, sting, or otherwise represent any threat to Katrina and Ward, coming ashore soaking wet and loaded up with gear. But they did light up the beach in a way that doomed any hopes of sneaking ashore.

"This whole incursion plan counted on the cover of darkness!" Ward fumed. "Having the beach covered in glowing blue fairy dust is gonna complicate this!"

Katrina had envisioned Amaja Rai waking up to find Katrina and Ward at the foot of her bed, and having a conversation where sheer shock and fear made it likely Rai would give honest answers. Alec had seemed convinced that the Transnistrian kid was the most likely suspect, but something about Rai stirred Katrina's suspicions. It may well have been the old file photos of Rai during her years as a corporate executive. Something in Amaja Rai's eyes declared that she was born to wield power.

They had gotten ashore, shed the scuba gear, and approached the deck when both Ward and Katrina heard the guards simultaneously. First over to the left, and then over to the right. And then up ahead. They heard the shouting and realized that with glowing aqua blue waters behind them, if they retreated, they would make a very easy target for any guards who wanted to take a shot at them.

"This went bad, quickly," Katrina sighed. "Maybe we are getting too old for this."

Ward lowered his weapon, a Glock with a suppressor, and placed it on the ground. He raised his hands.

"You think they're going to turn us over to the cops?"

"Folks this wealthy don't always want to get the authorities involved," she answered calculating the best odds of an escape and evasion.

The security guys were beefy and multilingual. Ward was pretty sure one was Filipino, one was German, one looked like he was either Argentinian or Chilean, and the other three were Indian. They stripped Katrina and Ward of their gear and anything they deemed useful as a weapon, and then ordered them to head into the house.

Once inside, the guards had a brief argument about where the zip-ties were supposed to be kept, and why they didn't have the zip-ties. Ward watched them and wondered if Amaja Rai had been assigned the worst team from one of the security contractors. Or maybe this team was made up of the rejects from other teams.

The Filipino disappeared down a hallway and returned with duct tape and used that to bind Ward's hands. Curiously, they didn't bind Katrina; both were led to the second floor, where Ward was told to sit on a couch, while Katrina was brought inside and told to wait.

***

Katrina stood in a luxurious combination home office and study. Katrina realized Raquel would have liked it, but she could never keep it so tidy. In fact, the room was almost a little too perfectly tidy, with everything at perfect 90-degree angles, down to the magazines on the coffee table.

After a few moments, the door on the other side opened.

Amaja Rai appeared, but she wasn't upset. Instead, she grinned a smile that lit up the room.

"I was hoping you would be the one who found me," Amaja Rai declared, in a voice as sensuous as velvet, that reminded Katrina of the sound of water splashing from a small waterfall. "Katrina Leonidivna."

Katrina couldn't completely hide her surprise at that statement. "How do you know who I am?"

Amaja Rai continued to offer a smile that was almost completely warm. "Please, take a seat."

Katrina remained standing, and Amaja furrowed her brow, but continued. "You're not just any senior case officer of the CIA. For years now, you've been something of an urban legend in the criminal and terrorist underworlds—the Central Asian–looking modern samurai. I understand in Islamist circles they call you 'Almar'at alshaytaniat alati tuasil qatl eayilatina.' Not that it's an easy nickname that rolls off the tongue."

Katrina tilted her head slightly as she tried to translate the words. "Sounds like, 'the devil who kills' ... "

Amaja nodded. "More like 'the devil woman who kills our brothers.' A woman cannot cut a path through the world the way you have without gaining some notoriety."

Katrina felt a weird surge of pride interrupt the tension of the moment. The work of the Dangerous Clique hadn't left many witnesses to its handiwork, but signals intercepts had indicated that their past missions had left stories and rumors, usually a description of a beautiful woman who appeared right before all the violence started.

"The fact that you know who I am means you expected me to show up at your door," Katrina surmised. "Which means I've found the person who hacked our systems ... Kobold."

Instead of denying it, Amaja just beamed with pride. "Katrina ... yes ... I am Kobold. And I didn't even have to hack the Agency's internal code name for me; my *nom de guerre* is being mentioned in various Discord servers."

Katrina shook her head, and wondered if hacking was superfluous considering how quickly the U.S. government spilled the beans on its own secrets.

"I wanted you to find me because I thought you might understand why I'm doing what I'm doing," Amaja continued. She sat and gestured to Katrina, and Katrina relented. She eyed the small sculptures on the table and wondered if they would be heavy enough to use as a weapon. An obsidian statuette of a falcon looked promising.

"Katrina, a few years ago, I picked up a *Forbes* magazine that ranked the world's most powerful people, and I noticed two consistent trends. First, almost no women."

Katrina nodded, unsure of where Amaja's conversation was going, but not finding much to disagree with, yet.

"Second, the men who kept atop the list year after year were usually autocrats, brutes, thugs, dictators. Vladimir Putin, Xi Jinping, MBS. Even the leaders of democracies like Trump and Modi were arrogant, narcissistic, reckless nationalists. The business world won't save us, with Sam Bankman-Fried and all the other egomaniacal tech bros. Last I checked, that walking Texas monument to megalomania named Jerry Jones is about the 180th-richest person in the world, ahead of George Soros. Silvio Berlusconi was still on the list, I guess it was his last year, ranked 336. Melinda Gates didn't even show up until 411. Democracy, communism, monarchies, business—it seems like, no matter how hard we try, the scum always rises to the top. We're ruled by insecure, power-hungry men who can only feel strong if they're dominating someone else."

Katrina stared at Amaja Rai, surprised at how the conversation had progressed. "This is my first confrontation with a suspected hacker of U.S. classified information where I feel like we should be having wine."

"Don't get me wrong, I can enjoy the company of a man. I'm sure there are good ones out there. But give a man power, and his worst traits come out—his ego, his need for control, his unwillingness to listen to others, his rage at criticism."

Katrina chuckled. "Yes, if only the world could be led by wise and compassionate women, like Kim Yo-jong or Elizabeth Holmes. Or maybe you're convinced you would be the benevolent dictator. You've hurt a lot of people."

"You notice I sat on the information for months before releasing it, right?" Amaja asked. "I'm not Julian Assange. I'm not a psychopath. I gave the Agency nearly half a year to get their people out of harm's way before releasing what my people hacked.

If any CIA assets got hurt, it was the Agency's fault for not getting them out of the country when they had ample opportunity."

Katrina furrowed her brow. Amaja Rai kept making frustratingly compelling arguments. "That doesn't mean there's a statute of limitations on your crimes."

"Katrina, my team cracked the CIA's firewalls because we've built a working quantum computer—or at least, mostly working, some of the time," Amaja declared, beaming with pride. "We haven't perfected it. But by breaking past the boundaries of known science, we've taken our first steps to changing the world."

"So did Robert Oppenheimer."

"Katrina, I want you to try to understand what my team and I are doing: we can fix the world," Amaja vowed, serious as a heart attack. "Quantum computing will give me access to all the world's secrets. All of them."

"That's what I'm afraid of," Katrina shot back.

"Katrina, with my quantum computer, I can build a real New World Order," Amaja boasted. "The U.S. government will never be able to hide any of its dirty little secrets."

Katrina couldn't stifle her laugh and blurted out, "Were you under the impression we're any good at hiding our dirty little secrets?" She realized that after all these years of marriage, Alec was indeed rubbing off on her.

Amaja shook her head at Katrina's sarcasm and gestured to an antique map of the world on the wall.

"The Chinese government would have you believe that less than ten thousand of its people died from Covid," Amaja sneered, in a tone that indicated she considered Beijing's official statement a sin on par with Holocaust denial. "It's just coincidence that since the pandemic started, they had two to three million more pneumonia deaths than usual. I can expose that secret. Why shouldn't I?"

Katrina thought for a moment. "You should have tried this pitch on my husband."

"Do you like the world the way it is, Katrina?" Amaja asked. "Are you so satisfied with the status quo that you see no room for improvement?"

"Your idea of an improvement is a power grab," Katrina replied icily.

Amaja quickly continued. "Putin's wealth can be tracked down and exposed to the last ruble. With the ability to hack into any banking system, I'll be able to bankrupt any man with the touch of a button. Eventually we'll be able to create deepfake video of anything. I can rewrite news reports in the time it takes them to travel from the camera to the screen. Russia's disinformation efforts might as well be sock puppets."

Katrina looked at her foe skeptically. "And what's to make sure you don't abuse that power?"

Amaja ignored the question.

"No coups, no seizing of power. Just quiet late-night phone calls, instructing world leaders on the decisions they will make. Just think, we could convert the world to green energy and steamroll the objections of the fossil fuel industries. Every religious extremist from Kabul to Texas will be shut down, shut up, shunted aside, forgotten. Your country's a xenophobic, homophobic, transphobic Orwellian nightmare state? Watch me expose all your secrets until you say 'uncle.'"

As Amaja described that vision, her face and voice revealed a deep-ridden hunger for revenge. Someone had done Amaja Rai wrong in her five decades on this planet, and she was going to make them pay dearly.

"We're going to put the whole world in order. Doing what's right will come first."

Katrina shot back a skeptical look. "If you're thinking of calling yourself the 'First Order,' I think Disney has the copyright on that."

Amala smirked a bit and studied Katrina closely.

"You've picked up your husband's habit of cracking jokes to dodge what's before you," Amaja observed. "My research indicates you're a mother now; you must be wondering what kind of world your sons will inherit. Who's going to shape that world? Your CIA? They have trouble managing their own parking lots. The only person who can really protect your children, and everyone's children, is me. Katrina, join me."

Katrina stepped closer and stared at Amaja for a long time. Amaja also rose and offered her hand.

And then Katrina took the offered hand and held it in a firm grip. Amaja smiled.

That smile disappeared a moment later as Katrina suddenly grabbed Amaja's wrist and bent her hand so far backward it sprained her wrist, tearing the ligaments in two places. Amaja howled in pain as Katrina wrestled the hand behind her back and threw her against the nearest table.

"What kind of an idiot do you think I am?" Katrina demanded. "You know that I took an oath when I joined the Agency, right? 'Support and defend the Constitution of the United States against all enemies, foreign and domestic, so help me God'? Just where do you think helping you blackmail my own government fits in there?"

Amaja's guards started pounding at the doors.

"You're breaking my arm!" Amaja cried.

"Yes, that's the point!" Katrina declared through gritted teeth. Amaja howled as Katrina gave her arm another awkward, intense twist, and shoulder ligaments tore as easily as tissue paper. And then she realized something about Amaja's global ambitions.

"Say, Amaja, by any chance do you hear the Voices?"

"What are the Voices?"

Katrina exhaled.

"Well, at least I don't have to worry about that."

Katrina realized the pounding at the doors had stopped.

"Ward?"

"All clear out here!"

Katrina gave Amaja Rai a shove into a chair, and Amaja, instead of fighting, gingerly held her shoulder and arm. Katrina went to the double doors she entered and opened them.

Ward stood with three men at his feet—two unconscious, the other groaning on the ground, holding his crotch. The shreds of duct tape around Ward's wrists indicated he had chewed his way through them and overtaken his captors.

"How did you—"

"Something's going on, they're freaked about some approaching aircraft," Ward reported. "They left fewer guys on me and . . . " His voice trailed off and he shook his hands, sore from punching. He noticed Amaja Rai in the chair in the corner of the room and gave her a little wave.

"Ma'am, I think you're getting ripped off by your security contractor, these are third-tier guys."

"Approaching aircraft?"

"Yeah, two helicopters, not ours. That wasn't part of the plan, and we don't have those kinds of assets in this area."

Katrina turned to Amaja.

"Where's the quantum computer?"

"Somewhere no one will ever find it," Ajama said with a laugh. "At the end of the earth."

Ward glared. "What are you, the Riddler? Lady, ain't nobody got time for that!" He paused. "Katrina, break her other arm."

"No time, we've got to get her out of here," Katrina declared. "Come on, let's see which one of her boats is the fastest."

CHAPTER EIGHTEEN

Ward had grabbed the guns of the security guys—he was unimpressed with their choice of firearms, too—and a walkie-talkie, but noticed the guards' chatter had reached a crescendo of panic about the helicopters and then everyone had just gone silent. Maybe the radio silence was a surprising burst of professionalism, but Ward and Katrina figured it meant that whoever was in those helicopters was taking out Rai's security team. Or the security team was resigning without two weeks' notice.

Which meant someone else had figured out Amaja Rai was Kobold, she was behind the hacks, had built a working quantum computer, and was arguably the most important human being on earth at that moment.

Katrina, Ward, and Amaja Rai had just gotten to the beach when two helicopters landed on either side of them—sleek civilian craft, both painted black.

"Airbus H175s, lot of countries use those, mostly Europe . . ." Ward observed.

Within a moment, a pair emerged from each helicopter—one man and one woman from each, all Chinese.

"And Airbus has a deal with China where they make it under another name," Ward realized.

Katrina hadn't met them, but she realized she had seen their photos recently.

William Yen Wen, the disappearing man nicknamed Waldo.

Chen Zhang, the beefy driver.

Peng Xiaodan, the cop.

Zeng Zongying, the interrogator.

The Nine Tailed Foxes, the Chinese government's version of the Dangerous Clique, apparently nowhere near as restricted to mainland China as the CIA believed.

Ward noticed a red dot on his chest and Katrina's.

"Two snipers on the perimeter," Ward winced, holding up his gun and moving slowly to place it on the ground. Katrina exhaled and did the same.

"A wise choice," Waldo declared. "And I'll bet my English is better than your Chinese."

"William Yen Wen," Katrina declared. "We meet at last. How do you feel about the nickname, 'Waldo'?"

"Flattering, once I understood its meaning, the man who can never be found," Waldo observed. "A month ago, no one knew who I was. Now it seems everyone in the world knows who we are."

"I guess I know what brings you to the neighborhood," Katrina quipped.

"You guys are interrupting a perfectly legitimate kidnapping," Ward added.

Surprisingly, that brought a smile to Waldo's face.

"The American version of the Nine-Tailed Foxes, the *Wéixiăn jítuán*, the Pernicious Assemblage," he greeted.

For a moment, Ward and Katrina thought about correcting the mistranslation of their team's nickname, but just shrugged and decided it was close enough.

"We will take Amaja Rai, thank you," Waldo declared. He took a hard look at the former executive.

Zhang and Peng forcefully grabbed Amaja and shoved her until she was face-to-face with Waldo.

"Your reckless actions have torn the world asunder," he spat. "One of the few satisfactions remaining to me will be watching you suffer the consequences for how you destroyed our lives."

"I exposed the truth," Amaja declared defiantly. "What happens next isn't my fault."

Waldo just lashed out and slapped her.

"Jiānzhà de biǎo zi!" he swore. "You destroyed our purpose! Until you leaked our secrets, we were the modern *Xia*—ancient, honorable warriors! We served our modern emperor, the state. We fought the injustice inflicted upon the great Chinese nation!"

Ward knew he should keep his mouth shut, but somehow, the Chinese operative's delusional self-image was too much to take, and he wondered if the angry Waldo might beat her even worse.

"Mmm, standing up to all those Tibetan, Uighur, and Taiwanese bullies, huh?"

Waldo turned to Ward, a bit surprised at the disrespectful outburst. Zhang looked at him like an angry dog itching to be let off his chain.

"You look military," Waldo observed. "Surely you relate, even if you don't want to admit it. We had a noble calling, a duty. And we performed those duties with excellence. And then one day—because of her—'Kobold!'" He spat the name. "It all disappears. We are exposed and disgraced. The Ministry of State Security says we are useless—even though it was their insecure servers that led to all this!"

"You're rogue!" Katrina realized. "This isn't a Chinese Ministry of State Security operation! You're doing this on your own!"

Waldo shrugged.

"What do you do when your own kingdom declares they no longer need you?" Waldo asked rhetorically, revealing a surprising bit of vulnerability. "What do you do when you're dismissed and told to spend the rest of your days in a retirement that is like a prison?"

There was an awkward bit of silence, as Katrina, Ward, and Amaja realized Waldo, one of China's most skilled and decorated foreign intelligence officers, was facing an identity crisis. He had dedicated his life to serving the Chinese state, and seemingly overnight, the state decided it no longer needed him.

Ward cleared his throat. "You know… we're hiring."

Katrina turned and glared at Ward. Clearly, Alec's personality had been rubbing off on him, too.

Much to their surprise, Waldo found that suggestion hilarious and laughed for a few moments. The other Nine-Tailed Foxes seemed to find it funny, too.

"Join you?" Waldo laughed, as if Ward had made the most ridiculous suggestion imaginable. "Why on earth would we ever want to work for the Americans?"

Ward and Katrina exchanged a slightly offended look.

Waldo kept giggling. "Throughout my life, we've looked across the Pacific at the so-called superpower, steadily growing fatter and lazier. Spoiled, weakening, arrogant. Starting wars it can't win, turning your economy into a giant roulette wheel, lecturing the rest of the world about democracy while angry mobs tear through your own Capitol."

Ward grimaced. "Yeah, not gonna lie, that last one really sucked, but at least we've got elections that people can argue about."

"When you spend your life working for Chinese State Security, I'm not buying that the integrity of free elections is your top priority," Katrina observed.

Her impudence amused Waldo. Chinese intelligence had determined that the CIA's "Pernicious Assemblage" was skilled, but there had been no indication of how reflexively, habitually, shamelessly disrespectful they were.

"My priority is China's greatness!" Waldo declared. "We're the heirs to a four-thousand-year-old empire that was the world's intellectual and innovative engine for millennia! We gave the world the gifts of paper, the compass, gunpowder and the printing press!"

"Hey, fellas, speaking of gifts from China, thanks a lot for Covid," Ward snarked. "Next time, wear gloves when you set up a bat petting zoo inside your virus research lab."

"You have a sharp tongue for a man in the crosshairs of my snipers," Waldo observed.

"If you planned on killing us, those snipers would have shot us by now," Katrina surmised. "You're disavowed. If you're supposed to be in some sort of Chinese state-monitored retirement home, you're not supposed to be in the Maldives grabbing the woman who invented a quantum computer. Beijing would never let you out of the country, too much risk of you getting grabbed by us or the Brits or even Russia and getting you to spill your secrets. That means you snuck out of China, which means you're fugitives."

Katrina took a bit of satisfaction in that last word.

"You're in enough trouble as is, which means from the moment you saw us and recognized us as CIA, you realized killing us would mean more trouble than you can handle," Katrina concluded. "After all, I'm not just any American. I'm . . . how does it go again? Almar'at alshaytaniat—"

"Yes, yes, the devil woman who kills the Islamists' brothers," Waldo recited, adding a little "big deal" gesture and rolling his eyes.

Ward shook his head. "I've killed more jihadists than cancer, but I don't get a nickname!"

Katrina ignored him. "Right now, I'll bet all of Chinese intelligence is looking for you, and if you kill us, you'll have the CIA, MI6, and every other Western intelligence hunting you down, too. Your Red Notice would go infrared. You want to turn Amaja Rai over to Beijing—"

Amaja Rai's eyes widened. "You can't do that! They'll torture me!"

Ward glared at Amaja. "Oh, suddenly CIA custody doesn't look so bad, huh? Should have come with us when you had the chance."

Waldo chuckled. "The Nine Tailed Foxes do not accept quiet retirement. We will have full reinstatement with new identities. Amaja Rai is an acceptable prize, but the real prize is the quantum computer."

Katrina's smug satisfaction evaporated.

He gestured, and Zhang and Peng took Amaja Rai toward the helicopters.

"You are correct, Katrina, I do not intend to kill you. But that doesn't mean I won't if you follow us," Waldo warned.

"Are you under the impression that I can fly?"

Waldo laughed. He gave her a little Robert DeNiro–esque satisfied nod with a pointed finger, as if to say, "You're good." As relieved as Katrina was that Waldo and the Nine-Tailed Foxes would not be leaving them dead on a beach on the Maldives, she was growing irritated with Waldo's unflappability. He and his team had somehow either independently tracked Amaja Rai or somehow followed herself and Ward, then waltzed in and taken Amaja Rai from them. And now, Waldo and his team of disavowed Chinese spies had an excellent chance of getting control of the single most powerful codebreaking machine on the planet, a breakthrough that made the Enigma codes look like a decoder ring from the bottom of a cereal box.

"We're in deep," Ward exhaled. "Playing catch-up to these guys is going to be a pain."

Katrina nodded. "But at least now we know we have Kobold. Let's just hope Alec and Patrick stayed out of trouble."

CHAPTER NINETEEN

TIRASPOL, TRANSNISTRIA
TECHNICALLY PART OF MOLDOVA
SEPTEMBER 8, 2023

The drive across the border was smooth enough; Alec Flanagan and Patrick Horne had gone through the border under the assumed identities of Aidan Flannery and Jerry Van Horne, a pair of Silicon Valley venture capitalists who were eager to dump a pile of American dollars onto anyone who promised they were on the verge of a breakthrough in a development of a working quantum computer. The not-quite-a-country of Transnistria wasn't exactly awash in foreign investment, so the local self-proclaimed technology innovation guru, Vadam Balan, was eager to meet with them when they inquired.

Before formally starting the meeting in his office around the corner from the Transnistrian national parliament, Balan insisted upon showing his American guests the national memorial in Surorov Square, across the street from the parliament. The site featured an Arc of Triumph, a Russian-made T-34-85 tank that had been imported from Hungary, and a memorial to those who had died in the Great Patriotic War—what Westerners called World War Two—as well as the short war that had left Transnistria in its state of semi-independence, as well as Chernobyl and another infamous war from the Soviet era.

"Afghanistan," Alec observed. "Boy, that place bites everyone in the ass eventually, huh?"

Once the trio returned to Balan's office, Alec and Patrick quickly learned that while Balan may have been an enthusiastic fan of the idea of quantum computing, he offered no sign that he knew how to actually build one. He argued that the need to keep the computer at super-cold temperatures could be easily overcome, that the "model" for a quantum computer he had designed looked like an hourglass or a woman's body, and, in what seemed to be a translation issue, Balan kept referring to the measurement of "qubits," or quantum bits, as "Q-berts," which made Alec think of the 1980s arcade game.

What Balan lacked in useful knowledge, he made up for in crazy conspiracy theories. He echoed Vladimir Putin in contending that a network of global elites, a "golden billion," secretly controlled the world's resources outside of Russia.

"That's roughly one out of every eight people on the planet," Alec observed. "Where do they hold their meetings?"

Balan ignored the question and added that Madeleine Albright was the head of a global project to dismember Russia and distribute its energy and mineral wealth to rapacious regimes around the globe. Alec cleared his throat and asked how Albright had been performing in this role since she passed away in 2022. Each time, Patrick gave Alec a disapproving glare and a nudge, wanting to keep Balan talking, in hopes he would say something useful. Alec felt confident within five minutes of meeting Balan that not only was he not Kobold, he doubted the fast-talking young man could spell Kobold.

When Balan told Alec and Patrick that he was certain the CIA had already developed a quantum computer, Alec had to swallow a spit-take.

At one point, the conversation drifted to the topic of the ongoing war next door, and Balan assured Alec that there were no civilian casualties in Ukraine; Russian bloggers had "proven" that the Ukrainians were hiring actors to lie down in front of sites that the Ukrainians had bombed themselves to create images to persuade world opinion.

"I don't know, I heard a friend of mine had a bomb land right in front of his car on the way to Kyiv," Alec said, deliberately using the Ukrainian "keev" pronunciation.

"All faked!" Balan scoffed. "Your friend is probably being influenced by the Nazis—or maybe the Jews."

Patrick glared at Alec, as Alec's hands in his lap subtly made fists.

"Mmm, indeed, those groups are known for working together," Alec concurred in a dry deadpan. "You think they hired the actors to be bodies in the mass graves too?"

Patrick kicked Alec under the table.

As they left the meeting, Alec and Patrick exchanged glances that admitted this trip had been a wild goose chase.

"I don't think he's the man organizing the most notorious, ingenious and destructive hacks in human history," Patrick sighed.

Alec stared back, frustrated that it had taken Patrick so long to acknowledge the obvious. "I don't think that guy could organize a sack lunch."

The two Americans sauntered over to a post-meeting lunch in the "Soviet Canteen," which was a small underground restaurant that looked like the Soviet Union had decided to launch its own chain of kitschy brand restaurants, akin to the Hard Rock Café or Planet Hollywood—except instead of guitars and movie props, the walls were adorned with pictures of Lenin, Stalin, Brezhnev and Khrushchev, Soviet military uniforms, and old Russian newspaper front pages.

"It's like the Rainforest Café of Red Square," Alec marveled.

Patrick and Alec ordered some traditional Russian dishes from the cafeteria-style setup and settled into a room off the cafeteria line with arched doorways and long tables and benches. A few other Transistrians slurped their borschts a few tables away.

"We're not going to find Kobold," Patrick lamented. "We're not going to stop him, and he's going to reveal everybody's secrets, and it's all going to come crashing down. All this work. All this effort."

Alec noticed that Patrick seemed to be taking it all personally—and that he had been so patient with Balan because he really wanted the Transnistrian to be Kobold.

"We'll find him," Alec declared, attempting to summon determination and certainty. "We find everybody eventually."

Alec's burner phone buzzed from an incoming call. Use of the phone was reserved for extreme emergencies, as the Agency couldn't guarantee that conversations on it would be secure—and in Transnistria, the assumption was that any kind of electronic communication—phone calls, texts, emails, social media—was intercepted by the Russian FSB.

Alec feared the worst about Katrina.

He answered and it was Dee, sounding breathless and panicked. Patrick furrowed his brow and started clearing the last of his food from one plate to another.

"Alec! Alec! NSA and FBI counterintelligence are running around with their hair on fire!" Dee shouted, almost screaming. "Kobold leaked the Swiss bank data two hours ago! It showed one account that had been slowly getting tens of millions of dollars in payments from Russians, Chinese, accounts that trace back to Atarsa, all kinds of hostile regimes and criminal groups going back almost two decades! You know that mole that we've been hiding from all these years? This is him! And when they tracked down who owned that account, they went through passport records to find a face to go with the fake name and found—"

Alec looked up and saw Patrick Horne swinging his now-empty lunch plate at him—the plate cracked across his forehead.

Alec slid off the bench and lay sprawled on the floor, holding his head. Patrick knocked over the table onto Alec on the floor, pinning Alec underneath it.

"You stupid son of bitch!" Patrick sneered, standing above Alec and pressing down on the table. "Do you have any idea how long I've waited to do that?"

Alec winced, groaned, and scrambled for his phone.

"Hey, Dee, great news, I found the mole, gonna have to call you back!"

Dee's voice through the phone was frantic. "It was Patrick's picture! Patrick is the mole! Patrick—"

Patrick brought his foot down upon the phone, cracking the screen.

"You?" Alec asked in confusion, head throbbing.

"If I had a gun, I'd put a bullet in your head, but I don't," Patrick sneered. He grabbed another plate and swung it down, cracking it over Alec's noggin like the first one.

The last thing Alec could remember before the throbbing in his head made him lapse into unconsciousness was Patrick insisting, to the other patrons and restaurant staff, *"Etot chelovek — Amerikanskiy shpion! Etot chelovek — Amerikanskiy shpion!"*

Right as Alec drifted off into dreamland, his remaining functioning neurons put the words together in English.

"This man is an American spy!"

CHAPTER TWENTY

Alec awoke in a small jail cell. Shortly after, he was informed that a man from the U.S. embassy was here to speak to him.

"I'm with the U.S. State Department. My name is Benjamin Tallmadge," the man said.

"Like hell it is," Alec snapped, rubbing his sore forehead. "You guys are getting a little cute with the aliases."

"Don't speak to anyone. You're going to get released in a few hours," Tallmadge instructed. "Raquel Holtz is on her way here—well, to Chisinau, Moldova—on a U.S. government jet. You're going to be transferred from Transnistrian custody to the Americans at the border."

Alec nodded appreciatively. "I don't suppose you know where Patrick Horne is, do you?"

"I have clear instructions to assure the release of the American citizen Aidan Flannery, which is the name on the passport with your face on it," Tallmadge declared evenly. "As far as I know, Jerry Van Horne, or this 'Patrick Horne' figure you just mentioned, has effectively vanished off the face of the earth."

***

A few hours later, at the border post that separated official Moldova and Transnistria, two police escorted Alec to the checkpoint. On the other side of the dividing line were Raquel, the American official calling himself "Talmadge," a Moldovan

Foreign Ministry official, and two Moldovan soldiers. One of the two soldiers held a cardboard banker's box. Not too far from the border post, a Russian armored personnel carrier with several Russian soldiers eyed Alec and the Transnistrian police warily.

"I was in Ukraine recently," Alec announced to the Transnistrian policemen, gesturing to the Russian armored personnel carrier. "Been a while since I've seen one of those in one piece."

A Moldovan soldier carried the box forward and opened the lid. One of the two Transnistrian cops looked inside, nodded, and accepted it. His partner gave Alec a little shove, and within a moment, the exchange was complete.

"How are you doing?" Raquel asked.

"All things considered, I'm fine, they never even moved me from the local lockup. How did you get me out so fast?"

"As soon as Dee's call went dead, we started looking. The moment they punched your alias name on your passport into the system, we knew it and had our people reach out demanding your release."

"I figured they would play hardball."

The man calling himself Tallmadge let out a little chuckle.

"The Transnistrian government blustered at first, but they had no evidence you're CIA," he explained. "Your only crime was getting into an altercation in a restaurant. They couldn't transfer you to the Russians easily, because Transnistria is landlocked, surrounded by uncooperative countries in Moldova and Ukraine—in fact, Ukraine hates their guts because they're mini-Russia. Our people communicated that holding you would be a lot more trouble than they can handle, and they asked for a trade."

Alec cringed, thinking of the Viktor Bout trade.

"Crap. Really? What did you have to give up for me?"

"A bottle of Pappy Van Wrinkle bourbon," Raquel revealed. "Retails at about a thousand bucks."

Alec stopped walking.

"Seriously? I don't know whether to be insulted or flattered."

"Just be glad you're free, a lot of our people in situations like yours have a much tougher time," Raquel declared. "Oh, other little bit of news, Katrina and Ward found Kobold, it was Amaja Rai, the Indian American tech entrepreneur."

Alec's eyes lit up. "Really? That's great!"

"No, not great," Raquel sighed. "Katrina and Ward couldn't hold onto her and now the Chinese Nine-Tailed Foxes have her."

"What?" Alec exclaimed in disappointment. "Oh, she is going to be so pissed. Dammit, China, stop pissing off my wife, that's my job."

He exhaled as they approached the State Department SUVs. "Please tell me we have a lead on Patrick. I really want to get my hands on him before the Department of Justice does."

Raquel's face communicated deep discontent.

"No sign of him. We think he made it downriver to the Black Sea, and if he got there, if we can dodge the mines in the sea, he can get anywhere."

She paused. "But right around when he disappeared, Patrick sent us a message to Katrina's non-classified e-mail account. It's a video. No one has watched it yet."

***

LIBERTY CAMPUS
SEPTEMBER 11, 2023

The image of Patrick Horne, clad in a tight black turtleneck, sitting calmly, in what appeared to be in some sort of home office, stared out from the screen.

"Are we ready for this?" Raquel asked.

The rest of the team nodded, but Raquel had her doubts. The team's mood was as morose and sullen as she had ever seen it, and the morning's brief ceremony, marking the twenty-second anniversary of the 9/11 attacks, had cast an additional pall over the mood of defeat. Katrina and Ward had both served in Afghanistan in different capacities. Both had spent the past year quietly coming to terms with the fact that the Taliban were now running the country from Kabul again. Neither one had ever openly asked whether all the sacrifice of blood and treasure had been worth it, but Alec had vented for them during a briefing a few months earlier. "It's like Hitler coming back in 1965 to run Berlin again."

And now, the team was bracing itself for the last message from Patrick Horne.

This morning, Alec paced. Katrina sat, arms folded, glaring at the screen. Dee stared at the floor. Elaine's fingers tapped impatiently; she had been the first to arrive. And Ward stirred coffee in a Styrofoam cup, rhythmically.

Raquel hit the "play" button.

"Don't bother trying to trace this message, I'll be long gone by the time you see it. Last year I asked Dee all her off-the-books tricks for tracing electronic messages. Thanks for the advice, Dee."

Dee stared in horror. "I helped teach the mole how to disappear."

"He fooled us all," Raquel said, trying to sound reassuring to Dee, but mostly sounding bitter.

From the screen, Patrick's smug smile faded, and he seemed thoughtful for a moment, looking offscreen. Then he turned his gaze back to the camera.

"Katrina. I've thought about how to tell you all of this for a long time. Because my betrayal of the Agency is now exposed,

I'm going to have to stay hidden for a long time. Don't worry, I've got safehouses, fake passports, allies in every country. You'll never mind me unless I want to find you. But before I disappear, I want to tell you all the things I've wanted to tell you for—God, it must be more than two decades now."

Patrick's face firmed up.

"I did all this because the world isn't fair."

From somewhere deep within Ward's lungs, like a distant rumble of thunder, a haiku of expletives started to bubble up and erupt from his frowning mouth.

"For the first twenty-some years of my life, I did the right thing," Patrick insisted. "I did what was expected of me. What would make everyone so proud of me. My high school transcripts glowed. Harvard. Columbia. Internship with the Senate intel committee. All the right mentors, all the right recommendations. The Agency accepted me, I cruised through the Farm, aced my first assignment in Poland." He paused.

"Yes, I remember, you bastard, we were friends!" Alec sneered the screen. "Once."

"And I met Alec, and we were the best of buddies. Alec, you were like a lesser version of me. You fit, because I needed a sidekick."

Alec's eyes bulged. "Sidekick?"

"But you talked about this girl you met at Georgetown who was so amazing, and I thought nobody could live up to the way you hyped her up. Neither of us knew that I'd already met her at the Farm, but she was using a different name then. 'Allison.' We didn't know each other well, but she was gorgeous and smart and sexy and just... the kind of woman a man meets, and he never forgets her face. And I flirted a bit, but she didn't seem interested, and I couldn't figure out why... "

Katrina stared at the screen. If Ward was a rumbling Mount Vesuvius of volcanic rage ready to erupt, Katrina's reaction to the video so far was a windswept frozen lake on the coldest winter night.

She seethed, "Oh, Patrick, there were so many reasons why..."

Before she could list any reasons, Patrick continued. "And then, months later, I finally get to meet this Katrina you've been raving about, and it's 'Allison.' And we're not supposed to acknowledge that we were in the same training class at the farm. Both of us have to act like we've never met before, but the one who got away is my best friend's girl."

"I was never the one who got away," Katrina whispered, pausing to grind her teeth. "I was never yours to begin with."

Patrick's video continued. "And then you and Harold Hare and Raquel have this crazy plan for a new team. And it's gonna have Katrina, and I'm thinking, 'Fine, here's my chance to show her what a mistake she's making.'"

"He was a member of our team for about twenty minutes!" Alec roared. "He quit on the drive to our first mission!"

"He left me on the side of the road!" Dee raged. "He was the opposite of leave no man behind! He left me behind at the first opportunity!"

"Yes, we were all there," Ward murmured.

On the screen, Patrick shook his head in frustration. "Right then, right there, the world spun off its axis. The CIA should have shut down your team, but they didn't, because apparently the thing with the kids in New York was some sort of 'great victory.'" Patrick sneered the final words.

Alec opened his mouth to argue that rescuing five kidnapped children and killing a slew of terrorists and mercenaries was indeed a great victory, but then he remembered he was arguing with a prerecorded video message that couldn't hear him.

"You guys ignored the rules, ignored protocol, never coordinated with anyone, just do whatever you want... and somehow, you always get away with it!" Patrick complained. "Everybody loves you anyway! I'm the one who's done everything right all his life, the golden boy, the one who always followed the rules! And I get *nothing*!"

On that last word, Patrick erupted in a frightening outburst of long-repressed rage.

"After a year or two of watching your team fall ass-backwards into success, I realize... this is all a joke! Everything I was ever taught was wrong. Nothing is fair. Nothing makes sense. There's no reward for being the good one, top of the class, doing what you're told, pleasing your superiors—at least, not the reward I wanted."

"He never saw me as a person," Katrina shook her head. "Just some prize to be won." Alec reached out to put a hand on her shoulder, but he could sense it wasn't doing any good.

"I transferred to counterintelligence to learn everything I could about how the CIA and FBI catch spies. Basically, the CIA was paying me to learn how to betray it and get away with it. By the end of two years, I knew exactly what we could and could not track—how to set up a fake identity with plausible paperwork, establish a Swiss bank account under a false name, how to conceal my communications, the works. Pretty soon the whole international criminal underground knew that for the right price, they could have any secret in the U.S. government."

Katrina, Alec, Dee, Ward, Raquel, and Elaine continued to stare at the screen.

"Aldrich Ames got caught after nine years. I started early in Bush's second term, so I'm not quite at Robert Hanssen level. My Swiss bank account's got... probably two hundred million by now. Honestly, I don't even care about the money, I haven't touched a cent yet, one of the many reasons I was never caught.... Mostly I did it because it made me happy. Everybody thought you guys were so smart."

Alec noticed Patrick hadn't mentioned Ward. Alec noticed that no matter how much of a jerk Patrick could be, he always steered clear of Ward. It felt good to have a friend who intimidated his rival.

"And right under your noses, sometimes on the same floor, sometimes just down the hall, I was there, sifting through our systems and top classified files, deciding which secrets I would reveal and which ones I would keep. Which operations I would ruin, and which ones I would protect. I sabotaged careers, ruined reputations."

Raquel's gaze shifted from the screen to the upper corner of the room.

"How many times did something go wrong for us, and Patrick was the reason why?" she asked.

Almost as if he had heard her, or had predicted her question, Patrick started to laugh, and went on his own trip down memory lane.

"Two thousand five, that big operation planned in Pakistan. They thought they knew where Zawahiri was. A lot of people wanted to know where the U.S. was looking for al-Qaeda and were willing to pay. You'll recall that at the last minute the Pentagon scrapped the mission because the operation was getting too big, and they weren't sure they still had the element of surprise."

The team stared at the screen, realizing that the number two leader in al-Qaeda might have been captured or killed just four years after 9/11, instead of in a drone strike in Afghanistan in 2022.

"That was a big one," Patrick said with a chuckle. "After that, I knew I could do this. Then in 2008, Bush is leaving, everybody knows Obama's coming in, and there's this talk he might pick Harold frigging Hare as the next director."

"Oh, no," Raquel murmured.

"Couldn't have that!" Patrick laughed to himself. "The old man loved you guys and let me walk out the door without a second glance. So, I made sure all the operations Hare was directing all went south at the same time. Really made him look bad, right as Obama was contemplating who he wanted running the Agency. People concluded Merlin had lost his touch, gotten old, couldn't keep up anymore."

"That bastard!" Alec put more pieces together. "He was always one of William Peck's favorites—he cleared a path for Peck to become director!"

On the screen, Patrick giggled. "Hare's career comes to a screeching halt. Then Trump put Peck in the big chair, and Peck made me Hamilton to his Washington—woo, man! After that, I really had access to everything!"

Raquel glared at the screen and spoke as if Patrick could hear her. "Yeah, well, too bad for you that somehow Atarsa figured out how to slip poison into Peck's coffee and ended his caree—" she froze.

Patrick's expression had changed, on the screen, from a burst of smug pride and nostalgia to a surprisingly sad look.

"Oh my God," Raquel gasped, realizing something. The rest of the team looked at her in confusion.

"Peck and I had a good run," Patrick murmured, almost wistfully. "Some Mexican named Jaguar reached out. Guaranteed the poison wasn't fatal, just a hallucinogen. When I agreed, I thought it was a simple job, somebody wanted to send a message to Peck, back down on something."

The team all exchanged horrified, disbelieving glances, putting the pieces together and solving a mystery that had nagged them for years. CIA director William Peck had been seriously poisoned by Patrick, his own right-hand man.

Alec stared, horrified, nauseous, still confused. "Peck never returned to work! He was never the same! The next year he was dead from Covid!"

For a moment, Patrick looked genuinely guilty. He started to speak, couldn't find the words, then tried again.

"Katrina, I want you to know I didn't realize Atarsa was about to try to burn down the country! What I did with Peck... He would have died anyway. Nothing to do with me."

"Jesus!" Ward roared, knocking his now-empty coffee cup to the floor in an explosion of anger. "Did this little punk ever have a conscience, or was he always Charles Manson on the inside? What, did he sell his soul on the black market along with all our secrets?"

Raquel grabbed the remote and hit pause. The team needed time to digest this—and as painful as it was to watch Patrick's message, they needed to see it.

Katrina stared at the screen.

"It's so clear in retrospect," she murmured. She remembered Dee passing along gossip from two of her girlfriends, that their relationships with Patrick started nice, but that he grew increasingly passive-aggressive, emotionally manipulative, and difficult to trust. It was a hazard of the profession, Katrina figured. Case officers had been trained to lie effectively.

But now, she realized, Patrick's antagonistic attitude reflected something much deeper and darker—an all-consuming, obsessive desire to hurt others who Patrick believed had wronged him. His "dark triad" personality traits—narcissism, Machiavellianism, and a lack of empathy were off the charts. Patrick nurtured his grievances the way most parents nurtured their children.

Alec was shaking. It was like finding an old friend had become a neo-Nazi, or that your neighbor was running a drug ring out of his well-kept suburban home on a cul-de-sac, or that your coworker kept human body parts in his freezer.

"You all right, buddy?" Ward asked. Raquel noticed that despite the sudden explosion of anger, Ward had quickly calmed and seemed to be taking the betrayal the best—he had never interacted much with Patrick, and never thought much of him.

Alec shook his head negative. He was enraged, stunned, and, he was surprised to discover, sad. He realized his memories of Patrick aligned with his nemesis's account in strange ways. When Alec first met Patrick, he was eager to hang out with a guy who seemed to be a rising star. Maybe Alec did seem like a sidekick back then. Alec's older brothers usually saw their youngest brother as an annoying tag-along, an unwanted burden. In Patrick, maybe Alec saw a surrogate older brother who would accept him. And then, yeah, sure, it was obvious early on that Patrick had a crush on Katrina, but lots of guys felt pangs of jealousy, desire, and lust for their buddies' girlfriends. Come to think of it, lots of men developed crushes on Katrina. And then Patrick went off to Poland for his assignment, and Alec thought it was water under the bridge.

And then Alec's mind jumped to what he thought was the indisputable worst-case scenario.

"I wonder if Patrick hears the Voices."

Raquel cleared her throat.

"There's just another minute or two, can you stand to finish it?" Everyone agreed that they could.

On the screen, Patrick started talking again.

"Did you like how I volunteered to lead the hunt for who poisoned Peck? And I'll bet you thought, when we closed the investigation with no serious leads or suspects, that it was such a defeat for me. Such a humiliation for me, that I couldn't find who did it! Every time I saw you in the hallways, or the elevator, or the parking lot, I was laughing on the inside."

"If you're wondering whether I'll try to come and kill you, I probably won't even try for a long while. If you're watching this,

I'm on the run, I probably have bigger problems. I just want that for the rest of your life, you to lie awake at night, knowing that when it really mattered the most, I beat you. I got away with it, despite everything you could muster. I want that thought to eat at you. I want it to make you miserable, to depress you, to enrage you, to make it impossible to enjoy anything. Alec, I want it to make you a bitter old man until you draw your last breath."

For a split second, Alec nearly lost control, but then he recomposed himself.

"It's possible that you'll never see me again. But I think it's more likely that you'll never see me until I want you to see me. And then that moment comes, my old friends… it will be far too late. Au revoir."

The message ended.

The team sat and stood in glowering silence for a solid minute. Even Alec didn't have any quip, until he had rubbed his eyes for a good thirty seconds, and then he stood up.

"Well, I guess I found my Belloq!"

For the first time in a long, long while, everyone understood Alec's reference.

"To hell with Patrick," Katrina declared. "Let's go find the Nine-Tailed Foxes."

CHAPTER TWENTY-ONE

LIBERTY CAMPUS
SEPTEMBER 12, 2023

An absolutely morose morning in the office was thankfully interrupted by Dee, positively bouncing through the vault office door, literally singing as she carried a folder.

Dee raised her eyebrows, pointed to Alec and the others, and sang, "Whenever there's trouble, we're there on the double—"

"... we're the Bloodhound Gang!" Alec answered. "Wait, are you telling me—"

Dee leaned over, pressed a few keys on her keyboard, and the opening chords of "Ode to Joy" started to play.

"This is big, she's playing the *Die Hard* music," Alec observed, growing giddy with anticipation.

Dee smiled the kind of joyous grin that was reserved for those rare days when your favorite sports team wins the championship. "Remember my program that Vanessa Barron and the Kobold Working Group had no faith in? Remember how, because it had never been done before, everybody thought I had built the world's dumbest and slowest tracer-oute program?"

"I remember!" Katrina smiled.

"I remember!" Raquel added, in excited anticipation.

"Pepperidge Farms remembers!" Alec added.

"Katrina, what did Amaja Rai tell you about where she had the quantum computer?" Dee settled into her workstation and began typing at a furious pace, bringing up a file.

"Somewhere no one will ever find it," Katrina quoted, carefully and deliberately. "At the end of the earth."

"Want to see the location that Amaja Rai and her team hacked the CIA from?" Dee asked gleefully. She pressed a button and a satellite photo appeared on her screen.

"Ushuaia, Tierra del Fuego, Argentina," Dee announced. "This is the end of the earth—or at least the Internet, or at least the landlines. Beyond that is Antarctica, and you need satellites to connect to the web. The southernmost city in the entire world. About as isolated a site as you can get on the entire planet, while still having access to a port, an airport, and the sorts of things you would need to build a research laboratory to develop a quantum computer."

The entire team simultaneously rose out of their seats in jubilation and joyous surprise as Ludwig van Beethoven's ninth symphony reached its emotional apex.

"Merry Christmas," Dee declared, beaming with satisfaction.

She typed a few more commands.

"Once I knew what to look for—unusual shipments or travel to Ushuaia, Argentina—I started finding tons of evidence—shipments for equipment of cryogenic facilities, processors, powerful portable generators. Also, I found Amaja Rai recruited and hired a team of about thirty people—dropouts, weirdos from Silicon Valley, frustrated academics. A handful from India and overseas."

"How did our search programs not catch this?" Raquel asked in disbelief. "How long have Barron and the Working Group been looking for—"

"Probably two-thirds of these people haven't done enough to pop up on our radars yet," Dee said with frustration. "We don't keep files on every promising undergrad. Rai found what appears to be brilliant kids studying theoretical physics in places like Rutgers, Penn State, Boston U. Everybody immediately thinks of Stanford, MIT, Harvard, Yale, but there are tons of smart people who get overlooked because they didn't go to the big-name schools... like, did you know that there's a Center for Quantum Information Science and Engineering at Ohio State University?"

"That's *THE* Ohio State University," Alec corrected her. "If you forget the 'the,' Brutus appears from behind a tree and throws buckeyes at you."

"She knew exactly how to recruit to stay under our radar screen," Katrina said, with begrudging respect. "And everybody else's."

"That woman knew that the moment she succeeded, she'd have powerful enemies," Ward added, nodding. "She'll never willingly tell Waldo and the Nine-Tailed Foxes where the quantum computer is, because once they know that, they won't need her anymore, and Waldo seemed pretty eager to kill her. But... they're a team of six demons with a professional interrogator in their ranks. Rai's gonna spill the beans, it's just a question of when."

They all exchanged grim glances. They knew that at that moment, Waldo and his team were likely doing terrible things to Amaja Rai to get her to reveal the location of her quantum computer.

After an awkward silent moment, Dee returned to what she had found.

"Each person on Rai's team only offered one piece of this puzzle," Dee continued. "Like, take this guy—In-Su John Kim, computer science and engineering professor at Ohio State. Wanted to leave after being passed over for head of that quantum center. He told his colleagues he was taking some private sector gig. Nobody knew he flew down to Argentina for the past year and a half. If we were a police state, and collected absolutely every last detail about everybody's life, then yes, maybe our algorithms would have connected him moving to a far-off corner of South America, along with the fifth-best professor on computer science in Bangladesh, and a grad student from the University of Waterloo, and an undergrad from the University of Maryland, and a teaching assistant from UC-Boulder and another from USC."

Raquel shook her head in disbelief. "And these guys working at the ass-end of South America figured out what China, Google, Microsoft, Honeywell—"

"When you're not answering to a Politburo or a board of directors, you're free to experiment in a lot more, higher-risk, higher-reward directions," Katrina surmised. "Innovation comes from the 'a-ha' moment when you're not thinking about something. When you're in the shower, or working out, that's when the idea comes to you. Then turning that moment of discovery into reality requires trying something new, which is often a consequence of how much patience you have for trying and failing. This was Amaja Rai's personal project, financed by her personal fortune. She could spend whatever it took on whatever crazy ideas her team suggested. She rolled the dice on some idea that everyone else thought was stupid... and hit the jackpot."

Raquel sighed twice, first in frustration, then in recognition. Rai assembled a team of overlooked, underestimated, crazy-but-bright scientists in a manner that mirrored Raquel's philosophy in assembling the team in front of her. And the benefits of operating separately from a cautious, risk-averse, slow-moving bureaucracy had been a key element of the team's success over the years.

"Through a whole bunch of cut-outs, Rai contracted with the local government in Ushuaia to build what was touted as a 'computer science research center,' on a little jut of land sticking off from the airport peninsula," Dee explained. "They just flew in all the equipment they needed and drove it about five minutes to this research center. Operated under everybody's noses since before Covid."

Raquel finally moved past her frustration that Rai's plot had evaded their attention for so long. "How fast can we or the Pentagon get a team to the southern tip of Argentina?"

"Not a lot of U.S. military equipment down there," Ward answered. "What we've got in South America is up on the other end, sticking around to help with drug smuggling interdiction. I can check, maybe the Navy's got someone in the area—"

"Wait!" Alec exclaimed, waving his arms. He took a dramatic pause.

"Guys, we now know the location of a working quantum computer," Alec pointed out. "In the past few months, this computer spanked us, the Chinese, and the Swiss bankers. Forget the Death Star plans, this thing *is* the Death Star! Whoever gets their hands on this computer gets an instant and permanent advantage against all enemies."

"Yes, and it's just a matter of time before Amaja Rai cracks under whatever Waldo and the Nine-Tailed Foxes are doing to her," Raquel shot back.

"I'm just saying I think we have to be extremely careful about who we share this with," Alec warned. "Sure, we're on relatively good terms with Argentina, but do we want the Argentinian government knowing there's a quantum computer on their soil?"

Katrina nodded. "The moment we tell Barron and the Kobold Working Group this, they'll tell Director Boyles, who will tell the White House, and the White House will begin putting together a plan to recover the computer. The odds of information this important leaking while traveling through those channels are . . . not small."

Raquel looked around the room.

"You think we should go get the quantum computer ourselves, don't you?"

Everyone looked around the room at each other.

"Let's get to Ushuaia, and when we're there, and we know it's there, we send the signal to the Kobold Working Group, Pentagon, everybody to come get it," Katrina suggested.

CHAPTER TWENTY-TWO

USHUAIA, ARGENTINA
SEPTEMBER 14, 2023

The raid was important enough for Raquel to call in the reserves.

Ward and Katrina led from the front; Alec and Elaine were behind them, Raquel and Dee were both armed but kept in the center, and Alejandro and Tom, the team's pilots, had been assigned to watch their backs. The two pilots joked that they had enjoyed sitting in the planes and helicopters and waiting for the rest of the team to finish their dirty work with gunfights and fistfights. But this evening, Ward had declared they needed at least eight members of the team.

"You guys keep taking me pretty far out of my jurisdiction," Elaine observed as they drove to the site in a pair of hot-wired four-by-fours liberated from the airport parking lot. "You also require me to turn a blind eye to one criminal act after another."

"I trust you and you shoot straight, so that pretty much makes you irreplaceable," Ward answered from the driver's seat.

"Operating in a foreign country, there's always a risk someone will attempt to track your vehicle," Katrina observed. "Hard for them to track you when they don't know which car you're going to steal."

Ward turned off the headlights and slowed as he approached the research facility, driving past it once.

The first obvious sign of trouble was that there were far too many cars in the parking lot for that late-night hour . . . and in the second-floor window, an electrical light was flickering.

"That's not good," Katrina whispered.

They doubled back and both cars parked near the entrance doors.

They could see one of the double doors at the entrance hadn't closed completely.

"Either they work nights, or somebody got here before we did," Ward warned.

Amaja Rai's quantum computing laboratory—operating under the name NEW HORIZONS RESEARCH FACILITY—was located on a peninsula, sticking out from the much larger peninsula that housed Ushuaia—Malvinas Argentinas International Airport. Upon landing, Alec observed that most Westerners knew the "Malvinas Argentinas" by another name, the Falkland Islands, the contested territory that was the focus of a ten-week undeclared war between the United Kingdom and Great Britain in 1982.

At the open gate to the research facility, the team could still hear the dull rumble of jet engines preparing for takeoff; the airport fence was about a mile or so behind them. The narrow, two-lane road extending along the peninsula coastline had been empty, lit only by the luminescent spillover from the airport runway lights.

The New Horizons Research Facility was a two-story building, designed with sleek, state-of-the-art modern architecture and a slanted roof. Dee had found and hacked the architectural plans and determined that the stylish but modest structure hid multi-floor research laboratories that extended three stories underground.

Ward's flashlight on the open door confirmed his worst suspicions. There were two bullet holes in the front door, and below it a blood stain indicating someone had been shot right on the doorstep, and then their body had been dragged inside.

"Somebody definitely got here before we did," Katrina confirmed.

They cracked open the door.

The entrance lobby was lit only by flickering lights, with a few long fluorescent bulbs hanging from the ceiling. What once had been a stylish but understated lobby and waiting area had turned into the O.K. Corral.

Katrina counted five dead bodies—what appeared to be a receptionist and, she guessed, three scientists. A local security guard stared at the ceiling with blank eyes. He had seemed to crawl toward the door, then back in a different direction, before rolling over. A gun had been left by the front door. The floor was a mess of blood and shell casings.

Ward picked one shell casing up off the floor and inspected it.

"I'd have to check to be one-hundred percent sure, but this sure looks like a five-point-eight by forty-two-millimeter cartridge, the sort of rifle ammunition used by the People's Liberation Army," he grumbled.

"The Nine-Tailed Foxes," Katrina exhaled. "Or did they get some Chinese military team in here instead?"

They methodically moved into the next rooms adjacent to the lobby, determining that the raid must have completed a few hours ago. There were no signs of any survivors, and many of the research scientists had head wounds consistent with deliberate close-range execution.

"Dee, you don't have to be here," Alec offered. "You can wait outside with Tom and Alejandro."

"This is what we're up against," Dee declared grimly. "The fact that I don't want to see this doesn't make it any less real."

Alec nodded, and he took a position behind Elaine as they carefully and quietly proceeded downstairs. Raquel and Dee stood among the bodies in the lobby for a minute, until Katrina emerged from an adjacent room, shaking her head in disgust and disappointment.

"You don't want to go in there," Ward warned, emerging behind her. "A whole line of these poor folks, all shot in the back of the head."

"A Chinese government team didn't do this," Katrina concluded. "All of these scientists are—were—potentially useful. A team on Beijing's orders would have wanted to bring them back alive. This was ruthless. This was almost... personal."

"Waldo sure seemed pissed enough at what Amaja Rai and her team had done," Ward whispered, his voice about an octave lower than usual. "He's psycho enough to do something like this. Remember him yelling she had stolen his purpose? That he had been a noble warrior?"

Katrina nodded.

"I'm sure the Nine-Tailed Foxes were used to not leaving witnesses," Raquel added. "They also probably want to give Beijing a quantum computer, and that thing is probably way too big to carry out of here."

Dee had already gotten out her laptop. "Wireless signal is still running. I'll be in their systems in a minute, but I'll bet the Nine-Tailed Foxes took what they needed and ran. A quantum computer is too big to carry out of here. But downloaded blueprints, schematics and system operating instructions aren't."

Alec's voice came through their earpieces:

"Hey guys, come on down here... we don't have to worry about this quantum computer anymore."

***

Whatever gunfight had started upstairs had continued downstairs, into the main laboratory.

What was left of the machine could still strike awe in the hearts of those who saw it—a three-story-tall, bizarre labyrinth of golden tubes and wires connecting complicated stacks of disks and transistors.

There was a vast interconnected ring of six smaller disks on the upper floor, and then one large disk in the center in the first level of the sub-basement, and then another slightly larger ring of six smaller disks below that one. Everything glistened yellow and orange, hues usually found in dandelions, honey, canaries, and brass, all gleaming a shine so bright that those who saw the massive machine felt compelled to squint. Alec's first thought was of a spectacular golden Christmas tree, all lit up for Santa's arrival.

But the gleaming, spectacular sight was interrupted by pieces broken, missing, smashed—and a closer look revealed that these broken parts were from some sort of heavy gunfire strafing the machine, too extensively to be accidental. The invaders wanted that machine broken and had fired enough rounds into it to make its repair long and costly.

Alec stepped back and realized that the overall form of the machine was wide at the top, narrow in the middle, and wide at the bottom again.

"Kind of like an hourglass, or a woman's figure," Alec marveled. "Go figure, that Transnistrian kid wasn't crazy about that part."

Katrina, Ward, Raquel, and Dee arrived downstairs, and all were similarly mesmerized by the three-story golden hourglass of wires and tubes.

"This is it," Raquel marveled. "Someday our grandkids are going to study this thing in a museum, sitting alongside the Enigma machine, and Deep Blue and Watson."

Katrina found herself disappointed when she spotted the sections that had been shot up. "All that work, to create the biggest computing breakthrough in human history, and these monsters just wanted to smash it."

"They're not pure Philistines," Dee lamented, holding up her laptop. "Network indicates that a few hours ago, someone came in and downloaded all the kinds of files—blueprints, operating instructions, research notes. Basically, everything you would need to build another one of these things." She gazed at Rai's masterpiece, and sighed, concurring that it would someday likely be displayed in a museum.

"It's so gold," Ward marveled. "It doesn't look like a computer, it's like some... giant tree and roots, or a sea anemone, unearthed from King Solomon's Mines, or some Mayan Temple, or..."

"Or the Ark of the Covenant," Alec suggested. "Except it's not going to melt the faces of our enemies. Nobody was ever going to steal this thing. It's three stories high and fragile as hell. You'd have an easier time stealing a bank vault or a nuclear reactor."

Raquel took it all in. Yes, her team had arrived several hours too late to stop a bloodbath. But they had gotten here, following a trail everyone else had ignored.

"Dee, is this thing fixable and salvageable?"

Dee was already taking lots of pictures. "Knowing the design of a machine that was proven to work, at least intermittently, will be a big step in the right direction. But it's more than just the design; you have to know how to operate it. Quantum computing is an attempt to operate on qubits, basically an artificial atom, and the super-cold temperatures isolate the qubits so they can be manipulated with an electromagnetic field and vibrate in unison to do the computing. But that's what's tripped up everyone else so far—achieving what they call 'coherence.'"

"I'm glad I'm not the only one who finds all of this incoherent," Alec chirped.

"Somehow this machine could achieve coherence more than any other, but we have no idea how this machine did it, or what it was doing differently from everyone else," Dee fumed. "Having this means we've got the tools and the ingredients in the kitchen, but don't yet know how to cook the recipe."

Ward didn't like the skepticism in Dee's voice. "Well, it's like we've got a banged-up car that we've never seen before, and just need to fix it, right?"

Dee shook her head. "More like we've got what's left of a Hadron Collider after a bunch of thugs shot up every part that looked important, and they appear to have killed everyone who ever designed it, built it, and operated it. Those Nine-Tailed idiots destroyed a lot of intellectual capital in their killing spree. I mean, the U.S. government's teams, the best guys from Google and IBM and the rest—they're smart guys. Give them this, and they'll figure it out, might take a lot of trial and error."

She sighed. "But by the time they get this one rebuilt and up and running, Beijing will probably have had theirs running for months, maybe a year."

Raquel nodded. "I'm calling it in anyway. Our station in Buenos Aires can get a team here, secure the site, prepare steps to take it apart and have it shipped back to the U.S."

Katrina stepped closer and noticed a plaque.

"Rai named this machine. 'The Giver of All Gifts.' She really believed she was going to completely change the world with this thing." She shook her head. "And it got her kidnapped and tortured."

"All gifts?" Alec chuckled grimly. "Do you know what 'all gifts' translates to in Greek?" He paused. "Pandora."

"As in the box? Real fitting," Ward grumbled. "Amaja Rai just opened something up and let out all the troubles in the world."

Their earpieces buzzed to life, with Tom's voice sounding uncharacteristically frantic. "Guys, we found something in the parking lot! You'd better come here quick!"

***

Tom and Alejandro had noticed a blood trail in the parking lot and followed it, finding one of the Nine-Tailed Foxes.

Zeng Zongying, the notorious interrogator of the team, lay bleeding between two cars. From the bloodstains on the car handle, she had tried to open one of the doors. But her desperate efforts had failed, as she had already lost a lot of blood. She looked pale and was breathing shallowly.

Tom held the Chinese agent at gunpoint and Alejandro had already patted her down and removed a knife.

"Gunshot to the lower abdomen, my best guess is somebody at this lab was armed and plugged her in the gut as her team was leaving," Alejandro reported. "She hasn't said much since we found her, but that could be stubbornness, or internal bleeding."

"She's got quite a bit of external bleeding, too," Alec observed. "No honor among thieves, huh? Waldo and the rest just left you behind?"

Zeng just gave them a defiant, angry stare.

"Talk to us and we'll save your life," Katrina offered. She attempted to repeat the phrase in Mandarin, but she knew Zeng Zongying spoke English—or at least that's what her hacked file had indicated. On the long plane ride to Argentina, Katrina had attempted to brush up on what little Mandarin and Cantonese she had picked up during her travels in Asia.

"Are we sure we want to do that?" Dee asked, flashing a surprising vindictiveness. "She and her team just killed a lot of innocent people. Bleeding to death on a cold night serves her right."

Zeng stared up at them, calculating her options.

Through a communications headset clipped to her belt, they could hear some desperate message in Chinese. Zeng was too weak to try to turn it off.

"Dee, tell me you can trace them through that," Katrina ordered.

"I can try." Dee removed the headset and transmission device.

"Can you tell what they're saying?" Raquel asked.

"I think it's something like, 'Tell us where you are,'" Katrina said. The Chinese phrase, spoken by the distinctive voice of William Yen Wen, or Waldo, was clearer. As Dee opened up the case of the personal communications device, Katrina picked up the headset and pressed a button.

"Hello, Waldo," Katrina spoke into the microphone coolly. "Do you know who this is?"

There was silence on the other end for twenty seconds, and then barely audible grumbling.

"Katrina, the slayer of the brothers, or whatever the hell it is they call you," Waldo sneered.

Katrina offered a quick smile to Alec. "Good to know I still make a lasting impression."

"Like any man could forget you," her husband answered.

"Waldo, I have come to bargain," Katrina declared. "I have your teammate Zeng Zongying here, but she's badly wounded. I can save her, and give her back to you, but it's going to cost you the plans to the quantum computer."

"Shoot her," Waldo answered.

From the ground, Zeng Zongying groaned and swore.

Alec looked down at Zeng. "Does he owe you a lot of money or something?"

Katrina visibly seethed. She was both surprised and unsurprised that Waldo didn't care a whit about his teammate's survival. Alive and in U.S. custody, she was a long-term security risk. Perhaps Waldo and Zeng had animosity behind their years of working together. Or maybe the Nine-Tailed Foxes had no loyalty to anyone left behind.

"For a man who talks of honor, you abandon comrades awfully casually," Katrina taunted.

"I can get other teammates," Waldo answered. "I cannot get another set of plans for a working quantum computer."

Katrina lowered the headset.

"Tom, go get the first aid kit and patch her up as best you can," she instructed.

Alec furrowed his brow. "Tom, take your time on that! No rush!"

Katrina glared at her husband. "We don't let anyone bleed to death in front of us, even an enemy."

Elaine cleared her throat. "Weren't you the woman who John Wick–ed her way through a dozen militia guys in the Freedom Tower?"

"That was totally different, Zeng's unarmed!" Katrina answered with a bit of irritation. Alec was about to object to what he was going to call a "kindler and gentler Katrina," but his wife shut him up with a glare.

Katrina shifted to a different approach with Waldo.

"Waldo, you've got the plans for a quantum computer now," Katrina said. "You can let Amaja Rai go now."

"We did exactly that, Katrina," Waldo declared. "I let her go from our helicopter, into the south Atlantic—a bit cold this time of year. Perhaps we should have untied her first."

Katrina found herself surprisingly saddened at the thought of Amaja Rai's murder at Waldo's hands.

"All right, Waldo," Katrina stalled for time. "What do you want?"

She heard a laugh on the other end of the connection.

"Nothing, Katrina," he said with a laugh. "There is nothing you have that I want. I have the world in my hands right now, in one portable external hard drive."

"With the Quantum codebreaker, China will turn 'the cloud' into the rain for the rest of the world—making everyone's secrets shower down like raindrops until it turns into a flood. Picture data breaches, everywhere, every day," Waldo boasted, with a chilling sense of satisfaction. "Everyone's e-mails, texts, those secret DMs to lovers. Everyone's complete medical history free to read. All electronic banking instantly insecure. People will need paper paychecks again. All electronic commerce insecure—we'll make the tech giants worthless overnight. No one will ever want to use a smartphone again. No more electronic trading at the stock markets."

Katrina and Dee exchanged unnerved looks. The technological nightmare Waldo described wouldn't happen overnight, but with one data breach after another, Beijing could destroy the Western world's faith in the security of anything saved on a computer network. It wouldn't quite bring back the pre-Internet age, but it would permanently hobble America's tech industry and give China an insurmountable advantage in all kinds of technological innovations.

"If they could do that . . . " Dee whispered.

"Would this kill off spam, too?" Ward asked.

Alec suddenly reached for the headset and pulled it from Katrina's hands.

"Hey, Waldo . . . by any chance, do you hear the Voices?"

Katrina glared at Alec, thinking that the question was at best a second-tier concern at that moment. She looked at Dee, who was shaking her head negatively—if she was going to be able to trace the signal in the Chinese team's headset, it was going to require more time or better equipment. But after a moment, everyone realized there had been a long and curious silence on the other end.

"Yes, I do hear them," Waldo answered.

Everyone's faces suddenly broke into expressions of shock and horror.

"I wondered if I was the only one," Waldo said with a surprising sense of curiosity. "Do you hear them too?"

Alec mouthed a slew of four-letter words without saying any of them aloud.

"I've heard them for years, but the doctors insisted it was all in my head!" Waldo's voice reverberated from the headset. The Chinese operative seemed excited, almost relieved to have someone to talk to about his secret. "I wondered if it was ghosts of my ancestors, but after a while I knew they were something different."

"Waldo, Yen, William, whatever you like being called, listen to me!" Alec's voice was as desperate as his teammates had ever heard it. "I know I'm CIA, you're former Chinese state security, and we don't have a lot in common, but you have to listen to me! We've been researching these Voices for a year! They're something like demons! They're trying to get you to do something terrible and destructive!"

"They're Yaoguai!" Katrina added, remembering the Chinese word for demon. "They're like . . . " She closed her eyes and tried to remember lessons about Chinese mythology from a college course decades ago. "Yama Kings, powerful and manipulative! They feed on pain and suffering and want to spread destruction!"

Yen only offered a sad little chuckle.

"Oh, Katrina . . . other man, whoever you are . . . " He laughed again. "I know. That's exactly what they are."

Everyone on the team—Katrina, Alec, Ward, Raquel, Dee, Elaine and Tom and Alejandro exchanged looks of horror. Their crisis—and the world's—had just managed to get exponentially worse. The task before them, tracking and hunting down one of the Chinese government's most notorious and slippery spies, had seemed daunting enough. Now Waldo seemed to be confirming he was hearing voices in his head that might be some sort of ancient demonic malevolent force hell-bent on spreading violent chaos and human misery whenever and wherever possible.

"Listening to them made me the most feared operative of my homeland," Waldo said, expressing what sounded like true gratitude. "Their path is true and has led me well. No, the true demon, the one who truly spread destruction, and fed on pain and suffering, was Amaja Rai. During our interrogation, she kept crying and saying she only wanted to save the world and help people. She couldn't see her great invention was just a force of chaos. And I suspect as she fell from our helicopter, into the frigid ocean waves below, she realized how wrong she was."

CHAPTER TWENTY-THREE

Dawn and sunlight had only physically brightened the situation around Katrina and the team. The mood was still dark as a moonless night.

The CIA Buenos Aires station had flown down a team as quickly as possible and secured the site. As far as anyone could tell, the Argentinian government had no idea that a massacre had been carried out at New Horizons Research Facility near Ushuaia-Malvinas International Airport. Besides the isolated, windswept seaside location, the noise from the airport and landing planes made it unlikely anyone would hear the gunfire inside.

Plans were already underway to dismantle Amaja Rai's quantum computer and bring it back to the United States. But the initial assessments echoed Dee's conclusion. It could be anywhere from three months to years before they could duplicate Rai's success. The absolute best-case scenario was that the U.S. would have a working quantum computer a few weeks after Beijing did and could launch retaliatory strikes against Chinese computer systems.

"About three or four weeks after Xi Jinping will gain the ability to expose any American secret he wants, from any U.S. government system, we'll be able to shoot back," Raquel grimly assessed. "That's kind of like having an atomic bomb a month after the Nazis got them."

But the team grappled with the unlikely odds of ever catching up to Waldo and his team, who were likely headed back to Beijing as quickly as humanly possible.

"Alec, I thought it was bad enough you had us hunting down some perfect, deadly, disappearing martial artist type, our own personal Storm Shadow," Ward grumbled. "Now you're telling us we've got the Exorcist on top of it, too?"

Alec shook his head grimly. "I don't know, man," he said, rubbing his eyes with the palms of his hands, convinced that coffee was no longer doing its magic on his body in the mornings.

Elaine approached, gestured for him to open his hand. She placed something in it.

Alec looked in his hand and realized it was a folded-up twenty-dollar bill.

"What's that for?" Alec asked.

"Almost a year ago, when we started this investigation, you said, 'Twenty bucks says I'm right,'" Elaine said with a grim smile. "I didn't formally take the bet, but I didn't forget you said it. I was really hoping you were crazy."

Alec chuckled, then shook his head.

"All we know is that Waldo thinks he's in touch with the Voices, or Yama Kings, or whatever you want to call it, or them," Alec muttered. "We don't know if it's real, although it's safe to assume he thinks they're real. And that, apparently, makes him capable of anything. You saw what he and his team did to those lab technicians."

Ward put a hand on Alec's shoulder and gave him a shake.

"Alec, I know this bastard feels really different from every other two-bit thug we've ever gone up against," Ward said. "But it's just the same old sons of bitches, with the same old wickedness in their hearts as always. We got into this business hunting down an old psycho who kidnapped kids. You said it yourself earlier, everybody who crosses us ends up six feet under or rotting in Supermax. This guy's gonna get his, too."

Alec nodded, attempting to appear reassured. Ward knew it was a lie.

"Sometime..." Katrina said, thinking aloud. "In a couple of months, we're going to start seeing our secrets spilled. It will be something bad. Every recent breakthrough at Los Alamos, or Sandia, or Livermore Labs. That will be how Beijing tests their new codebreaker. Then they'll go after private companies—Silicon Valley, Wall Street, the big banks. They'll start a financial panic. Maybe go after the markets themselves—convince everybody that their money's not safe."

Ward cleared his throat. "Damn. That wasn't what was worrying me. I was worried they'll post all the communications codes for the Pentagon, announce to the whole wide world that they're plugged into our comms—freak out our allies."

"Tank the markets, tank the dollar, make people afraid they won't be allowed to make withdrawals from the bank," Alec predicted. "Once you can hack into critical infrastructure, you can disrupt energy supplies. Blow up pipelines and distribution systems with overloads. Shut down water and waste treatment plants."

"You saw how well our country reacted to Covid and George Floyd," Elaine observed. "Now envision how everyone would react to this Chinese plan to use a quantum computer codebreaker to sow chaos in an election year. Flickering power grids, air traffic control systems going down, traffic lights all getting screwed up, hospitals finding all their computer systems failing. And all the while, every hostile foreign power pumping as much disinformation into Americans' social media feeds. By the end of the year, we'll all be at each other's throats as law enforcement and the National Guard hang on by their fingernails, trying to keep order."

"Our parents did so much to give us a better world," Katrina sighed. "And look at the world we're about to leave our kids."

"Pray for a miracle," Alec groaned.

CHAPTER TWENTY-FOUR

CIA HEADQUARTERS
LANGLEY, VIRGINIA
SEPTEMBER 21, 2023

The following week ranked as one of the most depressing in Katrina's life. Upon their return to northern Virginia, plenty of the Agency's seventh floor officials wanted additional briefings on what the team had found in Argentina. One of the few officials they didn't brief was Director Boyles, who was apparently still in intense negotiations with his hostile foreign counterparts, attempting to save foreign citizens who had helped the CIA for years.

But everyone else at the CIA's top levels proved all too comfortable scapegoating the Dangerous Clique for the fact that China now had the plans for a functional quantum computer. The deputy director of operations grumbled that the Dangerous Clique had always been too independent and too secretive, and that if everyone else within the Agency had been informed about their findings, the circumstances might be different. A few officials remembered to rake Vanessa Barron over the coals, for only investigating forty-five of the forty-seven suspects Dee and the NSA algorithm had identified. And the deputy director of analysis asked aloud if Alec Flanagan's freedom from prison had really been worth an entire bottle of Pappy Van Wrinkle bourbon.

"I'm just saying the Transnistrians don't know their bourbon, and would have settled for Buffalo Trace," he said, not caring that Alec was standing right in front of him.

Alec glared at him and conjured an appropriate curse: "I hope that for the rest of your life, every burrito you eat has a giant glob of sour cream at one end."

***

The week of gloom only ended when Raquel suddenly and mysteriously departed the office to meet with an unnamed friend on the staff of the Director of National Intelligence and returned in a state somewhere between shock and joy.

"Beijing doesn't have the plans for the quantum computer," Raquel announced to the assembled team.

"Say what?"

Alec exhaled for what felt like the first time in more than a week. "Tell me that God Himself struck down William Yen Wen and his merry band before they could get back to Beijing!"

Raquel scoffed, then paused.

"Crap, maybe He did."

Alec's eyes bulged, and Raquel explained how a series of bizarre events unfolded on the other side of the world, derailing the plans of the Nine-Tailed Foxes.

Raquel explained that the CIA's various stations across Asia and the NSA's intercepts had determined that after escaping Argentina, the remaining five members of the Nine Tailed Foxes hid for a couple of days, then managed to make it to Japan and reached out to Chinese spies there, telling them they had the plans for a working quantum computer.

"We've known for a while that there's a simmering rivalry between the Chinese Ministry of State Security—their civilian intelligence agency—and the People's Liberation Army's Second Department, their military intelligence," Raquel explained. "Apparently, in the past few years, between Covid, the economic slowdown, Taiwan, and everything else, that sibling rivalry has devolved into nonstop backstabbing."

"The Nine-Tailed Foxes were part of the Ministry of State Security, the civilian side," she continued. "When they got hacked, Xi Jinping was furious. He fired the old boss, and brought in a new boss from Second Department, General Fang Yu. Keep in mind, for years, Fang Yu had done everything possible to make the civilian side look incompetent."

"Fang Yu hated the Nine-Tailed Foxes and was the one who fired them and required their forced retirement to a state-run 'retirement community' that was basically Club Fed, a nicer-than-usual prison. Xi Jinping signed off on the decisions himself, although we don't know whether he had the whole story or was only getting Fang Yu's version of events."

Katrina impatiently interrupted. "Wait, so why doesn't Beijing have the quantum computer plans?"

"I'm getting to that!" Raquel insisted. "When the Nine-Tailed Foxes reached out to Beijing, telling them they had captured the quantum computer plans and wanted to bring it back, Fang Yu declared it was a trick and claimed that the Nine-Tailed Foxes had been double agents for years. He ordered Chinese military intelligence teams to try to track down the Nine-Tailed Foxes, with orders to execute them!"

Katrina and the rest of the team were dumbstruck.

"Wait... the Nine-Tailed Foxes steal the biggest technological breakthrough in years, and gift-wrap it and serve it on a silver platter to Beijing, and the Chinese government won't take it?" Katrina was stunned, elated, and confused.

"That's why I'm not entirely certain it wasn't the hand of God," Raquel said, shaking her head. "Then again, a phenomenal success by the Nine-Tailed Foxes would make Fang Yu look pretty stupid for firing them."

"He's backed into a corner!" Alec gleefully exclaimed. "Eff You, or Fang You, or whatever his name is, must do everything possible to make sure Xi Jinping never hears or believes that the Nine-Tailed Foxes actually have real plans for a quantum computer! He'll insist it's a trick or a trap or disinformation! Because the moment he says, 'Whoops, sorry boss, looks like the Nine-Tailed Foxes were right all along—'"

"It's a face-saving culture," Katrina declared dryly. "We saw it with Covid and the 'Zero Covid' policies! Better that millions of people die than you ever admit you were wrong!"

"You know, I've always had a hard time distinguishing face-saving from ass-covering," Ward quipped.

"Merlin thought something bad was out there, pushing us all towards a bad end, but there was something good out there, too, watching our backs and nudging us in the right direction," Raquel marveled. "Maybe the Good out there used the petty rivalries of the Chinese military bureaucracies to save the world—or at least give us a chance to save it."

"The point is, the Nine-Tailed Foxes are still on the run, still have plans for a quantum computer, and . . . are cut off from what they wanted most in this world, which is reinstatement to their previous lives," Katrina murmured, closing her eyes, trying to envision what her foes were thinking. "They're screwed. They can't get what they want. But they've got the plans to build the most powerful skeleton key in the world. What do they do?"

"Sell it to the highest bidder?" Ward asked.

"I don't think Waldo and the rest are really motivated by money," Katrina muttered, shaking her head. "Once they were disavowed and snuck out of China, they could have made a good living as top-tier mercenaries. You told them we were hiring.

They could have sold what they knew to us. None of that interested them. They don't want wealth, they want..." She rose and began to pace. "They want purpose, they want their sense of mission restored, to be back in a place where they feel they're doing what they're meant to be doing."

"They're never going to get that," Raquel said. "Everybody in the Chinese government thinks they're traitors. Fang Yu probably wants them dead so they can never tell their side of the story and expose that he's an idiot."

"May I remind you Waldo said he hears the Voices?" Alec exclaimed. "Everybody else who's heard the Voices turned out to be an aspiring mass murderer with the culinary tastes of Jeffrey Dahmer!"

He ran to his cubicle, and removed a four-foot by three-foot corkboard of Voices research, the sort of elaborate display that he knew might as well be a giant poster that asked, "I AM A CRAZY CONSPIRACY THEORIST, WOULD YOU LIKE TO SUBSCRIBE TO MY NEWSLETTER?"

"In Cyprus, Sarvar Rashin spent her last moments on earth trying to convince me my life was a joke, and everything is meaningless!" Alec began. "Murgen heard the Voices and was considered too messed-up for ISIS! Norman Fein killed his own grandmother! The Tattooed Man probably killed his own comrades in the middle of a battle in Ukraine!" Alec grew more and more excited. "People influenced by the Voices want chaos, anarchy, death and destruction on a massive scale. They're like the Joker, they just want the world to burn, they're—"

Alec paused. Katrina looked up, the couple's eyes locked, and they came to the same conclusion simultaneously.

"They're not going to sell the plans," she murmured. "They're going to just give it away... to everyone."

Elaine blurted out her skepticism first. "They've stolen the ultimate codebreaking weapon, and they're just going to give it away to everybody?"

"No, that's it!" Alec agreed. "They're going to share quantum computing with the world. Everybody. If they just put it up on the net, any country—hell, anybody with enough resources—can build a quantum computer and start breaking into other people's secure accounts."

"Depending upon resources, with a complete blueprint and instruction manual, people could whip up their own quantum computers in a matter of months, maybe weeks." Dee was now pacing as well. "Everybody with existing projects would just redirect their efforts into the proven directions. Russia, China, probably Iran and Pakistan, half of Europe—hell, you'd have dozens of quantum codebreakers in private hands. Remember when I said China having a quantum computer couldn't quite undo the computer and Internet revolutions? Well, this would pretty much do it—within a matter of months, no online database would be secure. We'd all go back to using bank tellers, paper ledgers—it would move us all back to the late eighties, early nineties, a world before the Internet."

"Are you sure that's such a bad idea?" Ward asked. "We'd finally get everybody to stop staring at their phones all the time." Off his teammates' disapproving looks, he added, "Kidding!"

"This is our second chance," Katrina declared. "We find them. Hunt them down. Get the plans from them, pry it from their cold dead hands if we have to—"

Ward cracked his knuckles. "Now you're talking! I'm in a mood to do some good old-fashioned prying."

Raquel nodded but still looked frustrated. "Okay, I'm all for that, but we've got to find these guys. Our team in Tokyo said that Waldo did his trademark move again, disappeared without a trace."

Katrina just nodded. "There's got to be some way we can find these guys. The big leak from Kobold had all their past aliases, known safe houses, known associates, known bank accounts. At some point, somebody on that team is going to slip up."

"Oh, we've got aliases for them—at least a dozen for each one," Dee exhaled.

CHAPTER TWENTY-FIVE

Dee had sprinted off to put in some requests with the NSA, and the rest of the team looked through anything in hacked files from Chinese State Security that could indicate where the Nine-Tailed Foxes were likely to hide.

"These guys are supposed to be the pro's pros, not going to use old aliases that are compromised," Ward groused. "Twenty bucks says they dropped all their old identities the moment Beijing got hacked."

"You're on," Katrina answered confidently. "Cover identities are a pain to maintain. A lot of China's best spies have been Chinese citizens, living abroad under their legal given name, conducting industrial espionage or seducing idiot members of Congress. Every one of those past aliases needs their own paperwork, passport, address, cell phone and landline numbers, legal records indicating they exist going back years—fake birth certificates, school records, employment records. If you're really diligent, you keep all of that information separate. If you get lazy, you start reusing it."

Within an hour, Dee and the NSA had come back with answers—too many answers.

"The good news is, yes, we have their aliases," Dee said, grimacing. "Unfortunately, in the past day, all those aliases booked dozens of flights and ferries from Tokyo to points out of the country, all over Asia, even to America. They're hiding by putting out a lot of chaff. William Yen Wen, Waldo, he's got twenty-six aliases going back more than a decade, and those identities booked flights to everywhere—Seoul, Hong Kong, Macau, Bangkok, Honolulu—the list goes on and on."

"That doesn't count, I'm not paying twenty bucks!" Ward exclaimed.

Katrina attempted to gently nudge Dee aside to examine the list on the screen. When that failed, she gave a not-so-gentle nudge, and started scrolling through the list of flagged ticket purchases by the alias identities, studying them intensely.

"Are you sure this is all of them?" Katrina asked.

"It's an electronic document, Katrina," Dee answered, a little annoyed. "I didn't drop one in the hallway."

Katrina nodded, deep in thought, oblivious to Dee's irritation. "Raquel, you went through everything in Waldo's file—in his career, was Taiwan the biggest objective?"

"Are you kidding me?" Raquel scoffed. "Unification with, or conquest of Taiwan is the biggest objective of the Chinese government, they've wanted it for generations. Xi Jinping calls reunifying with Taiwan the 'great rejuvenation of the Chinese nation.' Judging from the leak, Waldo worked on issues and missions related to Taiwan twice as much as any other place or issue."

Katrina scanned the list of red-flagged reservations again. "Did any of the aliases of Waldo or any other member of the Nine-Tailed Foxes book a flight to Taiwan?"

Now Dee nudged Katrina away from the keyboard and ran a few searches to confirm. "Nope. No flights to Taipei. Now that you mention it, that does look like an odd omission."

"If Waldo is ready to bring the world to an end, he's going to do it from the place he's spent his whole adult life obsessing about," Katrina declared. "Going back home to China's too dangerous. Blowing up the Internet age from inside enemy territory is going to be William Yen Wen's last middle finger to the so-called rogue province."

Raquel took one last review of the ticket reservations and nodded.

"Okay, so we've got a good theory that he's headed to Taipei. But that's a city that is almost as big as Rhode Island, with seven million people, how are we going to find him? Where's he hiding? Where's he going?"

Alec chuckled.

"Oh, I've got an idea," Alec said. "I mean, if Waldo just wants to put the quantum computer plans out there, he could do it from anywhere, including Japan. But he's got the Voices whispering inside his head, he's not just going to hit 'send' and wait for the world to end. We've got a guy who's had to be quiet and operate in the shadows his whole life. He's got pent-up rage and frustration and a sense of betrayal. He's going to turn this into a big extravaganza. Bin Laden had his videos, ISIS had their ceremonial beheadings, Putin's got his long-winded speeches. If you're gonna end the world, you're gonna make a statement. A manifesto."

"A suicide note," Ward added.

"Now, if I was in Taipei, and I wanted to make a big dramatic statement to the world, I know exactly where I'd say it. Remember, Waldo's going to want someplace big and bold and dramatic. Not a lot of places in Taiwan fit that. Their version of the White House was built by the Japanese, it looks like a college campus, nobody knows where it is."

Raquel and Katrina exchanged skeptical smirks. "Alec, I sent you there for a week after the whole thing with Hell-Summoner to give a non-classified briefing on the threat of genetically engineered viruses and shake hands and take pictures with Taiwanese officials. That was two years ago, and now you're acting like you're our team expert on the place."

"Hey, has anybody else in this room been there?" Alec asked. Off everyone else's look, he added, "No? Then that puts me one week ahead of the rest of you."

Alec typed and brought up an image from the web.

"Ever see the skyline of Taipei?" Alec asked. "It's got one really big skyscraper, a symbol of the country, the Taipei 101 building. It's like their Eiffel Tower, twice as big as any other building in the city. For about five years, it was the tallest skyscraper in the world."

"How many floors?" Dee asked.

"Well, it's called Taipei 101, that might be your first clue," Alec gently jabbed.

Raquel nodded, talking herself into trusting Alec and Katrina's instincts and analysis. "You think Waldo, to make a statement to the world, is going to do it at the top of some giant skyscraper?"

Ward chuckled. "Well, it's not like al-Qaeda's around to sue for copyright infringement."

"One last clue," Alec added. "Raquel, Katrina, you'll correct me if I'm wrong, the biggest success of the Nine-Tailed Foxes career came in Taiwan in 2021, right?"

"No, that's right," Katrina said with a nod. "We learned a year later that the Foxes, probably led by Ren Xiulan, penetrated the security detail assigned to protect Taiwanese President Tsai Ing-wen. They got a treasure trove—everything the detail does to prevent assassinations, the procedures in place for when the president is threatened, codes and passwords and evacuation routes. It was a mess."

"In the big Kobold hack of the Chinese, the Ministry of State Security file on the Nine-Tailed Foxes included just one photo of all six team members together." Alec brought up the file with the image, and it showed Waldo, Chen, Goh, Ren, Peng, and Zongying standing close together, their expressions ranging from Waldo's subtle smile, Chen's cocky smirk, Goh's goofy crooked grin, Ren's glamorous gaze directly into the camera, Peng's dutiful expression and strict posture, and Zongying's icy stare. The photo of the team's faces had been tightly cropped, and the only discernible background behind their heads was a row of thin metal slats, about four inches apart, and some sort of blurry green hills beyond the slats.

"I'll bet you a cheeseburger that picture is from 2021, and they're celebrating their big win," Alec declared.

"Okay, that's plausible enough," Raquel said with a nod. "What about it?"

Alec typed and brought up another photo from his own personnel file.

The photo showed Alec and a small group of Taiwanese officials giving a somewhat corny thumbs-up gesture, in front of an identical row of thin metal slats, once again four inches apart, taken two years ago. But this wider photo made it clear that the slats were the tall guardrails on the outdoor observation deck of Taipei 101.

"As far as we can tell, the only time the Foxes ever took a group photo—or at least one that ended up in the Ministry of State Security's electronic files—was there," Alec observed. "This place means something to them. It's where they celebrated their biggest win ever."

CHAPTER TWENTY-SIX

For the CIA, working in Taiwan represented a unique challenge, as the island represented the most coveted prize of the Chinese regime. Chinese spies were everywhere, and the CIA feared that almost every Taiwanese agency and branch of government was at risk of being compromised. The CIA and other branches of the U.S. intelligence community often wanted to share more information with the Taiwanese, but worried that anything shared with Taipei would end up in the hands of Beijing a short time later.

"New cover identities for you guys aren't the problem," Raquel concluded. "The real problem is that the moment we tell anybody over in Taipei that the Nine-Tailed Foxes are in their city, the Taiwanese will go to their highest alert, and probably within ten minutes, Chinese State Security will learn why. And if we're after the Foxes, they'll go after the Foxes, too. And who knows, maybe they stop to examine whatever files the Foxes are carrying."

"Any chance the Taiwanese can pick up the Foxes before we can find them, or before they get to the 101 Tower?" Ward asked. "Closed-circuit surveillance cameras, facial recognition, that sort of thing?"

"Well, there are rumors that the Taiwanese are using facial and biometric recognition equipment," Dee answered. "I say rumors because back in 2020, Taiwan banned the use of Chinese-made components in their surveillance systems, because they were afraid Chinese companies provided Beijing with a backdoor. They had supposedly switched over to components imported from Singapore and Thailand, but then they discovered those components were indeed made in China and just shipped elsewhere for resale under a new label, so they stopped using those systems. So, my guess is no, the Taiwanese will not be able to use facial recognition to find the Nine-Tailed Foxes."

Alec cleared his throat. "There are also some Taiwanese who don't like the idea of becoming a technologically advanced Orwellian surveillance state in order to fight off a potential conquest by a technologically advanced Orwellian surveillance state."

Ward shook his head. "I tell ya, being the good guys sucks sometimes."

"We go there, but we don't tell the Taiwanese who we're after," Elaine suggested. "Make up some Interpol notice or something."

"Taiwan isn't in Interpol because of pressure from China," Alec observed. "If the bunch of us looked Taiwanese, I'd say we should all be using Taiwanese passports. Because when they're stolen, no record of the theft ever goes into the Interpol database."

"Honestly, I think the best bet is tell the Taiwanese as little as possible," Katrina offered. "That we're in country and armed, investigating a lead on a Chinese spy ring, but no further details."

Raquel shook her head. "Boy, that won't sound suspicious at all."

CHAPTER TWENTY-SEVEN

NINGXIA NIGHT MARKET
NINGXIA RD, DATONG DISTRICT
TAIPEI CITY, TAIWAN
SEPTEMBER 25, 2023

Taiwan was everything that mainland China could be if the people were free to choose their own path. Both countries featured bustling crowded and noisy cities, but in Taiwan, the people chose their leaders in regularly scheduled elections. A long, ugly stretch of autocratic one-party rule under Chiang Kai-Shek ended in the 1980s, and Taiwan began a slow, steady evolution into a healthy, prosperous multiparty democracy. Taiwan's national police forces were bound by the rule of law, and their actions were subject to the review of an independent judiciary. The people enjoyed freedom of speech and freedom of the press, and enjoyed the benefits and frustrations of a multiparty system. Political pluralism was on display in every vote and the occasional parliamentary fistfight.

Perhaps most egregiously in the eyes of the Chinese Communist Party, Taiwan was a shining example that people—Chinese people—could live under democracy and liberty and thrive. Every day that Taiwan stood independently was another giant middle finger to Beijing's belief that it had discovered and perfected the one true shining path to prosperity and stability, and counterevidence that mainland China had to be ruled with an iron fist to guarantee its future. It was the equivalent of Staten Island declaring itself independent and Communist and figuring out a way to give its citizens a higher standard of living than the United States.

Upon arriving in Taiwan, the Dangerous Clique had proceeded to a CIA safehouse that was in a basement apartment just around the corner from the Ningxia night market—arriving after sundown, they squeezed past the crowds purchasing and enjoying squid-on-a-stick, sweet potato balls, pig intestine, stinky tofu, duck blood curd, one large hog on a leash that might have been some future night's dinner special, and the occasional poorly translated sign offering "chicken ass."

Being mostly underground, passersby never gave the apartment a second look—although if they had looked closer, they would have noticed surprisingly advanced locks, motion detectors, and security cameras and a reinforced steel door. The safehouse was about four miles from the Taipei 101 tower, about a fifteen-minute drive if traffic were cooperative, and only God knew how long if traffic was not cooperative.

Within the safehouse, the dining room table was covered with several sheets of blueprints on the observation deck levels. Ward had arranged various small objects that were used to represent the team, the likely route of the Foxes, and likely civilians on site. For his teammates he used Monopoly game pieces, five red hotels from the game to represent the Foxes, and pennies for the civilians.

"This is our plan?" Elaine asked as she examined the makeshift map.

"I thought it looked like Ward was playing Dungeons and Dragons, too," Dee answered.

"It's a work in progress," Ward grunted.

"You're going to have us sitting around with guns in our backpacks, waiting for God knows how long, hoping the Foxes show up," Elaine said, shaking her head.

Ward let out another frustrated grunt. "I'm trying to account for a bunch of variables."

"Trust me, they're going to come tomorrow night," Alec declared. "Raquel, their big score against the Taiwanese president's office was two years ago tomorrow, right?"

Raquel furrowed her brow. "Uh, something like that, I don't know if anyone ever nailed down a precise date."

Alec pointed to the photo of the six Foxes together, on the observation deck of the Taipei 101 tower.

"This photo was taken two years ago tomorrow," Alec declared.

Elaine looked at the photo closely. She had concurred that the slats behind them matched the observation deck, but she hadn't seen anything in the picture to indicate when it was taken.

"How can you be so certain?" Elaine asked, befuddled that Alec had somehow found some clue she hadn't. She stared at the printout of the photo closely.

"The position of the sun, it's obvious!" Alec answered.

Ward and Dee both gave Alec a quizzical look. Alec shrugged and silently mouthed, "I just made that up."

Katrina picked up a giant stapled stack of files—a printed-out translation of all the Ministry of State Security files hacked by Kobold—and flipped through it furiously.

"No, I think you're right, I think tomorrow night is most likely," Katrina concluded. She pointed to one line on one of the hacked personnel files. "Tomorrow is Ren Xiulan's thirty-ninth birthday."

Ward couldn't help herself. "Thirty-nine? She looks like she's in her twenties!"

"Maybe she's born with it," Alec chirped. "Maybe it's Maybelline."

"Point is, if you're on the run, your own government wants to kill you, you've got one of the biggest secrets in the world, and your team leader wants to set off a technological Ragnarok . . . " Katrina said, staring at the photos of Ren in the file and trying to see the world through her eyes. " . . . you don't want to spend your last birthday before you turn forty just sitting and hiding somewhere. She's going to mark the occasion with her team's most daring operation yet."

"Is that insight, or projection?" Raquel asked. Off Katrina's adamant look, she sighed and turned her attention to the table. "Ward, why don't you walk us through what you've got so far?"

Ward nodded and moved around the red hotel pieces on the blueprint.

"We strongly suspect that at some point in the next twenty-four hours, the five remaining members of the Nine-Tailed Foxes will travel to the observation deck of the Taipei 101 tower and reveal the plans to the quantum computer to the world. It is reasonable to surmise that Jin Goh, the team hacker, will arrange for some sort of live broadcast and uploading of the plans."

He moved the Monopoly pieces back to their starting positions. "This is us."

"Why do I get the feeling you made me the shoe?" Alec asked.

Ward ignored him.

"Most people reach the observation deck by the elevator bank; this spot here is for ascent, the spot one floor below is for descent. There are four stairways. There are no metal detectors. The security presence at the tower is standard for that of a major tourist attraction, which is to say insufficient if you're dealing with a team of highly trained Chinese spies. Or us, for that matter."

Ward shook his head.

"It is reasonable to assume that the five remaining members of the Nine-Tailed Foxes will be armed, and based upon what we saw in Argentina, these bastards are not afraid to make the lead fly. In a perfect world, we would take them down the moment we see them, but that might cause some heartburn if we can't evade the Taiwanese authorities. You never know if some security guard or off-duty cop might see us and think we're the terrorists."

Elaine shook her head skeptically. "Any chance we can take them down as they're approaching or entering the building?"

Ward unrolled another blueprint, this one of the skyscraper's ground floor.

"Four sides of the skyscraper, four long banks of entry doors, massive lobby, shopping mall adjacent and underneath, lots of tourists and Taiwanese civilians," he answered, as dissatisfied as she was. "We would need dozens of personnel to cover every possible entry point. If they're throwing their end of the world party on the observation deck, I think that's where we've got to crash it."

He stepped away from the table and turned to a corner of the room with heavy lockboxes. He opened a case that had been retrieved from a locked closet in the CIA safehouse.

"Because I always prefer to be more heavily armed than whoever is trying to kill me, some of us will go to the Taipei tower carrying Heckler & Koch MP7s, with suppressors," Ward announced, holding up one of the compact but intimidating-looking submachine guns. "Probably the pinnacle of submachine guns right now. Used these plenty in Afghanistan. When you absolutely need to put hot lead through the internal organs of your enemy, accept no substitutes. Less than five pounds and only twenty-five inches, relatively light for its power, it will fit in our backpacks. But—and I will speak slowly so that everyone understands the importance of this—we will only use the MP7s if things get ugly. Say it with me."

"We will only use the MP7s if things get ugly," his teammates recited in unison, with all the enthusiasm of office workers singing happy birthday to the guy who keeps stealing pens from their desk.

Ward put the MP7 down and removed another weapon from the lockbox.

"Because we will be in a public place with potential for panicking civilians around, our first choice will be to use these—Glock 19s with suppressors," Ward said, holding up the sleek black pistol and the suppressor. "Allow me to remind you that these weapons have *suppressors*, not *silencers*. It will still be loud. Do not envision those quiet, cool 'PIF PIF' sounds you see in the movies."

Raquel had brought a secured satellite phone, and it emitted a subtle beep and a light went on, indicating an incoming call. She stepped away and answered it, but Ward continued.

"I think our best bet is get there early, the observation deck opens at ten. We hang around and hope we see them before they see us; Waldo would probably recognize Katrina or me. He might try to Hans Gruber everyone up there as hostages to ensure his escape, or maybe the Foxes see this as a one-way trip. Either way, ideally, as they're setting up to do their big 'we're gonna end the world' broadcast, we catch 'em by surprise and take them down. And hopefully nobody's got any suicide vests. Based on their history, that's not their style, but we're in uncharted waters here."

Ward shook his head. While he and Katrina had roughly equivalent training and had been in about the same number of tight scrapes, he often took the lead in the tactical planning of a situation like this. The Dangerous Clique's only leader on paper was Raquel, but each team member sort of naturally took the lead when addressing their realm of expertise. Ward had been shaped by the U.S. Army Rangers, and long since gotten used to jumping headfirst into dangerous situations with a motley crew—the sharp-as-a-knife CIA case officer, the wisecracking analyst, the brilliant but comparably innocent NSA hacker, the cool and collected FBI agent. He loved them all on some level, and that manifested in an abiding desire to protect them, even though they had volunteered for the same dangerous duty he had. In Ward's mind, he was the only one who had specifically been trained to kill any threat that faced them, and he should be the first one bursting through the door when they didn't know what was on the other side.

He shifted a group of pennies around the blueprint.

"Based on how they massacred those unarmed scientists in Argentina, the Foxes might well show up guns blazing, putting a lot of civilians on the ground," Ward said gravely. "We may well be stepping into the equivalent of four or five mass shooters rampaging through the tower."

Elaine nodded, recognizing that Ward was putting together a plan that represented the least-bad option, although not necessarily a good option.

"There's only six of us unless we want to drag Alejandro and Tom out. They're reliable, but I don't know if I want to put them into a situation they haven't trained for." He paused and rubbed his eyes, as the jet lag caught up with him for a moment. "I just feel like I'm bringing us into this with a half-assed plan, and somebody's going to die because I didn't account for something."

"Hey, buddy, this is a good plan," Alec said, putting a hand on Ward's shoulder. "They have no idea we're going to be there. A wise man once taught me that on the periodic table of victory, the most important element is surprise."

Ward smiled. "I taught you that."

Alec shook his head. "No, you taught me that knowing is half the battle."

That got a laugh out of Ward. "That was G.I. Joe!"

Alec played it straight. "No, G.I. Joe taught me that you can shoot a million red and blue lasers and never hit a single human being. You can be America's daring, highly trained special mission force, defending human freedom against a ruthless terrorist organization determined to rule the world, and never actually kill anyone in years of combat."

The team's mood had brightened a little, but Alec wasn't finished. He pointed to a corner of the blueprint. "The only thing I would change about this plan is that I would make *me* the racecar."

Ward let out a short laugh and shook his head. "Alec, you're not the racecar. Maybe on a good day, you're the Scottie dog. Katrina's the racecar."

Alec begrudgingly nodded. "Okay, I'll give you that one. But then which one are you?"

Ward pointed. "Well, it kills me to give the Navy any credit, but I'm the battleship. Raquel's the top hat, Elaine's the wheelbarrow—"

"Because I carry the heaviest load," Elaine concluded.

"Dee's the iron."

"I'm the iron? Housework?" Dee asked with a bit of indignation.

"No, because you make everything smooth," Ward answered to Dee's satisfaction.

Katrina noticed that while Alec and Ward playfully bickered about which Monopoly game piece should represent each team member, Raquel had steadily grown more agitated during her phone call.

"No, that's fine, my team is going to love this!" Raquel finally barked with seething sarcasm. She pressed the button to end the call and was momentarily frustrated that she couldn't dramatically hang up on a satellite phone.

Katrina looked at her with expectation. "What are we going to love?"

Raquel's body language shifted from outrage to disappointment.

"That was a friend on the seventh floor of Langley. Boyles reached his deals to get our agents out of Russia, Syria, and Iran.

The good news is he saved probably a hundred, maybe two hundred of our sources from execution."

"Wait, that's great news!" Katrina insisted. "What's the bad news?"

"Dozens of captured terrorists are getting out of prison and shipped to those countries in exchange for our agents... including our old enemies Fabrice Vuscovi, Allen Pittman and Shakira Eribat."

The team erupted in a series of groans, swear words, and exclamations of disbelief.

"Vuscovi's getting shipped off to Tehran, Pittman to Moscow and Eribat to Damascus," Raquel continued, seething. "Best-case scenario for us, they're going to live quiet, comfortable lives as consultants to their host governments. Worst-case scenario, their host governments let them loose to attack Americans again."

Alec pounded his fist against the wall of the basement apartment, and then winced as the impact hurt his hand.

"Alec, get ahold of yourself!" Katrina warned her husband. "I hate this as much as anybody, but there's nothing we can do about this right now."

And then, it seemed, Alec suddenly calmed. But then he looked up with an unnerving smile.

"Oh, I'm fine, honey," Alec said, grinning a bit madly, and he started to pace. "In fact, I'm peachy. You're right, in a situation like this, I shouldn't focus on what I *can't* control. I should focus on what I *can* control. And then, I should kill someone."

"Oh, crap," Ward whispered. "I've seen this look in Alec's eye before."

Dee sidled up alongside him and quietly asked, "When?"

"Hunting Hell-Summoner right after the pandemic ended," Ward grimaced and muttered under his breath.

Alec stopped pacing on the other side of the room, and stepped to the dining room table, peering at the maps and Monopoly pieces and pennies.

"New plan, everybody!" Alec announced with the smile and enthusiasm of a game show host. "Since apparently anyone we capture and turn over to law enforcement—thanks for opposing the death penalty, Elaine, that turned out just swell for all of us!—gets let out on the street at the drop of a hat, there's no point in capturing anybody anymore! Apparently, Gitmo and ADX Florence are about as reliable at keeping people behind bars as Arkham Asylum!"

Ward leaned over to Dee. "You see, Batman's villains keep escaping—"

"Yes, I get it, thank you!"

"When we meet up with Waldo and his merry band of nihilists, there's no point in taking any prisoners!" Alec announced. "We see 'em, we shoot to kill!" He picked up all of the red hotel pieces that represented the Nine-Tailed Foxes.

"Where's Waldo? Six feet under, once we've found him!"

He dropped a red hotel piece onto the floor and immediately stomped the plastic with his boot.

"That hot babe Ren? Wrap her up like Laura Palmer!" Alec repeated the ritual of dropping the red hotel and stomping on it.

"Their big driver? Death on the highway!" *Stomp!* "The dweeb hacker? Deleted!" *Stomp!*

"Their secret police ex-cop? End of watch!" *Stomp!*

"The only way we end the threat that these five represent is by bringing them to room temperature! Otherwise, someday some other idiot CIA director will just trade them away for a hostage and a Pokemon card!"

Katrina looked at her husband in concern. "Alec—"

"No, my Wonder Woman, this time, to protect our kids and the world they're going to grow up in, we have no choice but to treat this the way all the great ones did—Dirty Harry, John McLane, Murtaugh and Riggs! We're breaking out the Punisher playbook, executing the Wolverine protocols! We're going hunting for some Nine-Tailed Foxes, and every last one of them is going to take a swan dive into the dead pool! Either they're going down . . . or we are!"

CHAPTER TWENTY-EIGHT

OBSERVATION DECK
EIGHTY-NINTH FLOOR
TAIPEI 101 TOWER
SEPTEMBER 26, 2023

Even as Asian cities competed to build the world's tallest and most spectacular skyscraper, the Taipei 101 tower stood apart from the other slender architectural knives pointing to the heavens. The Taipei 101 featured a design of eight sections or steps that looked a little like a traditional pagoda. Because the number eight was considered lucky in Chinese culture, the architectural plans kept using groups of eight. The green glass was selected to make the building look natural, almost like a stalk of bamboo. It remained the world's eleventh-tallest building.

At the top, just off from the indoor observation deck, the Taipei 101 allowed visitors to see the world's largest tuned mass damper. Most visitors had never heard the term, but most quickly grasped the purpose of the massive yellow sphere, eighteen feet in diameter. Most skyscrapers sway; one of the ways to minimize that swaying was to build a giant counterweight attached to the building on springs. When the wind pushed the building in a certain direction, the mass damper took a moment to sway with it, acting as a brake upon the initial sway. When the wind stopped and the building swayed back, the mass damper then minimized it in the other direction. Mass dampers acted as a brake that stabilized tall skyscrapers, diminishing the swaying sensation for everyone inside.

And that two-story circular inner chamber, focused on a giant yellow ball that to the naked eye, didn't appear to move and the building didn't seem to move either, was one of the building's major attractions. And that, Alec and Ward had agreed, was the best place for most of the team to hang out and wait, hoping no one found them or their backpacks suspicious.

"I still think we should spread out. It increases our odds of spotting them early," Elaine suggested. The team had brought tourist guides and scrolled through their phones, and as far as they could tell, no one had taken a second glance at them.

"Okay, if you want to walk around the observation deck again, go ahead. But keep in mind, we stand out in this crowd. Except for Katrina, we're all pretty Gaijin-looking," Alec answered.

Elaine nodded and departed the mass damper chamber, into the main indoor observation deck, which formed a circle around the eighty-ninth floor.

Just around the corner from the stairwell entrance leading to the mass damper, Katrina was browsing through the gift shop for the third time today. She had already bought two refrigerator magnets to maintain her cover.

"I'm a Bukharan Jew, I don't look particularly Taiwanese or Chinese," she said under her breath.

"Eurasian is more Asian than the rest of us," Alec answered. He listened to the sounds through his earpiece. "If we had time, we would have gotten wigs, or—wait, are you buying *another* refrigerator magnet?"

Inside the gift shop, the woman behind the register, wearing a disposable mask, sweetly asked Katrina for her credit card. Katrina pretended she was talking into her smartphone.

"It's not like we lack friends who wouldn't like souvenirs!"

"Keep your magnets away from my computers," Dee warned.

One wall away, Alec looked at Ward and rolled his eyes.

"We're gonna go home and get asked, 'Did you save the world?' And we're gonna say, 'No, but we brought home some nice souvenirs!'"

***

The Voices had warned William Yen Wen, a.k.a. Waldo, that he and his team would likely encounter resistance once they had reached the observation deck of Taipei 101. Luckily, years of working in Taiwan had left Waldo and his team's muscle, Chen Zhang, with plenty of contacts on the wrong side of the law. The Chinese spies had worked with one crew of a half-dozen thugs, who Waldo had nicknamed the "Bamboo Six." The men were loosely affiliated with the Bamboo Union, the largest of Taiwan's three main criminal triads, involved in illegal gambling, drug trafficking, and all manner of crimes. The Bamboo Six were intimidating, ruthless, greedy, not particularly smart, didn't ask a lot of questions, and brought their own firearms. Waldo told them this was a quick hostage operation—go up, take hostages, demand a ransom of roughly $15 million in cryptocurrency. This came out to about $1.3 million each for the perpetrators. Once the ransom was paid, Jin Goh would disable all the elevators except one, take the team down to the first floor, where they would use access hallways to the adjacent shopping mall, Taipei Trade Center, Taipei convention center, and Grand Hyatt. No matter how far the police extended their perimeter, little-used corridors behind storefronts and lobbies, designed for maintenance crews, would offer Nine-Tailed Foxes a quick escape route.

The Bamboo Six didn't know that there would be no ransom demand, and that the true plan was to leave them behind without warning after uploading the quantum computer plans and announcing to the world that the Information Age was about to come to a crashing end.

Waldo wasn't afraid to die, but he didn't intend to, and as far as he could tell, all his teammates felt the same. But he wondered if everyone on the team was hoping tonight would be their last mission together. Under the stress of being disavowed and becoming fugitives, the team's bonds were fraying rapidly.

The files that had been hacked by Kobold had thankfully left out most of their personal details. The Nine-Tailed Foxes were not quite the well-oiled machine that their official records or fearsome reputation suggested. Waldo and the team's beautiful seductress, Ren Xiulan, had been having a passionate, tempestuous, on-again off-again affair for years. They had initially believed that only someone else in their odd and dangerous profession could understand the pressures and challenges in their life. But their teammates, particularly Chen Zhang and Zeng Zongying, contended the turbulent relationship clouded their judgment and endangered the team on missions.

So, Waldo and Ren broke up, only to discover that as exes, they were even worse for each other. Whenever Waldo or Ren started another relationship, jealousy would drive one to seduce the other and break up the other's burgeoning relationship—and then the affair would begin again, until the next massive fight. Chen Zhang complained that he felt like he was working in a soap opera, while Zeng Zongying berated Waldo and Ren for putting their personal desires above the needs of the state.

The drama only got worse after Waldo and Zeng Zongying got drunk and had an impassioned one-night stand that might have been more easily hidden if Zeng's fingernails hadn't left scratches all over Waldo's back, arms, and neck. Ren discovered their tryst and, with justification, exploded in rage, berated Zeng Zongying as an insufferable hypocrite and Waldo as a shameless womanizer. This epic fight did not stop her from reconnecting with Waldo a few weeks later.

Meanwhile, the team's hacker, Jin Go, had been asking to play a larger role in the team's missions for years. Alas, every time he stepped away from a keyboard, Jin Go proved to be clumsy, out of shape, awkward, and a liability in every sense of the word. Waldo wondered if Jin Go had some mental disorder; the Westerners apparently used the term "on the spectrum." Everyone else on the team resented Jin Go and angrily told the hacker to stay in his lane, but Waldo saw Jin Go as a hapless kid brother who wanted to play with the older kids.

The latest revelation to crack the team's already fragile chemistry was the revelation that Peng Xiaodan, allegedly a devoted agent of Chinese State Security, had actually been leaking information about the team to her old bosses at the Second Department, China's military intelligence, for years. And now, instead of rewarding his inside source, Peng, General Fang Yu had left his star agent out to dry.

Their final gathering in their hotel room, before the night's operation, turned into a volcanic eruption of long-simmering resentments and grievances.

Waldo had tried to convince his team that once the proliferating quantum computers had destroyed the entire concept of online security, the world's superpowers would be in a race to adapt to a new world where the computer revolution had suddenly been reversed. Only paper records would be secure, and any computer connected to the Internet would be too dangerous to use. The entire Orwellian surveillance state that the Chinese government had built would crumble under its own weight and insecurity. Beijing would find itself blinded, having grown far too dependent upon technology and desperate for good old-fashioned human intelligence agents. And then, Waldo argued, the

Ministry of State Security would have no choice but to welcome them back with open arms.

Ren Xiulan was livid when she realized what Waldo's ultimate objective had been all this time. She screamed at Waldo that she had wasted the best years of her life with a man who had always loved his duties and his job more than her. She listed off the men who had begged her to marry them—a member of the Politburo Standing Committee, a billionaire, an up-and-coming tech company CEO, and seemingly every handsome leading man in the Chinese film industry. Ren cried that she had given up the life of a princess to be a Nine-Tailed Fox—and now, after all these years, on the eve of her thirty-ninth birthday, what did she have?

Chen Zhang barked at both to shut their mouths, spitting that their emotions had first complicated and then ruined everything. He growled that he had always pulled the team through danger by keeping it simple—drive the car, get to the target, come in guns blazing, break some necks, grab whatever asset or prisoner the Ministry wanted, and then get out.

"The two of you have sucked the rest of us into your vortex! If it isn't the affair, it's the bickering!" Chen sneered. "You're adults in the field but teenagers with each other! It has always been left to me to be your babysitter!"

Jin Goh jumped to his feet and attempted to stand up for Waldo, who, he felt, was one of the few people who had ever seen him as more than an awkward hacking machine.

"That man has led us to our greatest victories!" the short and pudgy Jin Goh insisted, standing toe-to-toe with the much larger Chen. "Where would we be without him? You curse at him because you know you're too dumb to—"

Chen just slapped Jin Goh and knocked him off his feet, and his glasses off his face.

"Challenge me again, little ant, and I'll hit you like a man, and then you won't get back up again."

Peng Xiaodan shouted at them to stop. "After all these years, and all those missions, this is what we have left? Fighting among ourselves in some hotel room in Taipei?" But her teammates just glared at her.

"So sorry to hear that Fang Yu's puppet thinks we're not showing enough *loyalty*," Ren hissed.

Waldo noticed that no one on the team had objected to leaving Zeng Zongying behind in Argentina.

The Nine-Tailed Foxes were devolving into any one of the bands featured on VH1's *Behind the Music*—their long run of success had come to its inevitable end, and in the face of unexpected adversity, the team's cohesion was rapidly unraveling. To an objective outside observer, the team's sudden collapse from the heights of the espionage world hadn't been the fault of any of them. Amaja Rai's groundbreaking innovation had enabled hacking the most secure systems of the Ministry of State Security, a development that none of them could have foreseen or prevented. But killing Rai hadn't made them feel better or solved the problems caused by the team's exposure. In frustration, the team was turning on each other, looking for scapegoats.

Waldo looked at his team and declared, "Destiny requires us to work in harmony for one more night."

CHAPTER TWENTY-NINE

TAIPEI 101 TOWER
SEPTEMBER 26, 2023

The five remaining members of the Nine-Tailed Foxes approached one elevator; the Bamboo Six waited to take another one.

A cheerful, sweet elevator attendant greeted the Foxes, welcomed them in, pressed the close-door button.

"You are riding in the Toshiba Ultra High Speed Elevator, which can ascend at a top speed of more than one thousand meters in one minute," she explained in a girlish tone so highly pitched one would wonder if she had completed puberty. "You are now ascending close to sixty kilometers per hour. For twelve years, this was the fastest elevator in the world, until it was surpassed by the Shanghai Tower."

Jin Goh was working with a tablet. Besides the laptop in his backpack, he carried an external hard drive with a handle that held the team's most precious advantage, the purloined blueprints and operating instructions to Amaja Rai's quantum computer.

"The Bamboo Six are in the other elevator," Jin Goh reported. "Security cameras disabled." He looked at Chen Zhang and felt his cheek still sore from last night's slap.

"Good work, ant," Chen answered with begrudging respect.

With one beefy hand, Chen grabbed the head of the sweet elevator attendant and brutally slammed it against the wall of the elevator. She let out a short yelp and then dropped like a stone, likely suffering the effect of a concussion.

Jin Goh excitedly removed his phone and held it up, as if to take a picture of Waldo.

"Whenever you're ready," Jin Goh said with excitement.

Waldo looked at his four teammates. "Let's change the course of history."

He checked his hair in the mirrored back wall of the elevator, ran his hand through his thick black mane, and turned and stared into the camera on Jin Goh's phone. His hacker teammate nodded, indicating that he was livestreaming.

"You do not know my name, but you will remember my works for generations," Waldo declared.

"We are the Nine-Tailed Foxes. Only the highest levels of your governments have heard our name, but they tremble in fear when they hear it. For many years, we served our great nation and tried to build a better, orderly world. But now it is clear that the forces of chaos will not allow it. Our mission and purpose were detailed by a demonic, infernal device—but one that, in just a matter of moments, will stop being our problem. We are going to make it everyone's problem."

He smiled.

"If you've ever wanted to build a quantum computer, and gain the ability to hack anyone, anywhere, at any time, we're about to show you how."

***

Inside the tuned mass damper chamber, Dee's eyes widened and she reached out and shook Ward's sleeve at the shoulder.

"My search programs just pinged! Someone just set up a live feed that's going out on several social media platforms at once, referring to a quantum—"

The audio feed from the live feed piped through Dee's laptop.

They heard a familiar voice announce: "You do not know my name, but you will remember my works for generations."

Alec grinned. "That's our Waldo."

"I don't even need to run a traceroute program, I recognize it," Dee said, pointing to the screen. "That's one of the elevators we used to come up here."

"The curtain on our show goes up in about thirty seconds," Katrina announced, putting the shopping bag with tourist magnets into her backpack, and reaching for the Glock-19. She wondered whether she could take more of the soon-to-arrive assailants out, faster, with the MP7 submachine gun, but realized there were simply too many tourists around on the observation deck.

"Ward, you've got job one," Raquel reconfirmed. "We may want to kill the Nine-Tailed Foxes, but we need to stop those quantum computer plans from getting uploaded!"

"They both feel like needs to me!" Alec quipped.

***

The elevator doors opened, and the five Foxes stepped out. Even after all these years and all these deadly assignments, they still felt adrenaline coursing through their body. A few moments later, the other elevator opened and the Bamboo Six split into groups of three—one group heading to the left, the other to the right.

"The quantum plans are a lot of data—it will take several minutes to complete the upload," Jin Goh reported.

"Stay close to me, our dutiful, diligent ant," Waldo said with a wink and smile. Jin Goh smiled and straightened his posture. As if through magical alchemy, Waldo had turned Chen's insult into a proud nickname.

In perfectly timed coordination, every member of the Foxes and Bamboo Six reached into their jackets, purses, and satchels and removed handguns. The Bamboo Six carried Chinese-made QSZ-92 pistols, one of the standard sidearms of the People's Liberation Army. A day earlier, Waldo had gone to one of his old lockers in a Taipei self-storage business and retrieved a stash of CS/LP5s, slightly more compact and concealable versions. The guns hadn't been fired since before the pandemic, Waldo had wondered whether being in storage for years would make the guns less accurate than he remembered, but there hadn't been time, or a safe place, to test-fire them.

But the Voices reminded Waldo that the observation deck offered plenty of civilians around for target practice.

***

The 89th floor observation deck featured floor-to-ceiling UV windows, cleaned every day, offered jaw-dropping views in all four directions—well beyond the spectacular sprawl of Taipei to the green hills and small mountains beyond. Even the 56-story Sky Taipei, the second-tallest skyscraper in the city that resembled a cross between the Citibank tower in Manhattan and a shard of jade, looked small from the observation deck. More than two million visitors, mostly foreign tourists, visited the observation deck in 2015, but the numbers plunged during the pandemic and had slowly been climbing back up. This evening, as the sun set in the West, dozens of families, couples, small groups and lone gawkers took selfies with the sweeping expanse of the city behind them.

The Bamboo Six fired their first shots into the two security guards and other observation tower tour guides and employees—anyone in any position of authority or responsibility who could help get people away from the attackers. The tourists screamed and began scrambling, panicking, ducking, diving behind the couches and benches and coffee shop and ice-cream parlor.

One shot missed and shattered the glass, opening a terrifying expanse into the cold air beyond the window.

Waldo turned to Jin Goh and gestured for him to start livestreaming again. Jin Goh nodded and raised his phone again.

"Do you hear that, world?" Waldo asked, with a disturbingly comfortable smile, raising his voice to be heard over the gunfire and screams and sounds of chaos behind him. "That is the sound of Pandora's box being opened. That is the sound of our vengeance upon all of you. That is the sound of chaos being unleashed, and your world coming tumbling down around you, an inevitable consequence of your arrogance and defiance of the natural order."

***

The gunfire and screams had begun just a moment earlier, and now they were getting louder—whatever trouble had started was steadily getting closer. Dee noticed Alec smiling.

"Why are you smiling?" she asked.

"You're about to see," Alec said with a laugh.

"Let's go!" Ward ordered in an insistent whisper, and he, Alec, and Dee moved out of the mass damper chamber, emerging from around the corner of the entryway, weapons drawn.

Ward saw them first, and in a fluid motion he declined to one knee, as if genuflecting before the power of the weapon in his hand.

The fleeing tourists parted like the Red Sea, giving Ward the sort of clear shot on an unprepared foe that he saw in his dreams.

The three members of the Bamboo Six had no idea who Ward was, only that a burly American with a beard approaching ZZ Top length had appeared out of nowhere, leveling a compact submachine gun at them, quickly flanked by some other tall American grinning like a madman and a wincing blond Cuban-American holding her handgun and suppressor like it was a bomb that could go off in her hands at any time.

But behind them, Waldo recognized Ward from their run-in in the Maldives, and his eyes suddenly widened in aghast astonishment as he realized that somehow, some way, the Dangerous Clique had anticipated his moves. For one millisecond, it was as if time stood still. Waldo thought he and his team would have several minutes before they encountered any serious resistance. They had barely started their operation and now these Americans, like ghosts, were here to haunt them.

"Timber," Ward growled.

And in a barrage of bullets, the Bamboo Six were reduced by three. Dee rose to the occasion, and at least some her shots hit the gangster thugs in their legs, and Alec actually shot a round through the neck of the Bamboo thug to the left. But those shots were almost superfluous, as Ward had used his MP7 to strafe the three thugs in a giant Z pattern across their chests and torsos. They fell to the ground with horrified expressions on their faces.

Waldo and Jin Goh watched the Bamboo three get cut down, and ran. The pudgy hacker scrambled and ducked behind a couch; Waldo disappeared behind the nearest corner.

"Did you see that?" Alec said, exploding in glee. "Did you see that? Waldo's eyes were the size of pie plates! God, I'm going to miss this feeling when I retire!"

Dee breathed heavily. "I thought we were only using the MP7 if it gets ugly!"

Ward shook his head. "No, I only wanted you guys using the MP7s if it got ugly, I trust myself!"

"Ya hear that, Waldo?" Alec shouted, riding the high of adrenaline and a victorious first strike. "Bet you can't hear those Voices over the sound of my gun!"

Waldo popped back around the corner and fired more shots in their direction. Alec and Dee scrambled and ducked back into the doorway to the mass damper chamber, while Ward clambered behind a pillar just barely wide enough to protect him.

***

On the other side of the observation deck, closer to the gift shop, Katrina, Elaine, and Raquel had unknowingly drawn the more difficult assignment—three remaining Bamboo Union thugs, along with the bruiser Chen Zhang, the seductress Ren Xiulan, and the military cop Peng Xiaodan had left them outnumbered two to one. But the attackers had expected rent-a-cops and quickly overwhelmed security guards. The crowds of panicking tourists had obscured that three women were not frightened at all, almost as if they had expected the attack, and that they were reaching into their backpacks.

In fact, Katrina, finding herself square in the sights of one of the Bamboo Union thugs, simply held her backpack in front of her with one hand and used that to obscure the fact that she was pointing her gun right at him with her other hand. By the time he realized where the shots were coming from, one of her shots pierced his heart.

Waldo and Ren had brought the Bamboo Union thugs on this mission to hide the Foxes' escape, but within the first minute of the gunfight, they were serving another, even more important role: cannon fodder.

Chen, Ren, and Peng had all been shocked to see their Bamboo Union muscle—who they had sent ahead of them—suddenly getting shot—all center mass, two from a Western woman and one Eurasian. The three remembered seeing the Eurasian woman from the Maldives.

"FBI!" Elaine had yelled, out of instinct, and then she realized she was roughly one hemisphere out of her jurisdiction. "Drop the gun! Let me see those hands!"

Instead, Chen, Ren, and Peng raised their handguns and fired back. But, as Waldo had worried, the old guns almost seemed startled when they discharged their rounds. More glass shattered, the stuffing of the couches exploded as rounds pierced them, and the tourists screamed as the exchange of shots grew more intense.

Elaine and Raquel could see each other; the FBI agent had ducked behind a pillar and Raquel had ducked in a doorway leading to an inner room displaying an elaborate model of the tower and the building's former certification as the world's tallest building and current certification for Leadership in Energy and Environmental Design. The panicked tourists seemed to be screaming from every direction, making it tough to tell where they were hiding; some had simply hit the floor, crouched and covered their heads. Neither Elaine nor Raquel had trained on the MP7, and neither one wanted to use it with so many civilians around.

Katrina realized that Chen, Ren, and Peng were focusing all their fire on Elaine and Raquel; in all the commotion, none of the Nine-Tailed Foxes had noticed she had shot one of the Bamboo Union thugs.

She dropped to a crouch, scrambled to the window, and inched closer as the three Foxes fired at where Elaine and Raquel had been, keeping her gun hidden within her backpack.

Peng was closest, and she seemed furious, blasting away at where Raquel had been. But her handgun seemed to jam after firing five rounds. She looked at it and hit the side in anguished frustration.

Rising slightly, pressed against the glass wall overlooking the city, Katrina took shallow breaths, lined up her shot.

Squeezed, and squeezed again.

And two rounds went through the neck and jaw of Peng—blood from a carotid artery suddenly spurted out upon the floor.

With the Bamboo Union thugs dead and Peng bleeding out in front of them, Chen and Ren instantly changed priorities: escape.

***

"Katrina just took down Peng!" Raquel's voice reported through their communications system.

Alec and Dee were still crouched in the doorway to the mass damper chamber. Alec had been trying to provide cover fire for Ward, who had made himself as narrow as possible behind a pillar. Bullets fired from somewhere just around the corner kept hitting the pillar. Alec and Ward could still see Jin Goh hiding behind a big green plush couch.

"That guy's got way too much faith in that couch," Alec surmised.

"He's not shooting at us, Waldo is!" Ward shouted from behind the pillar. While he was scrambling, his earwig had slipped out. "I'm okay back here, but you guys have got to figure out if Fat Boy is uploading the computer plans!"

Dee had checked out of the gunfight to consult her laptop. "No sign of an upload yet!" She typed. "If he starts, I can try to take it down, attack it, but all I'll probably do is delay the inevitable!"

Alec's manic grin started to fade. He looked over at Ward behind the pillar, and then down at Dee, crouched over her laptop.

"Whole fate of the world depends upon this, right?" Alec asked to no one in particular.

Alec crouched down and swung his backpack off his back. He reached in and raised the MP7 that Ward had reluctantly given him, flicked off the safety.

"Alec, put that down," Ward said.

"On the count of three, I want you to fire at the spot that Waldo's firing from!" Alec said, taking a deep breath.

"Alec, I don't have a good angle, and neither do you!" Ward fumed, knowing that somewhere in his gut, he knew his subpar plan would lead to a desperate situation like this. "Waldo could shoot either one of us!"

"But not both," Alec said, raising his eyebrows. "Whichever one he shoots at, the other one of us finishes him off."

"None of our kids are losing a dad today!" Ward barked.

"One," Alec began.

And then, one beat too early, Alec popped out from around the corner and let loose in the direction of Jin Goh and what he was carrying.

Alec would later brag that he had demonstrated remarkable marksmanship, but the simple fact of the matter was that when a reasonably competent adult male fires thirty rounds from an MP7 submachine gun at a crouching target who is poorly hidden behind an object that cannot deflect bullets, at least some of those rounds are likely to hit the target.

Two rounds pierced the external hard drive, and three more tore through Jin Goh's left hand, and one more through the wrist. The Chinese hacker howled in pain, and flailed his bloody hand, sending little droplets of blood all around the floor.

"*Yes!*" Alec shouted with glee, pumping his fist.

Then Alec looked to the corner where Waldo had been, and realized, with thanks, that he wasn't shot. He turned to Ward, who was enraged that Alec had gone early, wanting to draw Waldo's fire and give Ward a clear shot.

"The bastard never popped up!" Ward roared. "I fired in his direction, but I don't think he's there anymore!"

Off in the distance, they saw the wailing Jin Goh slowly rise to his feet, cradling the bloody mess of what was left of his hand, and scrambling further away.

Alec put down the MP7 and picked up the lighter, easier handgun.

"Everybody, the hard drive he's got is shot to pieces, I think that eliminates the threat of him uploading the plans. And their hacker is, uh ... " Alec paused. "Shorthanded."

"He seems like the kind of guy who's experienced typing with one hand," Dee quipped.

Katrina ducked through the mass driver chamber and emerged by Dee and Alec.

"They're cutting and running," Katrina reported. "Raquel and Elaine are laying down fire, trying to keep them away from the elevators."

"Tell them to relax, because I just shut down all the building's elevators," Dee said, with a look of satisfaction. "Nobody's going to get away from us tonight."

"They could go down the stairwells," Katrina warned.

Dee shook her head. "Building security, with guns, is coming up those stairwells," she reported. "Big beefy guys in bulletproof vests, coming up from the security office, climbing, eighty-eight floors. They'll be here by ... " She checked her watch. "Next Tuesday."

"There's thousands of people on the lower floors, they're going to try to ditch their guns, look like hostages, slip out with everyone else," Katrina warned, trying to think like her enemies. She pressed her earwig in. "Elaine, Raquel, can you guys keep them from getting past you?"

"Roger that," Elaine responded.

"We're gonna close in, they may come running to you," Katrina said.

"Pincer movement," Ward nodded.

CHAPTER THIRTY

Chen and Ren were disturbed to find Waldo slowly retreating in their direction.

"Where's Peng?" Waldo demanded.

"Your friend Katrina turned her into a blood donor!" Chen spat. "How did they know we were coming here?"

"Doesn't matter, Jin Goh can't upload the plans," Waldo raged and burst forth with a slew of Chinese swears, that roughly translated to "stupid inbred stack of meat" and "son of a drooling whore and a monkey."

"Wait for me!" Jin Goh cried, attempting to run while holding what was left of his hand in his armpit to apply pressure to the wound. He was leaving a steady blood trail behind him.

Waldo turned and glared at Jin Goh, who was, he realized, as hapless and pathetic as his teammates had claimed.

"Didn't bring your laptop or the external hard drive, did you?" Waldo snapped.

"I have one hand!" Jin Goh cried back. "I couldn't even carry my cell phone!"

And Waldo suddenly realized that the live stream of their assault had never stopped. For all he knew, the whole world was still watching.

***

For those watching the live stream, the chaotic image had shifted to the ceiling of the observation deck, and then the floor. And then the phone moved, and it rose to just see a quartet of people's feet, and the barrels of two MP7 submachine guns.

"Ladies. Gentlemen, I'm sure what you just saw was frightening," a woman's voice said in an even, calm tone. Only a handful of people around the world would recognize the voice of Katrina Leonidivna. Katrina realized she was creating an audio file of her voice that could someday become a headache, but she felt there was a greater need, and greater opportunity, at this moment.

"The world has no shortage of evil men—and women—who see bloodshed and mayhem as just another way to get what they want," she continued. "They have thrived in chaos and fear. They've acted arrogantly, leaving death and destruction in their wake, believing no one could ever catch them. But you should know someone else is out there, hunting them as relentlessly and mercilessly as they prey upon the innocent. My friends and I have a message to them, a message that is the same as the one that the terrorist group Atarsa delivered to all of us, all those years ago." Katrina paused.

"None of you are safe from us."

Katrina stopped the recording. Behind her, Alec smiled. "We're the Dangerous Clique, and we approved this message."

***

Dee typed a few more commands.

"Jin Goh had disabled the security cameras on the observation deck right before they arrived, and I'm giving us access, but not the building security team," Dee said. She scrolled through several feeds, showing groups of tourists hiding in corners, or starting to move more openly toward the emergency stairwells, now that no gunfire had been heard for a few moments.

"There they are," Dee noted. "Or at least three of them—the muscle, the model, and the one-handed hacker are hiding behind the counter in the ice-cream shop."

Alec fumed and rolled his eyes. "I can't believe I'm about to say this, but . . ." He sighed. "Where's Waldo?"

"I don't think he's on this floor," Dee said in frustration. "I've got facial recognition software running, either he's not here or he's not showing his face near any camera."

"Let's bag those three foxes while we can!" Ward declared.

"Wait—I've got him," Dee interrupted. "Two floors up, on the outdoor observation deck level."

"Dibs," Alec and Katrina said simultaneously.

***

Chen, Ren, and the bleeding Jin Goh had scrambled behind the counter of the ice cream shop. Chen and Ren kept their guns at their sides but intended to drop them the moment police or security guards arrived. Jin Goh, they figured, would also be initially mistaken as a shot hostage. If they played their cards right, they would be taken to a hospital and discharged and never suspected as the perpetrators; Jin Goh had insisted his software had already scrubbed the building's video footage.

If those crazy Americans found them, Chen and Ren figured they could surrender. The CIA was always looking for defecting Chinese spies, and they knew plenty of secrets that Beijing would hate to see revealed. Their past crimes, their slaughter of the lab technicians in Argentina, their murder of Amaja Rai, their short-lived terrorist attack on the Taipei 101 tower—all of it would be forgiven and forgotten in exchange for detailed debriefings. Chen and Ren, in conversations separate from the others, wondered if the Americans' offer might have been a better deal, one that Waldo had rashly rejected without even consulting with the rest of the team. Both thought of themselves as patriotic Chinese, but their own government had rejected and disavowed them, all because the Ministry of State Security couldn't secure its own servers. After that humiliation and betrayal, what did they owe China? Chen had always dreamed of living a life of fast cars and wild fun, straight out of one of the *Fast and the Furious* movies. Ren realized that America had an endless supply of wealthy men who would treat a gorgeous Chinese woman like an empress. The pair had done their part to restore China to its former glory; now both believed it was time for them to cash in and enjoy the good life.

If their old enemy, the Central Intelligence Agency, was willing to underwrite their new lives and give them new identities, it would be a perfect satisfying irony.

What Chen and Ren had not expected was for Ward to strafe the ice cream parlor counter with thirty rounds from his MP7, without any verbal warning. They died instantly.

Jin Goh scrambled out and raised his hands—well, hand—and begged for mercy.

Ward was surprised when Dee stepped forward, holding her Glock-19 and pointing it straight at Jin Goh's head.

"How much mercy did you and your teammates show to all those computer scientists and programmers and designers down in Argentina?" Dee asked coolly.

Jin Goh just stammered. "It was the mission!"

This answer just enraged Dee even more. "What threat could they possibly have presented to your team? They were computer people, just like you and me! They weren't commandos! They weren't spies! They were just trying to make the world a better place by building something amazing, inventing something no one else ever had! And you guys just stormed into the place and slaughtered them!"

Dee stepped closer, and surprised Ward by putting her Glock right up against Jin Goh's forehead.

"Did you even object?" Dee demanded. "Did you even pause, for a moment, to realize that all those people in that lab were no different from you and me, people who spent most of their waking hours behind a keyboard, trying to solve problems, looking for the glitch in a line of code?" She admitted that pressing the gun against the Chinese hacker's forehead, and seeing his terror and regret, and the tears coming to his eyes, felt satisfying.

"I never said anything to anyone on my team," Jin Goh admitted, weeping. "They would never listen to me anyway."

After a long moment, Dee pulled away the gun.

"I'm not going to kill you," Dee announced, to the relief of Ward. He had suspected that the sight of the slaughter in Argentina had affected his friend much more than she had let on.

"But it's not because you don't deserve it," Dee seethed. "It's because I don't kill unarmed men."

Ward removed a zip-tie from his backpack, and realized Jin Goh was no threat, and instead put it around the forearm of the hacker's bleeding limb.

"I'm using this as a tourniquet," Ward growled. He pulled it tight and turned to Dee.

"You alright?"

Dee pressed her finger to her ear.

"Katrina and Alec found Waldo!"

CHAPTER THIRTY-ONE

Waldo had determined that the observation deck level didn't have a good place to hide and was about to descend the stairwell when Katrina and Alec greeted him with sixty rounds from the MP7s. Katrina had methodically and precisely put two rounds through Waldo's right kneecap; she felt confident he couldn't pull one of his trademark disappearing acts when he couldn't walk and was bleeding profusely. As promised, Alec had gone for the kill shot—and grazed Waldo's scalp, put a round through his side by his rib cage, and managed to shoot Waldo's gun. Waldo staggered for a moment, then fell forward, down the half-flight of stairs to the landing.

When his body stopped tumbling, he coughed and wheezed—alive, but too pained to move.

"Uncharacteristically good shot." Katrina offered her husband a backhanded compliment.

"Well, I was aiming for his face," Alec admitted. "You want to zip-tie him?"

***

Katrina and Alec bound Waldo and dragged him down the remaining one and a half flights of stairs. The indoor observation deck had grown cold with one of the floor-to-ceiling windows shattered, and a chill wind started to whip through the floor. Elaine was telling people to descend the stairs, and enough tourists and visitors seemed to understand her English and gestures: the threat was gone.

"I figure we've got three or four minutes before the Taiwan cops and building security get up the stairs," Dee reported. "When we're ready, we can use the elevator to the basement. To the central control room, the elevator system is going to look like nothing's moving."

Upon seeing Katrina and Alec dragging Waldo, Ward let out a low-pitched and satisfied "hooah!" He had just pulled out the bodies of Ren and Chen from behind the counter and taken photos for verification.

"Good hunting, my friends," Ward said, saddling up to Waldo. "Right now, you're realizing you should have just stayed in bed this morning."

Waldo attempted to spit on Ward's face, but it just got on his shirt. Ward just laughed.

Raquel looked at the bloodied, beaten, and bound Jin Goh and Waldo.

"As much as I'd love to take these guys with us, we're going to have to leave them for Taiwan's National Investigative Bureau," Raquel declared, shaking her head. "There's just no way we can get these guys out of the country, under the Taiwanese's noses, with them in this condition."

Dee examined the makeshift tourniquet around Jin Goh's arm, tightened it a little, and gestured to the empty space where the window had been.

"You want to know the difference between you and me?" Dee said to Jin Goh. "I'm making sure you don't bleed to death. All of my kindness gets taken for weakness."

Alec turned to Waldo and asked a question that surprised even himself.

"You got kids, Waldo?"

"Procreation is a distraction from the mission," the Chinese spy answered.

"If you'd had them, everything would look different," Alec said with genuine sympathy for Waldo. "Maybe the Voices never would have gotten their claws into you. You have a kid—or two, like us—you've suddenly got a real big reason to leave the world in better shape than how you found it. Doesn't really leave any room for nihilism."

Waldo looked at Alec in sadness, then horror. Then Waldo's body suddenly wriggled and writhed, as if he was having a seizure. After several spasms, he seemed to regain control.

"We do not lack for easy prey," Waldo—or something within him—whispered. "Slay my vessel, dispel me, matters not. My siblings will just strike on some other battlefield. As my ancestor said, 'We are legion.'"

Alec laughed. "Yeah, well, right now the score is Dangerous Clique twelve, Legion, nothing."

Waldo chuckled. "You can be certain that the Voices were there, whispering in Vladimir Putin's ear, when he chose to invade Ukraine."

Alec felt his knees go weak, and for a moment wondered if Taiwan was experiencing an earthquake. After a moment, he shook it off and tightened his grip on Waldo.

"I can't wait until some Taiwanese scientist dissects your brain," Alec sneered back.

Waldo sneered, wriggled, and glared at Katrina and Alec. Finally, he let out one deep snarl in English:

"Next time, I'll go after your kids."

Before Alec could speak, with one swift motion, Katrina shoved Waldo through the open space where the floor-to-ceiling window had been.

Katrina, Alec, Elaine, Dee, Raquel, and Ward could see, in Waldo's eyes, that he had never believed Katrina could do something like that—and he belatedly realized it was the last mistake he would ever make.

CHAPTER THIRTY-TWO

William Yen Wen, a.k.a. Waldo, plummeted down eighty-nine stories, hitting the side of the Taipei tower several times, before slamming into the pavement of the surrounding courtyard so hard that his abdominal cavity ruptured. He left a crimson splatter of brain and blood and ruptured organs in at least a two-foot radius around the spot of impact.

***

Ward hoisted up Jin Goh, speechless and in shock from seeing Waldo shoved through the empty space and carried to his doom by gravity.

"What are you going to tell the Taiwanese, Jingo?"

"Before my teammates could kill any more people, some outsiders appeared out of nowhere like ghosts and shot us up like American Old West cowboys!"

"That'll do," Ward concluded with a nod to Katrina, and Ward let go of him, and he dropped to the floor with a thud.

The four women and two men of the Dangerous Clique headed to the elevators. Dee double-checked to make sure the security camera video feeds of the past half-hour would be permanently erased. She couldn't erase Waldo's livestream, but as far as she could tell, the Clique did not appear on it other than their shoes and pant legs, and Katrina's warning to the evildoers of the world that they would never be safe. The elevator doors closed, and less than a minute later, the Taiwanese National Police Agency's SWAT Team, named Thunder Squad, emerged from the stairwells—exhausted from climbing eighty-eight flights of stairs.

***

So many officers, inspectors, detectives, and senior officials from the Taiwanese national Criminal Investigation Bureau had rushed to the scene that an officer jokingly asked if anyone had stayed back at the CIB headquarters building. When Thunder Squad breached the doors to the observation deck floor, they indeed found a bloodbath, as the initial terrified reports had claimed, but casualties were much lower than expected—three dead security guards and two wounded, one dead civilian tourist, and about a dozen injured. The dead civilian tourist hadn't been shot but had suffered a heart attack upon the onset of the panic.

And then there were the ten dead who, eyewitnesses claimed, had perpetuated the attack, aligned with the ominous live stream about "Nine-Tailed Foxes" and "forces of chaos" and "a quantum computer." The unseen woman who had said the hunted had become the hunted had spoken English, but that didn't necessarily stand out in the crowd; almost 30 percent of Taiwanese spoke at least some English. Almost every Taiwanese policeman had heard about a Chinese team called the "Nine-Tailed Foxes" after last year, and three of the dead matched the description of the Nine-Tailed Foxes in the hack from weeks ago.

What's more, Jin Goh, the team's hacker, was now in custody, with a hand that was so badly shot up it was likely to require amputation. Goh was crying and already begging the policemen around him for a deal. Taiwan still had the death penalty for numerous crimes, including murder, robbery, and hijacking.

CIB investigators noted that the man in the video, William Yen Wen, had not been among the dead on the observation deck. They believed that the man who had fell from the observation deck was also a potential hostile, and was possibly Wen, but identifying what was left of his body was going to take some time.

The witnesses claimed that a handful of Westerners had slain the Nine-Tailed Foxes. When these reports reached Taiwan's National Security Bureau, the director-general sighed, removed his glasses, and rubbed his eyes. He didn't know precisely what had happened, but he had strong suspicions that whatever had happened at the Taipei 101 tower was connected to the cursory notification from the local CIA station chief that an agency team was arriving in-country to investigate a report about a Chinese spy ring. And the director-general remembered two pieces of advice from one of his predecessors, a retired general who was now a top official at the Taiwanese Ministry of Defense. The first was that when things go unexpectedly right in the world of intelligence, don't ask too many questions about why they went right, just accept it as good fortune and move on. And the second piece of advice was that when the Americans offer a gift, take it and don't look back.

***

The police barricades kept being pushed back, extending the circumference of the police-controlled zone in the heart of Taipei. When the six members of the Dangerous Clique emerged from the Taipei international convention center, they pushed their way through the growing crowds of curious gawkers behind the police barricade, crossed Keelung Road, and walked a block west, to settle into an Australian restaurant and bar with the unusual name of "Woolloomooloo."

The patrons at the bar were abuzz about the emergency situation at the skyscraper just up the road, shouting out news that they read from their phones. Above the bar, a television played Mandarin-language news coverage, which kept replaying the short video of William Yen Wen, and then the even shorter section of the video of the team's feet, and then back to footage of the police cars, fire trucks, ambulances and military police vehicles and a sea of flashing lights on the streets around the Taipei 101 tower.

"Why did you pick this place?" Alec asked as they settled into the table.

"Vibe just felt like ours," Katrina said, gesturing. A Ukrainian flag hung in one window, as well as a rainbow flag and several banners, including one in English demanding, "Liberate Hong Kong, Revolution for Our Times." Copies of English-language newspapers hung from a long rung.

"Good to see ordinary people are willing to stand up for something," Raquel observed.

"No one likes bullies," Dee observed.

"Autocrats, terrorists... they look at free peoples and they think we're all pushovers," Katrina declared, just starting to smile. "They look at their armies, their propaganda videos, their foot soldiers pledging to die, and they think they're so intimidating. And they can be, no doubt. But these big overconfident men underestimate their foes, every time."

"They're blind to the strength in their enemies," Raquel concurred. "Democracies and republics don't run around pounding their chests and trash-talking."

"Speak for yourself," Ward said with a smile.

Raquel smirked, then continued. "A figure like Putin or Xi looks at happy people here in Taiwan, or in America or Europe or Japan, and thinks that just because the society isn't austere and militaristic, it can't fight. They can't perceive strength that looks different from theirs. Just sucks that we share the same era and the same planet with the likes of them."

Katrina shook her head. "We can lament living in the time of Xi and Putin, but there are always men like that. Our parents had to live with Khrushchev and Mao, and our grandparents had to live with Stalin and Hitler."

Ward let out a chuckle. "Well, with Hitler, our grandparents lived with him until they didn't."

"You notice there's always a Russian?" Alec quipped. "Every generation, in the Evil Bastard Olympics, somebody from Moscow makes the medal platform." He wondered if the Voices had always had a nest, or infestation, in the Russian capital.

Ward greeted the beer that the waitress placed in front of him. "Well, William Yen Wen wanted to take gold in the Evil Bastard Olympic sprint, and we fired the starter's pistol into his ear. My guess is that in a couple of weeks, almost everyone will have forgotten about him. Honestly, considering their notorious reputations, I expected more of a fight from those Nine-Tailed Foxes. They saw us, crapped their pants, and cut and ran."

"Waldo's spent his life working for the Ministry of State Security, which is not an institution that cultivates improvisation and creative thinking," Katrina observed. "He and his crew drew up the plan and executed the plan—they couldn't change on the fly or call audibles."

"We work for a flawed institution," Katrina continued, looking at Elaine and adding, "institutions. Within a flawed government, in a flawed country. But we get a lot of the big things right."

Elaine noticed Dee had seemed quiet and thoughtful during the conversation, or pensive.

"What's on your mind, Dee?" she asked. "Should we be worried that Jin Goh might have studied those plans for a quantum computer well enough to use them as a bargaining chip in Taiwanese custody?"

Dee thought for a moment and offered a skeptical shake of the head. "Even if he's got a photographic memory, he'd have to redraw the blueprints, rewrite the programming code, a million little details. That's a really complicated machine to build. I think that, at least for now, the U.S. has the lead in the race for a working quantum computer."

"Because of what's left from the machine from Argentina," Raquel added.

"That . . . and my friends at the NSA are among the best in the world at data recovery."

She reached into her backpack and removed Jin Goh's external hard drive, that had once looked sleek and black, but that was now cracked in two places where two bullets had torn through it.

CHAPTER THIRTY-THREE

CIA HEADQUARTERS
LANGLEY, VIRGINIA
OCTOBER 2, 2023

About a week later, Raquel was summoned to the office of Director Boyles on the seventh floor of the CIA headquarters building.

"How is your team recovering?" Boyles asked. Ever the diplomat, he had the good sense to at least appear concerned about those who worked underneath him.

"Thankfully, just minor bumps and bruises," Raquel answered with a gentle shake of her head. "We lucked out in lot of ways. Merlin—Harold Hare—used to say somebody up there's looking out for us. Maybe he was right." *Maybe it's that equivalent of the Voices on the other side*, she thought to herself.

"Glad to hear it," Boyles said, tapping the desk. He cleared his throat and turned to the real reason he had summoned Raquel.

"The good news is that between the equipment we suck out of Argentina and that damaged external hard drive, the National Security Council feels good that we're leading the race to build another working quantum computer," the director declared. "You and your people had a lot to do with that."

"Sir, as I see it, that's our job," Raquel said. She couldn't resist adding a satisfied smile.

Boyles's smile faded. "There's some bad news, too. When I brought the NSC up to speed about what happened in Taiwan, everybody from the SecDef to the DNI to Homeland was spitting hot fire about being kept in the dark," Boyles began. "Your team took some awfully big risks. Quite a few people think you should have looped them in."

He waited for an answer, and when none came, Boyles added, "Myself included."

Mm-hmm, Raquel nodded. "Sir, which recent event is supposed to make my team feel better about sharing information, the worst hack in our history by Kobold, or the revelation that Patrick Horne, the guy down the hall from us for the past twenty years, has been a mole selling our agency's secrets this whole time?"

Boyles frowned and nodded. "Point taken."

"Sir, you're fairly new to the Agency, and my team and I have been doing this since Iraq started. We have a system that works, most of the time," Raquel asserted. "And it looks like, at least for a while, that system is going to have to stay in place. Our plans to start developing a younger backup team are back to square one—"

"I've assured all our exposed case officers that they're not out of a job," Boyles interrupted, with just a touch of defensiveness. "They're smart people, we'll find something for them to do. Although I understand Ravid has already applied to Quantico."

"He'll probably fit in there like a glove," Raquel said, with a half-smile. "I'd like to get another crew of recruits in place, but with nearly two hundred of our youngest case officers pushed into involuntary retirement, I'm at the back of the line. And I'm not even going to ask you to push me closer to the front of the line—"

Boyles laughed at the thought, held up a memo on the recruiting crisis. "It's a long line, Raquel!" He rattled off the parts of the clandestine service scrambling to fill holes, counting on his fingers. "Counterterrorism, counterproliferation, China desk, Russia, Iran, North Korea, transnational crime, cybercrime—yeah, I'm so unreasonable to give them priority." He shook his head.

"Either you guys keep going with your current team, or we close up shop."

Raquel responded with a grim nod. "We figured you would say that. Katrina and Alec are going to try to balance the risks of the job with parenthood as best they can."

"I understand Rutledge has enough children for a prime-time sitcom," Boyles remarked, eager to demonstrate he had reviewed the team's files.

Raquel shook her head. "He's wired differently, Army Ranger. His family always knew the risks, always accepted the risks."

Boyles tapped his desk with his fingertips. "I suppose you think I'm going to say, 'Job well done, keep doing what you're doing, keep me out of the loop, your budget requests will continue to get approved, and you only need to see me when you need something.'" Boyle's wrinkled eyebrows indicated he believed the team's past arrangements were unacceptable.

Raquel gave Boyles a carefully calibrated stare of determination that never quite crossed into hostility. "Sir, your predecessor and I had a lot of friction, and while I'm not narcissistic enough to say that's what got her fired, it certainly didn't help. As far as I can tell, you're doing the best job you can in the toughest of circumstances. The president threw you into the deep end and hoped you could swim. I want to be your ally. This agency's facing way too many emerging threats to waste time on infighting. But if we're going to be allies, my team needs to keep having that long leash. And that means trusting my judgment on when to keep things close to the vest and when to loop you in."

Boyles glared across the desk.

"Give me one good reason why I should stake my career on you and your team operating with your traditional level of minimal oversight," he demanded, without raising his voice.

"Let's start with, you just put three of my team's worst enemies back on the streets of Russia, Iran and Syria," Raquel shot back.

CHAPTER THIRTY-FOUR

SOMEWHERE IN NORTHERN VIRGINIA
OCTOBER 6, 2023

It had been a few years since Katrina and Alec had thrown a party.

"Do you remember when we threw the party after coming back from Cyprus?" Alec laughed. "God, we were so hung over. It took a lot of drinking to get everyone singing karaoke."

Katrina was still cooking up a Bukhari feast, turning their kitchen into a plethora of exotic scents, a busy stove, oven, and a slew of pots and pans—lamb and mutton, rice and grain, dumplings and flatbreads, in addition to the usual spreads of party vegetables and chips and dip. Will and Harry were being relatively cooperative, and this time Dee had come over early, eager to play with the twins, getting more verbose and less shy around new faces with every passing week, and seemingly fine with the departure of the four grandparents. Ward and his wife, Marie, had made the journey from Williamsburg, and Marie set about pouring glasses of wine and perusing the house's cocktail ingredients.

"We're going to have to hire a nanny," Alec sighed. Ward had asked for a beer, and Alec responded to his nonspecific request by removing bottle after bottle from the refrigerator, each one a weirder and more obscure microbrew than the previous one.

Ward examined the options like they were elixirs from an alien planet. "Mole spicy chocolate, coffee bourbon porter, triple Trappist ale, blueberry hefeweizen . . . Don't you have any beer-flavored beer?"

"Try the Trappist ale," Alec recommended, handing him a bottle opener. Ward shook his head and twisted the bottle cap off with a brief grunt.

"That wasn't a twist-off," Alec observed.

"When you're strong enough, everything's a twist-off," Ward boasted with a smile.

Sensing an implicit challenge, Alec took a bottle of the blueberry hefeweizen and held it up, alongside a bottle of the coffee bourbon porter. "You're the brawn on this team, I'm the brains." Alec turned the porter upside down, latched the bottle cap of the porter as a lever, and with one quick gesture, popped off the blueberry bottle cap, spilling only a few drops of purplish foam.

"Smooth move, Archimedes!" Ward laughed.

Katrina shook her head in disapproval. "I don't understand how you guys can worry about getting older. The moment I leave you two alone together, you guys act like teenagers."

Marie chuckled. "Katrina, are you getting the nanny for Will and Harry, or for Alec and Ward?"

Alec reached for a paper towel and remembered where his train of thought had derailed.

"Even with team coverage, our parents are getting too old for taking care of the little guys for long stretches," he lamented. "They love the bejeezus out of Harry and Will, but it's a lot of pressure on them—any little raised temperature or potential ear infection. And that's on top of their usual worry whenever Katrina and I are overseas."

"I know how they feel," Ward jabbed.

Within the hour, the Leonidivna-Flanagan household started feeling just short of crowded with the arrival of Raquel and her husband, Vaughn, then Elaine and her husband Joe, Alejandro and Tom and their wives, Minnie Black from the Treasury Department, and her husband Ted, as well as all seven members of the short-lived TNG team, eager to trade dark jokes about the little-known upsides of being exposed in a massive hack.

"My waiter at the Chinese restaurant was really attentive, and he said if I ever wanted to talk, he was there to listen," O'Connell began. "Like, *really* listen."

Benedict went next. "You know, when we were exposed, I was warned about how the Russians use these honeypot agents, incredibly gorgeous women, to seduce American agents and get them to spill their secrets. So, I've kept my eyes open, on the lookout. But dang it, I can't find a single one of 'em!"

"I'm not feeling bad, my career with the CIA is derailed, but I've already gotten offers from S.H.I.E.L.D., the Kingsmen, Section 31, and Omega Sector," Emma said with a shrug.

"The Syrian embassy in Washington is following me on Twitter ... " Belina announced. "In an unmarked car."

"I've got the Iranians following me ... in the car in front of me," her sister Sonia added. "Their vengeance upon me is driving really slowly."

"I've got two guys following me—one's all black, one's all white, and they both have long, triangular faces," Chip Brauer added, hoping his friends had ever read *MAD* magazine. "I think they're trying to kill each other. They keep using bombs that look like dark bowling balls with long fuses."

Ravid was picking Elaine's brain on what it was like to work in the FBI's counterintelligence division, when everyone told him it was his turn for a joke about being exposed. It took him just a moment to think of one.

"The other day, I was nearly the victim of identity theft," Ravid lamented, but raising a finger. "I say nearly. It wasn't that they caught the guy, but because when the guy realized he might get mistaken for me, he changed his mind. 'An exposed CIA officer? The hell with that! Everybody's trying to kill that guy! I'll steal the identity of someone in less danger, like a narc at a Hell's Angels rally!'"

About ninety minutes into the party, the twins needed to be put to bed, and only their parents had really perfected the "five s" approach—swaddle, side or stomach, shushing, swaying, and sucking. Alec noted that singing was also an "s" word and sometimes worked, and Katrina teased that he should never mistake swaying for shaking. The idea, as Alec understood it, was to re-create the sensations Will and Harry felt within the womb, to calm them and help them fall asleep.

Alec found himself holding and swaying Will, and Katrina found herself holding and swaying Harry. They stood in the twins' room, with the door closed, hidden away at the party they were hosting, in an odd slow dance, each one rhythmically swaying a near one-year-old in their arms.

"That's why the memory of our party after Turkmenistan feels so weird now—it was life in B.C., Before Children," Alec joked in a whisper. He shook his head. "I can't believe how we think of that as the good old days now."

"You never know you're in the good old days until they're gone, and you're in some new days," Katrina whispered back. "But all in all, these are the good new days. The world's still spinning, we've got the twins, we've got our friends, our families, we've got a whole lot of good and smart people watching our backs. And we've got each other."

Alec nodded, but Katrina could tell he wasn't quite convinced.

"We kept the plates spinning, this time," he said, thinking of the old variety show guests on television who could keep so many plates spinning on the heads of sticks simultaneously. "There's a whole world of trouble out there, and I know it isn't entirely rational, but some days I feel like one day... it's just going to come knocking at our door."

Despite the ominous thought he had just expressed, Will had fallen asleep, his face the perfect persona of peace. Katrina gave Harry one last sway, and he, too, had drifted off into dreamland.

They gently placed each twin in the adjacent cribs. Then Katrina reached up and turned her husband's head to his.

"Alec, who did you marry?"

Alec gave a "good point" nod to her.

"A whole lot of men and women from that whole world of trouble have come right at us, looking for a fight," Katrina stated, and Alec could see that gleam of satisfaction. "And a whole lot of them ended up dead. You're right, Alec, you don't have a Belloq, and I've never had a true nemesis. At least not for very long. Don't say Patrick, either, because we both know he won't be around long enough to claim that title. You and I live full lives—and these headaches and curveballs and bumps in the road are the price we willingly pay for these full lives. And I wouldn't have it any other way."

Alec nodded, and they headed for the door, to rejoin the party.

"We are blessed," he agreed.

CHAPTER THIRTY-FIVE

PLEINMONT HEADLAND
TORTEVAL, GUERNSEY
THE CHANNEL ISLANDS
SIX MONTHS LATER

None of the three prisoners had any idea why they were being transferred, or where. About a half-year earlier, the U.S. government had extradited them to a trio of hostile countries, despite the prisoners having little or no connection to those countries. Once they were transferred, their imprisonment barely met the definition of the word, and each prisoner enjoyed a state-provided stay at a luxury hotel in the capital city. They lived under constant surveillance and escort, and were required to wear an ankle bracelet with a tracking device, but it was a much more enjoyable way to live than the grim fate of those residing in ADX Florence in Colorado.

Every few days, representatives from the host countries' intelligence services subjected them to thorough debriefings on their areas of expertise and past crimes. All the prisoners were forthcoming and cooperative, partially out of a sense of gratitude for getting them out of American custody, and partially because there wasn't much point in lying.

And then, with zero warning, one morning two diplomatic security agents gave each prisoner a terse, hostile announcement: "You're being transferred." Each prisoner was dressed, and taken, with no possessions, not even a toothbrush, to the capital city's airport. The guards escorted them on a flight to London, and then a connecting flight to the English Channel Island of Guernsey. The diplomatic security agents refused to answer any questions, and gruffly discouraged any inquiries.

Once they had landed, the diplomatic security agents took the prisoners to a reserved rental car, put zip tie wrist restraints onto the prisoner, and the moment they left the airport, the agent who wasn't driving placed an opaque black hood over each prisoner's head. One of the prisoners, a British citizen, scoffed, "I'm not sure I see the point of this! I know I'm in Guernsey. and this is not a particularly large island!"

The six diplomatic security agents drove their cars, and the three prisoners, to the Pleinmont Observation Tower, a massive, ominous, dark seven-story naval observation tower. Built and used by the Nazis from 1942 to 1945, the tower was part of an elaborate defense system during their occupation. After the war the menacing tower was turned into a museum, but the year-long interruption of tourism during the pandemic had forced its closure.

The only light on the stairs was the red of the exit signs, making the whole structure appear vaguely demonic. As a particular American intelligence analyst would observe in the near future, "If Sauron and the Galactic Empire built condominiums, they would look like this."

A large sign outside the entrance indicated the Pleinmont Observation Tower was "CLOSED FOR RENOVATIONS." There was no sign of any construction equipment or vehicles.

After being marched up six flights of stairs, the three prisoners were shoved into seats and had their zip ties cut and removed. They heard the agents speaking briefly to someone—each time in the agents' native language—and then the footsteps of the agents leaving.

Two women and a man had their black hoods yanked off their heads simultaneously. One man and one woman recognized each other. They had been seated around a rough-hewn table, with five other people seated, and one empty seat.

"Pittman?"

"Eribat? What are you doing here?"

"You're here because I've decided I want you on my team," said an American man, standing dressed in a sharp black suit. "I've spent the past two decades doing business with, and favors for, the Russian, Iranian, and Syrian governments. I asked nicely and gave them a sense of what I want to do with you, and *voila*—I checked you guys out like a library book. And trust me, if you don't help me, I can kill you without the slightest consequence."

The three new prisoners looked at their new captor, and the motley crew assembled around the table.

"Let's get these introductions out of the way," the American began. Pittman found him oddly cheerful, but then he realized it wasn't cheer that their host emanated in every word and gesture. It was self-satisfaction. The American pointed at Pittman.

"Doctor Allen Pittman, known by the *nom de guerre* 'Hell-Summoner,' the notorious virologist who flipped from saving lives to cooking up bioweapons in spring 2021." He pointed to Pittman's right. "Your former client, Shakira Eribat, former leader of the Shedim, a European secret society dedicated to eradicating Jews. The woman to your left is Fabrice Vuscovi, chief recruiter for Atarsa, that terrorist group that terrified America back in 2019."

They looked around the table.

"The Barbie twins across from you are Madison and Tiffany Reed, who are facing charges of attempting to blow up the Freedom Tower back in August 2021. Through intermediaries, I posted the several million dollars' worth of bail for them and got them out of the country on fake passports." He paused and offered a conceited smile. "The U.S. Department of Justice is really pissed about that."

"The Mexican Bonnie and Clyde next to them are Juan Comillo, a.k.a. the Jaguar, and his lovely partner in crime, Esmerelda. Two of the most notorious mercenaries in Mexico, and arguably the world's foremost experts on how to cross America's southern border."

"Let's get one thing straight," Jaguar declared with an indignant glare at the American. "You didn't break us out; no one's ever been able to catch us. We're here because you promised a payday of generational wealth."

"He also promised us revenge," Esmerelda reminded.

"Yes, yes, I'm getting to that," the American said, rolling his eyes. "And finally, the hardest man on the planet to find and recruit, Arslanbek Murgen. Formerly of ISIS, formerly of al-Aswat, or the Voices, who's been living under a new identity for years."

Murgen wore a black turban, long, flowing robes. His face a long beard with streaks of gray in it. Pittman noticed that the Turkman's hands were badly scarred.

"*'Akhbaratni al'aswat 'an 'antazir al'iishara*," he answered. The American knew enough Arabic to understand—"the Voices told me to wait for a signal."

Pittman stared in incredulous concern over the notorious collection seated around the table.

"How did you—"

The American cut him off. "I found all of you because I after twenty years of selling CIA secrets on the black market, I have arguably the world's best Rolodex of rogue state intelligence agents, criminals, mercenaries and assorted riffraff. I had another strong prospect to recruit, but after what happened in Taiwan ... he dropped off the list."

The figures around the table exchanged confused glances; no one had any idea what the American had meant by the phrase "what happened in Taiwan."

Pittman already didn't like this American and seethed at the man's insufferable arrogance. Pittman would be no man's lackey. He turned and gave the man an icy, contemptuous stare. "Just who—"

"My name is Patrick Horne, and the only reason my name isn't on an Interpol Red Notice is because the CIA is too embarrassed to reveal what I did. But rest assured, I am the most wanted man you've never heard of."

Everyone around the table exchanged glances, wondering if anyone recognized the name.

"If you're really that wanted, shouldn't we have heard of you?" Jaguar asked.

"What, are you on, like, double secret probation?" Tiffany asked.

Patrick ignored them.

"For the past few years, I've had a front row seat as one particular CIA team kicked your asses from one side of the globe to the next," Patrick said, needling his guests. "They ruined your plans, left the corpses of your comrades bleeding in the dirt, and left a bunch of you to rot in jail. All of you have plentiful motivation to help me."

Shakira Eribat noticed that two of her tablemates had made eye contact and seemed to be staring at each other, as if communicating silently: Fabrice Vuscovi, chief recruiter for Atarsa, and the terrifying Arslanbek Murgen. For a brief moment, Eribat had a vision of a giant, woman-sized termite and a man-sized cockroach sitting across the table from each other.

Whatever she was seeing, Pittman didn't see it. He sneered at Patrick.

"So, what are we supposed to be, some sort of terrorist all-star team? The Legion of Doom? Spectre?"

"Well, seeing as you're all out for blood," Patrick began, quite pleased with how much he knew. "I've been referring to our collective effort as the Blood Pact."

Everyone around the table seemed underwhelmed.

"That makes us sound like part of the Red Cross," Esmerelda said skeptically. "Maybe we're the Bad Blood? The Cold Blooded?"

"I didn't bring you here to workshop the name," Patrick fumed.

"Well then, just what do you have in mind?" Pittman demanded.

Patrick chuckled. "Well, doctor, I think the plan is pretty clear." He smiled. "We're going to murder every last member of the Dangerous Clique."

ABOUT THE AUTHOR

Jim Geraghty is the senior political correspondent of *National Review* and a contributing columnist to *The Washington Post*. In recent years, he's reported from notorious trouble spots like wartime Ukraine, Taiwan, Transnistria, and Des Moines, Iowa.

Made in United States
Troutdale, OR
07/16/2024

21265977R00136